# BETWEEN HEAVEN
## AND HERE

For Kevin + Jammy~

# BETWEEN HEAVEN AND HERE

I'm so glad to have met you....

*Susan Straight*

## SUSAN STRAIGHT

2016

## McSWEENEY'S BOOKS
### SAN FRANCISCO

McSweeney's and colophon are registered trademarks
of McSweeney's, a privately held company with
wildly fluctuating resources.

ISBN: 978-1-936365-75-3
www.mcsweeneys.net

*To my city, my hometown, everyone
who left and everyone who stayed.*

"It's a thin line between heaven and here."
—Bubbles, *The Wire*

# HER ROYAL HIGHNESS

WHEN SIDNEY CAME out of the taqueria and headed down the alley, he saw Glorette Picard on her knees, her back to a shopping cart parked near the fence, her face held up toward the shadows made by two wild tobacco trees that grew along the chainlink. Sidney flattened himself against the wall, holding the bag of tacos like a school lunch, and waited for the sound of a man's voice.

She must be on her knees waiting. The man would be against the fence, getting his money. Or the drugs. Glorette had been sprung for years, living here on the Westside, moving from apartment to apartment just ahead of the rent. She and her friend Sisia worked regular rounds near the Launderland because that's where one crew sold rock from a dryer.

But he didn't hear anything except the back of his shirt rubbing against the stucco, loosening a few rough grains. Glorette's eyes were open. She was about twenty feet away. Her face was upturned, her lips parted like she was having trouble breathing, and her neck curved long and golden.

Her neck. That made his nature rise. How the hell was he hearing his father? *Boy, when your nature rise, you gotta watch who you with.*

Sidney had never been with Glorette. Why was it always her neck he'd wanted, when they were young? Who kissed her neck now? None of the men along Palm Avenue who stopped in cars and trucks or brought her back here to the alley cared about her neck. Throat was inside the neck. Sidney had danced with her once in high school and let his lips brush down along the side of her neck as if it were an accident when he shifted, and she'd shivered.

But she was with Chess then. After that, she met a musician from Detroit, an older guy named Sere Dakar, and when he disappeared, she was seventeen and pregnant.

Sidney stepped away from the wall, but she didn't turn her head. She was focused on the shadows. She didn't see him. Or she did, and she didn't care. Hey—Sidney Chabert. Remember?

The alley lit up like heat lightning flashed, but it was August. It wouldn't rain for months in Rio Seco. The silver flashes were from a huge SUV coming down the other part of the alley, behind the Launderland. The glare turned her into a small crouched figure behind the cart. Sidney slid around the corner of the taqueria. Those boys. The ones who sold the rock. They had a brand new Navigator, the sound system pounding so hard the drum shock collected in his sternum.

Spongy marrow inside. Sidney walked quickly around to the front doorway of the taqueria. Now his heart beat hard behind the sternum. Surgeons cracked open the sternum to get to the heart. Back when he worked at the hospital, he listened to the doctors in the hallways and the cafeteria. The neck and the throat—the first time he'd thought of the difference, he was nineteen, a brand new custodian, and the words floated all around his cart. Inflamed throat. Broken neck.

His father-in-law had gotten him the job. Jinelle's daddy had been in maintenance at County General for twenty years, since he arrived from Shreveport. Jinelle was already working at her mother's beauty salon. She was good. But she'd never touched Glorette's hair, not even in high school when all the girls cornrowed and braided during lunch. No one looked like Glorette. Long neck, perfect eyebrows, her waist-length black hair in a crown on top of her head. No one ever saw it down, and that was part of her beauty. They would pay for her hair. Jinelle always said angrily, "Hair is dead. Just keratin, okay? I can make every woman's hair look the same. Just a lotta product."

Had Glorette's hair been down, just now?

The Navigator paused. The boys must have seen her. But then the car turned down the small cross street, away from the avenue.

The man would be in a hurry, with the interruption. Sidney didn't want to see that shadow move toward Glorette, where she waited patiently because she felt she had no choice.

*Because she didn't choose me.*

The taqueria's glass door was covered with hand-painted phrases. Tacos de lengua. Tacos de cabeza.

Tongue and brain. He didn't want to see the man, but he wanted to wait for her. He pushed open the door.

Glorette was from Sarrat. It wasn't even a neighborhood, like the Westside. It was another world—one long dirt road that led to a small bridge over the Rio Seco canal, and then a narrow gravel road wound through tunnels of orange trees to one white house and ten smaller wooden bungalows. Sidney had been there twice, when his father worked on a refrigerator for Mrs. Antoine.

The groves and houses all belonged to Enrique Antoine and Gustave Picard. Sidney's father was from New Orleans—Treme—but those men were from out in Louisiana cane country past Baton Rouge, he told Sidney that day in the truck, bringing back a new coil for the refrigerator. Sidney's father had come to California after he got out of the war, and in 1958 he'd met five beautiful girls at a church dance. The girls had just come from Louisiana, some place out in the fields called Sarrat. A rich white man was hunting them, some old woman told his father, and they were sent to live with her.

His father said, "Few years after that, here come Enrique Antoine. I heard he killed that white man and headed out. He brought his brother—Gustave. He stay right there." His father pointed to a small porch across the street from the yard where they'd pulled out the refrigerator, and Sidney saw Glorette on the steps, drying her hair.

Sidney sat at the table he'd just vacated. His plastic container of hot sauce was still there. A straw. He'd forgotten to leave her a straw that night, five years ago. He'd found her in the ER when he wheeled his cart past, collecting predawn trash. Glorette peered at him from the bank of plastic chairs. "Ain't you—?" Her huge purple-brown eyes shimmered with fever, and she coughed so deep in her chest it sounded like cellophane crackled behind her ribs.

Lungs black from crack smoke and torn from coughing, Sidney thought. He'd frozen there while she stared at him. Lungs didn't weigh much, when the surgeon cut one out and left it in the medical waste bag. The red bag.

She'd said, "Sidney, right? You graduated, huh? I missed the last three months. Learned all I needed to learn by then." She coughed again, then grinned up at him. Even with all the smoking and the streets, her teeth were still white as mints, her neck marked with only one creased line like faint jewelry. "Learned when a brotha say he got protection, that don't mean he know how to use it."

Sidney had looked away, at the old man in the wheelchair by the door, his foot hugely swollen and bare. At a Mexican woman's braid hanging over the back of her chair, almost to the floor.

"You want to marry me?" Glorette had whispered then.

Sidney felt his forehead crease, tight and dry from the heat of the hospital basement and the incinerators. He was ashamed at what he carried in his cart. What he had to burn for extra money, down there in the basement with Raoul Moreno.

"What?"

"That's what all y'all used to say in school. You Westside fools. Just marry me, baby," she murmured, and coughed again until her eyes watered. She raised her face to him and said, "But you wanted to put me in your crib and then trip, like do I think about you all day while you at work, or am I studyin some fool. Right? Ain't you asked me back then?"

Brothers had all asked her something—marry me, baby; come on over here by the lockers with me, baby; help me out with this pain I got, baby; take down that hair and let me see it on your back, baby. Gimme some a that, I swear I give you every dollar I got in the world.

But nobody had any dollars back then, because they were all teenagers. In the ER now, he and Glorette were thirty years old. "I ain't never asked you that," Sidney told her, bending nearer so the intake nurses wouldn't hear. They were staring at him since he wasn't moving along.

Glorette had never even looked at him, except sometimes in math class when she and her friends teased him about his name.

She coughed again, so hard her body bent like a question mark over her cupped palms, the admissions form sliding to the floor. When she raised her head, she said, "No. You asked Jinelle. You still married?"

Sidney shook his head, and she stood up unsteadily, her hand slapped to the wall. "I always said, Hell no. Any a you fools be the same. Want to lock me in some house. Tie up my time. Always talkin bout Wrap that pretty hair around me, baby, I want to see how it feel. Shit. Any woman same as me when y'all eyes shut."

Then she'd fallen to the dirty linoleum floor, and Sidney didn't even think before he squatted down and picked her up. Regulations. Call an orderly. No. She was longer and heavier than his daughter, but not dead weight like a sleeping child. The creases at the backs of her knees hot over his right wrist. The shoulderblades sharp from her halter top, digging into his own shoulder. Her hair fell out of the loose bun and draped over his arm. No, it didn't. This wasn't a damn movie. The intake nurses started yelling at him from the Triage window. "What the hell are you doing? You're Chabert, right? Put her down!"

He pushed through the double doors and went down the gray tunnel of hallway through their voices until he saw an empty gurney. White and clean. He lay Glorette on her side and her eyelids trembled violently as if boiling water were underneath.


AT THE TABLE closest to the register, three Mexican guys had beer and tacos. Their t-shirts and jeans were covered with slivers of palm frond. Guys working off the street. They looked up, then dismissed him. *Must think I went outside to check my car.*

He usually saw Glorette and Sisia from a distance, because Excellent

Video was four blocks up on Palm. But he hadn't had a car for a week now. The brakes had gone out on his old Cavalier and he thought that rather than spend a few hundred on new ones, he'd send the money to Jinelle in Shreveport. His daughter Sarena was twelve now, and she needed braces. Orthodontia, the doctors had called it when Sidney worked at County General.

At the video store, he had three-to-eleven shift. All this week he'd taken his break at nine so he could watch anime in the back room while opening boxes of new DVDs. He needed a break from the trailers blaring all night on the TV above him. Tonight he'd helped Mr. Jae close up, then picked out two new anime videos and walked to the taqueria. His apartment building was only six blocks from here anyway, and he figured he'd be fine walking until fall, since all he did was go to work, then go home and watch movies.

Behind the counter, the mop bucket propped open the back door to the alley. The taqueria closed at midnight. Sidney got up and walked toward the register, listening to the slice of darkness past the door. No Navigator. No voices.

The woman who worked in the taqueria came back to the counter and nodded warily at Sidney. He couldn't think in here for free. But the man would leave. A car would start up. Sidney could go back to the alley and offer Glorette tamales. He'd heard she loved the taqueria. Someone at Sundown Liquor had joked that she would do you for shrimp tacos and a Coke, if she was hungry enough.

The woman frowned at him. He said, "Got hungry again. Two tamales. Por favor. Pollo." Her eyes were shadowed with light blue. Eyelids like two baby oceans, but when she looked down to write, Sidney saw creases where the makeup had heated into crescents. Frosty second brows.

Before he could stop it, the vision came. Eyebrows and eyelashes on fire when the woman looked down at the order pad. The leg hairs burning, glistening purple-gold. Red fingernails when she handed him the can of Coke. Pure varnish. Nails would flare up intense in the incinerator. Flames shooting blue-hot from the fingers, like the hands belonged to some cartoon.

She paused and tore the sheet from the pad, and then said something in Spanish to the men at the table.

Sidney leaned against the wall, staring at the back door. It had been so hard not to look at Jinelle like that, when he came home from the hospital and saw her cheeks with downy hair on them, her neck where the hair grew into a point at the nape. When he saw their daughter Sarena's boneless-looking body in the crib, legs bowed and soft. Because that one time when he carried a red bag of medical waste from the cart to the incinerator, a finger had fallen to the floor from the tangled bundle of surgical bandages and needles. He saw hair between the knuckles. Raoul Moreno, his supervisor in the basement, had laughed and said, "Come on, carnal, you knew they lost some shit in there now and then!"

Sidney stared at the poster on the taqueria wall. Aztec gods. But they looked like the two gargoyles carved above the front entrance of County General. The hospital was so damn old the walls were stone.

"Quit playin. We ain't got time." The rough voice carried through the back door.

Sidney moved down the short hallway, closer to the rectangle of dark. He heard the smudge of dragged heels in the gravel, someone walking toward Glorette. "Stop trippin, Glorette. Jazen and them looking for us." Sidney glanced outside, feeling like a fool. Like a child, listening to something he wasn't supposed to hear. Sisia stalked down the dirt, wobbling in her heels, her extensions swaying, like a drunk model on a bad Tyra Banks special.

Sisia and Glorette had been sprung together all these years. Sisia was tall and built, opposite of Glorette. "Brick house," brothers used to laugh, "and somebody done shut the window on her face." Sisia's cheeks were round and full and pitted like dark oranges. Her hair was jheri-curled back then, with those stray ends waving up in unfortunate ways, like horns, no matter how she tamped them down. Now she always had braids, even if her shoes were taped together. "Percy and Harry and Sidney," Sisia had sneered at Sidney in math class. "All them old-time names. Like a old man."

"Name after Sidney Poitier," he had answered, cocking his head like Chess and Lafayette and the cool brothers did.

Sisia laughed loud. "Who in the hell gon watch some Sidney Poitier but my country-ass uncles? Give me some Blair Underwood. Some Denzel."  .

Now Sidney smelled bleach from the mop bucket. Behind him the woman from the counter said, "No. No baño!" He turned. She looked up at him, her eyes black as licorice in the dim light, and he saw that the three men in the taqueria were standing now, watching him intently.

He held up his hands in surrender and said, "No, no baño. I got it." They think I'm fixin to rob this place, he realized.

Outside, Sisia said, "Oh, shit, Glorette. Why you had to pick the one I wanted? Why you always gotta be the queen?" It sounded like Sisia was crying. Sidney closed his eyes. She said, "I wouldna left your ass. Why you had to talk yang?"

The woman from behind the counter went past him, breathing hard, and closed the door. She said, "Two tamales."

Sidney walked slowly back to the counter, the men still standing, their mouths wide and long and clamped shut. Not chewing. The plastic plate held two tamales bundled up in cornhusks, like kids in sleeping bags. Sidney sat at the table again, his tacos making translucent clouds of grease on the paper bag. The tamales. The Coke so cold that when he pushed in the tab, fog seemed to rise from the darkness underneath his finger.

Sisia wouldn't talk long.

The imprint of husk on the corn dough—lines like fingerprints. Was each cornhusk different? On *Law & Order SVU*, they were always resurrecting prints—from dead fingers, from beer bottles and walls, and even buried under electrical tape.

Who burned all the body parts they were always weighing on that show? Who disposed of their medical waste? The hearts they liked to hold up, the severed digits?

Sidney looked out at Palm Avenue, past the backward Spanish words. The men were speaking softly now. They were waiting to see what he would do. Whether he was a thief. Muslims cut off the right hand of a thief.

What the hell they do with all them hands? In the paper you saw them standing around in a courtyard, all the sentenced men. Who chopped off the hands, in a row?

Chess always said to him, "You seen Archuleta's leg and you ain't figured it out? Damn, Sidney, you that stupid? You sure as hell looked lost when your picture was in the paper right in front of the furnace."

Sidney looked over at the men. They had finished eating. They were merely watching him now. Chess and them didn't know. The cops had brought all that marijuana to burn in the incinerator. The smoke was heavy and sweet as magic fog in some slasher movie. No one knew the leg was in there until the bag fell away and they saw the thickness of the thigh. The round eye of bone.

He checked his watch. Eleven-thirty. Too early for Glorette and Sisia to quit Palm Avenue. When he had started working at Excellent Video a few years ago, after the hospital closed, he'd seen that all the women were as predictable as the older white security guards stationed in front of the drugstore. Strolling and patrolling were mindlessly the same. Guarding something inside, or looking for customers, they paced in patterns every night. Like the zoo. He'd thought he would see Glorette close up. Maybe she'd come into the video store. Twice or three times she passed by the front window—her back, her elbow when she kept walking. She carried a bag of what looked like paperbacks.

He didn't want to get with her. He just wanted to see her, talk to her long enough to know whether she remembered that night in the ER. If she remembered him. If she'd ever done that to anyone else. Ever.

But why would she come to the video store? Chess said she didn't even have a TV.


WHEN CHESS CAME in for videos, he acted like Glorette was still his girlfriend. Not like she'd ignored him after she met Dakar. Not like he'd had a daughter with some other girl. He'd come up to the counter and say, "Man, she stay at Jacaranda Gardens now, them gray apartments. Her and her boy. Ain't a damn thing in there but a futon and a glass-top table. Her and Sisa let them sprung fools party up in there all the time, and they walk off with everything. Her son's seventeen, and he can't even keep a CD player or no shoes."

"What you doin up there?" Sidney said, putting the videos in a bag. Mindless shit like *Xtreme* and *Fast and Furious*. Chess didn't even know what anime was.

Chess lifted his chin so Sidney saw his neck, where a thin green wash of Magic Shave remained near his ears. He still wore a fade. "I hang up there sometimes with her. Talk about the old days. Gold days." Chess looked out at his car, a Bronco with the hood crazed by the sun. He leaned over the counter and said, "So you miss County General? They closed that shit down. After what y'all did."

Chess laughed and lifted his chin again, and Sidney slammed the cash register closed. "Wasn't just me workin in the basement, okay? Was two or three other dudes." Really it had just been him and Moreno. They were the only ones whose names made the newspaper.

"Least I don't take advantage of somebody like Glorette," he said.

Chess shrugged. "When I leave, homegirl's fine."

FRIDAY NIGHT—CHESS and the Antoine brothers were probably hanging out under the huge pepper tree in the parking lot of Sundown Liquor, three blocks up Palm. The Antoine brothers were Enrique's sons, big guys who played football in junior college. They drove in from the groves to buy beer and play dominoes. Card table, some folding chairs, and too much talking shit, under the tree. Sidney never hung out. He stayed away unless Archuleta's customized van wasn't in the parking lot. He hated seeing the leg, in his mind, whenever he saw the handpainted sunset on the van doors.

Sidney picked up the tamales and Coke and walked slowly out the door. *Don't wanna alarm nobody.* He turned the corner. Crickets were loud in the weeds along the sidewalk, but with each step he took they all stopped singing but one—suddenly it wasn't music but a single scraping. Fingernail on a plastic comb. His father used to joke, "Even that bug gotta get him a woman."

Sidney felt himself hard. Nature rising. He'd always hated how country his father sounded. Even from New Orleans, he sounded as country as the Sarrat people. After he'd finished the refrigerator, he'd installed a window swamp cooler for Mrs. Antoine. He'd said in the truck, "Man, they got they own church out there. They own cemetery. They own chickens. Don't need nobody or nothin."

Sidney pushed his palm hard against the stucco wall to distract himself with the rough grains. No voices in the alley. No shopping cart wheels. The crickets began again.

That night in the ER, he'd come back. The intake nurses were distracted by the old man screaming about his inflamed foot. Sidney carried two cartons of chocolate milk on his cart. Glorette was in one of the curtained-off exam rooms. He said the words quickly. "Why you waste yourself like this? Look how sick you are."

She'd opened her eyes. "Waste?" she'd said, drawing out the word, her lips darkened from the way she kept licking them. He put the chocolate milk on the silver tray. "How I'm a waste?" she whispered. "All y'all want is to look at my face while you gettin off. Leave me lone."

"How you feel?" he said, bending closer, and he saw her amber eyes, one fleck of brown like a piece of leaf floating in the left eye.

She said, "You got a shirt under that one?"

"No."

She pulled at Sidney's shoulder, then said, "Undo them buttons." She said, "Help me up. Why you so hot?" She stood before him, small and perfect, even after years of walking the streets. Her hair was pushed up at the back where she'd been lying down, but it looked purposeful. What did Jinelle call it? Teased. Bouffant. Like Audrey Hepburn.

Don't think of Jinelle.

Glorette pushed his shirt aside and leaned close to his chest. He felt something brush against his nipples. Not her lips. Soft and tickling. Eyelashes. She moved them slowly, again and again, her breath heating his skin.

She said, "You smell like smoke and somethin else."

Outside in the hallway someone called, "Why's that medical waste cart here? We just had a pickup."

Sidney jumped away from Glorette and buttoned his shirt. He batted at himself, in his pants, and she said, "What they said about you? Somethin about the basement. Lord, that's you. When they talk about Archuleta's leg."

"You okay?" he whispered.

"I'm fine," she said, distant, as if she were in a tower. A turret. The princess bride. "Just fine."

Fine as wine and just my kind, they all said every time they saw her. Every brother on the Westside had fallen in love with Glorette, and even though she'd been on the street for ten years, as far as he knew, no one had ever fallen out.

WHAT HE WANTED to ask her was whether she'd ever done that to anyone else. How had she known to do it? Nothing Jinelle did to him had ever made him feel that way. Not sex. Not even hot. But shaking and trembling inside, just under the layer of his skin.

What if that was just an experiment? What if he was the only one she'd ever touched with her lashes?

In all these years he'd driven up Palm to work and thought he'd seen her—the red sandals she always wore, the high crown of her hair—he couldn't stop. It wasn't something you could lean out the open window and ask. Not when she was used to men asking how much?

*What you did to me—you did that before?*

No one spoke. He went around the corner, no slipping and sliding, and walked down the alley. The shopping cart had moved closer to the wild tobacco trees. Curled inside was a shape.

Glorette was sleeping. Homeless people never slept inside a cart. Even if it was their hooptie, the only transportation they had, no one fit inside a cart. But Glorette was small. He moved closer, along the chain-link, and in the light from the single yellow streetlamp he saw something glittering at her bare toe.

She must be damn tired to sleep like that, take a nap slumped with one arm across her chest and her feet up awkwardly.

He couldn't see her face yet. Her long black hair fell through the slats at the back of the cart and lay in the dirt. He felt the shock inside his jeans. All that hair.

The Navigator. The drums. Sidney flattened himself against the fence. The plastic slats through the diamonds of chainlink danced and shimmered with the vibration. The world leapt with the drums. The yellow flowers, like macaroni, dangled from the wild tobacco tree hiding him. They shook until the car turned away.

Glorette didn't stir. Her hair poured from the cart like black ferns, cascading from a cave wall. The cave where the hero hid out while he rested, got himself together, and made his plans. "Hair is dead," Jinelle used to say in annoyance whenever the brothers brought it up, at a house party or barbecue. She'd been working at the beauty salon years then. "Glorette should get her a style and stop wearin that old bun like a grandma." But Chess would say, "She don't have to get a style. Get anybody she want the way she is."

Now Sidney didn't want to wake her. She wouldn't remember him if she was this high, and that would kill him on a night like tonight. Nothing to do but tacos and anime.

Damn. He'd left the videos on the table, next to the hot sauce.

What was in the plastic bag at the back wheels? It was tied shut. Looked like that same stack of books. Sidney crouched down and flattened the plastic. Maruchan Ramen. Ten for a dollar. That must be what her son ate, because she was always carrying it.

The wind moved the palm fronds suddenly, the sweet whispering, and a rat shot across the phone line above him. The rat scrabbled for a moment on the taqueria roof and disappeared. The night was warm and dry, but rats would be working. Sidney couldn't leave the tamales, like he'd left the chocolate milk. Glorette hadn't moved; her arm curved around her waist. She was small, but rounded breasts and perfect behind. The foolish sprung wardrobe of yoga pants, exercise bra, and red high heels. Sidney came closer. The left heel pushed out from the cart like a stick. The toe ring was a sparkly flower of red jewels. He could pick her up and move her to—no, she couldn't sleep in Launderland, or the bushes, or the taqueria.

He reached into the cart and moved her hair from her face. Her eyes were open. She wasn't sleeping. Her neck was bent too far to the left, and two small half-moons filled with blood marked her collarbone.

SIDNEY THREW UP against the fence. He steadied himself, fingers in the wire. Red chunks of tomato, white flags of tortilla chip. The tamales were on the ground. His fingerprints were everywhere on the plastic. His body fluids were here. He smeared his foot over the tomatoes, crushed the sour smell into the soft dirt by the fence, pushed the mess into the weeds.

He could hear the conversation he'd have with the cops when they came.

"I was walkin cause the brakes are out on my car."

"I got off work at Excellent Video at eleven. Bought some tacos and headed home."

"It ain't in the shop cause I sent my paycheck to my ex-wife for my daughter's teeth. Yeah, all the rest of her body, too. Bite expanders. Teeth are too big for her jaw. Like mine."

"Four years. That's how long I been divorced."

"Yeah, I know her, but from when we were kids. Long time ago. No, I ain't seen her for years. Well, yeah, everybody sees her on the street, but I haven't seen her close up. Yeah, she's close up right now."

"No, I ain't paid her nothin. I ain't touched her. No, I ain't remarried. Come on. No. Yeah, I walked over here to see if it was her."

"Glorette Picard."

HE COULDN'T CALL the cops. Not a brother walking through the alley near midnight, a loser with no car, no woman, only a couple of anime videos. Shit. Which were in the restaurant. Which meant everyone had seen him looking all nervous and jumpy. Buying two meals.

Can't leave her here. Not with the rats, and the Navigator, and the crickets. Cops would come eventually, in the morning, and find everything. Including his vomit. What did they always say on *SVU*? Something's always left behind—the dead tell us the truth. The story.

Mexican music came from the taqueria when someone opened the door. Sidney was tired. He backed into the trees again, and water was flung across the alley, a white plume of water that hit the fence and washed his tomatoes back into the dirt.

Hell, no. Wasn't no *SVU: Rio Seco*. The city had closed County General years ago and built a new medical center out in the wilds, but the morgue was an ancient brick building downtown, covered with ivy; you could smell it sometimes from the street, it was so inefficient. The city wanted to build a new morgue by the medical center, but there was no budget. And the cops wouldn't be women with tight sweaters and boots and long hair. They'd be Rio Seco PD. He'd be the brother with no car—what a loser—who just found the body. Uh-huh.

"No, it didn't bother me to pick her up. I've seen bodies before. I worked at County General."

"I picked her up because I thought she was sleeping."

"I don't know CPR. I was a custodian at the hospital."

"I wanted to help her."

"She didn't love anybody but her son, from what I heard."

"No, she didn't tell me."

Nobody would drop liquids into revolving machines or find stray red needles from a bottlebrush plant or take a fallen eyelash from her shoulder and extract the DNA.

Nobody would care about Glorette. No cops or technicians. They'd laugh about her clothes, find multiple kinds of semen inside her, make fun of her apartment, pull Ramen from the cupboard, scare the shit out of her son. Well, hell, someone killed a crack addict. Top priority. What did they used to call it? No Human Involved.

The left leg of her pants had been dragged up when she'd been put in the cart, and her knee was pressed so awkwardly that her skin pushed through the metal mesh. Five squares of flesh.

The scratch marks were from small fingernails. Not Sisia's, because she had hands like a man, and long square fake nails. He picked up

Glorette's hands. No blood. No nails. They'd been bitten into soft invisible edges.

Glorette had been kneeling by the cart. Sisia had to have put her inside, or she climbed in herself. And died? Her neck wasn't bruised. Heart attack, from smoking too much rock?

Sidney had come into his father's yard one day to find him sitting straight up in an old recliner—a washing machine dismantled beside him—and dead. Heart stopped, mouth closed. Fists on his legs.

Now he unbuttoned his shirt. *Come here.* He draped it over her body and picked her up. She was not stiff. She was not soft. A layer of something was forming under her skin. A river spreading over banks and then leaving silt and mud just below the surface. Her head fell back over his wrist and her hair fell across his thighs.

No. No. He couldn't carry her down the alley like this, couldn't carry her anywhere. Save a dead body? Nobody died of solitude. *You can't save her.* The wind prickled on his bare back, and a door slammed behind the fence. A lighter scratched, push tab snapped, and smoke drifted into the alley.

Sidney paused in the trees. He could hear the man sucking the smoke into his lungs. Hear his shoes moving on the concrete. Patio. His wife made him smoke outside. Not weed. Strong cigarette like a Camel. "Jesús, mira, you better not stay out there all night," she called, and the sliding glass door slammed shut.

*I can hear him, he might hear me.* Yes, officer. Black male. About thirty-five. Carrying a woman.

One car was parked on the side street. An ancient Nissan Sentra. Mexican flag in the back window. The taqueria woman, or the men.

The smoke released from the man's lungs and lifted in a dancing skein over the alley fence, like a bad detective movie. Fake fog. Blue. Glorette's body was no heavier than his daughter Sarena's. He had called her last week. She talked for five minutes, and then her cell phone went off. Her ringtone was loud. Some dude sang, "My body, your body, my body, your body." *Who the hell is that?* Sidney said. *Pretty Ricky,* she said. *I have to go, Dad. That's my friend. Mom's at work.*

"She told me you carried her one night at the hospital," Jinelle said, furious. "I ran into her at Rite Aid and she said you rescued her and shit. You some kinda knight? You got feelings for her? Why she couldn't walk? What you mean I didn't need savin? I ain't never needed savin. You did. And I ain't the one now. No. Go get her. Her royal highness. I'm gone."

The beer can landed in a pile near the fence. The sliding glass door clanked shut. Sidney looked down at Glorette's face in the streetlight. Her eyes amber, frozen. Helen of Troy. Her lips were etched sharply into her face without makeup. He curved her body onto its side, in the workshirt, and lay her in the cart again. He pushed it through the soft sand and gravel and onto the sidewalk. He wouldn't look down the narrow side streets. The Antoine brothers would be at Sundown Liquor. They had to be there.

He didn't care who heard the wheels grinding on the asphalt when he crossed the streets and headed down the next alley. The light was dimmer here, behind the shoe repair shop and the Botanica San Salvador. More smoke came from the open back door of the botanica—candles and marijuana. When the cops had brought all the black plastic bags of weed to the basement, Moreno had crowed like a bird. "Contact high, carnal!" he said, and the cops shook their heads. But they were smiling. Ten bags. Homegrown sinsemillia.

"Authorized to dispose," one cop said, peering into the incinerator. "Damn, this place is old."

Moreno sailed two bags into the glowing door while plastic hissed and the smoke filled the basement with a sweet-burnt blackness. In the dim basement Moreno said, "The government checks the smoke, man, you know. For emissions or whatever. It can't be too thick or black out there, in the air. So burn some bags off that last cart, Sidney."

"Damn, this one's heavy," the cop said, helping him lift two red waste bags from the cart. When they threw it in, the plastic disappeared, and Archuleta's leg lay in the burning bright branches of sinsemillia.

"What the hell are you guys doing?" the older cop yelled. "You're not supposed to burn body parts!"

"I didn't know it was there!" Sidney remembered his eyes burning, tearing. But Moreno didn't care. "Man, them surgeons throw all kinda stuff in the bags. We can't check em all. Lotta wombs in there. You know? I'm glad the doctors don't decide guys don't need our equipment no more."

The young cop stared inside the flames, and Moreno closed the door.

In the newspaper, after they interviewed surgeons and cops and administrators, they came to the basement and Moreno told them everything. He didn't care. He didn't care about emissions and airborne viruses and gangrene. The photographer thought Moreno was hilarious, with his huge mustache, and Sidney didn't notice the flash until it was too late.

Behind Sundown Liquor were empty boxes in a pile. He wasn't going to talk to Glorette. He wasn't an idiot. He left her there and went around to the parking lot.

Four men were under the pepper tree. Two red embers floating in the darkness, one set of white teeth laughing when he walked forward under the bright light from Sundown. Archuleta's van, with wheelchair lifts at the back, with gaudy desert sunsets glowing on the doors, parked near the door. Sidney didn't care. Chess hollered, "Hey, brotha, you lose your shirt?" Some other fool he didn't even recognize said, "He still hot years after workin that basement." Lafayette and Reynaldo Antoine wore plaster-spattered black Dickies; they didn't move anything except their eyes. They never had to say much. Lafayette slammed down a three-six and said, "Fitteen."

Chess opened his mouth and Sidney said, "Back up off me tonight, man, I ain't in the mood. Just walk away. I gotta talk to Lafayette."

"What the fuck wrong with you?" Chess said. "You never come to Sundown cause you don't want to make chit-chat with—"

Sidney said, "I see Archuleta in there behind the counter, okay? I know—I burned up his leg. Now get in your Bronco with this fool and go. We got business." Lafayette stood up and Sidney remembered his father speaking French to Enrique Antoine out in Sarrat, carrying the swamp cooler. Sidney said to Lafayette, "Li cousine. Mouri. Pas moi." He shrugged to say he didn't know who'd killed her.

Chess said, "You just babblin."

"Lousana brothers crazy and shit," the other man said, but he followed Chess to the Bronco. Sidney waited until it started up. Not the alley. Down Palm. Uh-huh.

Sidney took the Antoine brothers to the alley. "Glorette," he said. "I saw her in the alley when I came out the taco place. Then I heard her friend Sisia talkin to her."

"They fightin?" Lafayette said.

"No, like—sad." Sidney nodded. "Sisia had to been who put her in the cart. But I don't know how she died. Maybe a heart attack. All that rock."

"Why you bring her here?" Reynaldo said, toothpick like a catfish barb at the side of his mouth. He looked like he didn't believe Sidney hadn't been the one, maybe, to kill her.

Sidney folded his arms over his chest. The air brushed his collarbone. "What the cops gon do but laugh? What the morgue gon do but cut her up? Don't y'all want her back in Sarrat? You got that cemetery." He paused. "I heard her father wish she was home."

Lafayette nodded. "He keep her son sometime. Feed him." He stared at Sidney, his eyes that strange green, like he was making up his mind. Lafayette loved to fight. He'd broken jaws and noses in high school. Sidney kept his eyes hard. He didn't blink until Lafayette moved his hand to Reynaldo. "Get the truck."

The truck rumbled up the alley, and Lafayette said quickly, "Qui sais?" Who knows?

Sidney said, "Only me. And Sisia. If she did it, she won't say nothin. All she want is rock or money." He looked down at Glorette's hair, the wild strands he'd smoothed when he put her inside his shirt. "I never saw a purse or keys or nothin. Just this bag."

He handed Lafayette the bag of ramen and Lafayette said, "Glorette live on air. But she try to feed that boy."

They glanced around the alley and then lifted her into the truckbed, among the plastering tools and tarps. Lafayette covered her with a thick tarp, and when her face was gone Sidney leapt up into the truckbed beside her. "What you gon do?" Reynaldo said.

"Cops see us, tell the truth. They don't, tell her dad when we get out to your place." *And hope I don't see your pops,* he thought. *Cause my pops made him sound like a stone cold killer—the way he did that white man.*

The truck swayed around the corner and headed down Palm. Sidney rested his head against the cab window. He didn't want to see Sisia, or the Navigator, so he closed his eyes until he felt the dirt road that led to Sarrat. Then he reached down slowly, so Reynaldo wouldn't see the movement, and uncovered her left foot.

*Marry me.* He felt her toe cold and smooth as plastic.

Her toenails had no polish. Her heels were cracked and dirty, like someone had drawn designs there with black pen. Puckered scar—as if from a cigarette burn—near her ankle, pink as gum.

They crossed the canal bridge, the water sliding metallic beneath, and then in the tunnel of orange trees he slipped the toe ring into his pocket and breathed in the scent of white blossoms on the dark branches.

# EL OJO DE AGUA

IT WASN'T DREAMING, because he wasn't in his bed and he wasn't asleep. He was in his chair, before the fire in winter, or before the screen door in summer, and it was always near midnight.

He was sleeping on the levee, during the flood of 1927, the way they had all curled in on themselves to keep warm there on the mud—even the grown men and women, if they were small and flexible. The big woman called Net couldn't sleep like that. She lay on her back, her stomach to the moon, three children tethered to her by strong fingers in their hair or an arm over their bodies. Gustave watched them in the moonlight, like animal babies angling for food.

But there was no food, after three days. They had been working in the cane when the water came like a carpet unrolling before them. They carried only their hoes and lunch buckets.

His mother had been stung by something in the field the day before. A spider? Her ankle was huge and swollen. She stayed in their room to sleep. The water erased all ten houses near Bayou Becasse, farthest from the fields.

They waited for a boat. The water stopped rising about ten feet from the top of the levee. In the daytime, all they could see was the yellow-brown water, dirty and surging up near the people. The water slapped itself in wavelets and sucked on itself in circles. An entire world was under the water.

Far away, near the edge of sight, he saw two roof spires. The church and the school. The rest of the scattered houses of Sarrat and Bayou Becasse were gone. Oak and pecan trees showed only their crowns, branches laid like veins atop the water. Snakes waited in the branches, measuring the distance to the levee.

Gustave heard the voices: "I ain't eat no snake, me. Ain't no Indian. I want some meat but not no snake."

It was not a dream, but he was not awake. He slept in his chair, upright, before the open screen door.

On the levee, he had curled himself so hard against the cold he felt his backbone bend like wet willow. Dogs and cats covered their faces with their tails, but he had nothing. Just a shirt and pants dirty from cane. No lunch. He'd been hoping to share with someone. Two men sat on boxes, keeping watch. He didn't know them. They were from another place.

They were watching for a boat, for soldiers, for someone.

Sometimes a dead pig or cow floated past. The ears so small. The hooves like gray plates.

THE PHONE WAS a black cricket in the kitchen, but by the time he realized it was not a cricket and he'd gotten up from his chair and made his way to the back, the noise stopped. Gustave watched the phone's circular dial. His daughter Glorette always made fun of the phone, when she was young and had gone to the houses of school friends in Rio Seco, away from where they lived in Sarrat, the place he and Enrique had made here in California. Princess phones were pink and gold, she said. Wall phones were like house slippers.

Gustave leaned on the counter near the phone, in case it rang again. It would not be Glorette. His daughter had never called him, not in the five years since her mother died. He couldn't give her anything but money, and she only wanted money to buy drugs. But her son Victor may have called. In the moving every three months from apartment to apartment, just ahead of eviction, and in the way Glorette lived with thieves and fools, now and then Victor was hungry and desperate. Gustave had bought him a cell phone for emergencies.

He opened the lid on the pot of beans he'd made earlier. The beans breathed when he blew on them to see if they were soft. He thought of his mother, standing over the embers of the cook-fire, making cornbread.

Victor used to stay for a week or so with Gustave and his wife back when he was six or seven, when things got bad. Gustave could still drive and he'd stop by the rented house and find the boy sitting in the kitchen with his schoolbooks and paper and a mask like Mardi Gras on his face, but not a smiling mask. Only his eyes moved. His mother had been gone all night. He'd eaten Corn Pops dry in a bowl, the yellow dust clinging to his lips.

Anjolie made corn bread every night. Cush-cush in the morning, the corn mush laced with molasses. And on Saturday, beans and rice. Meat attached to a bone. Rib meat. Chicken backs. Neck bones floating like a puzzle on top of the water. His grandson would put the neck bones into his mouth and frown until Gustave said, "Fish them out with your finger, oui, they just the taste now. The meat cook down."

Victor had called three months before. He had the flu, and his mother hadn't been home in three days. He had tests in school. Gustave found the apartment called The Riviera and brought money and medicine. TheraFlu and Advil. That was what his grandson asked for. In the cupboards there were packets of noodles that looked like clumsy lace, and in the refrigerator there was soda. Gustave said, "Come and stay with me. Eat some meat and oranges. We get you a ride to that school, there."

His grandson lay on a mattress and said, "I'ma graduate in June. I can walk now. I'm cool, Grandpère. Thanks."

Gustave heard voices now through the open kitchen window, someone talking up the road near Enrique's house. The window was open to catch the cool night air. All the houses except Enrique's were three rooms, shotgun style, like Louisiana. The scent of orange blossoms was stronger back here, closer to the trees. When Enrique had brought him here, in the winter of 1957, there were flowers and fruit on the trees at the same time. January. They picked the oranges the next morning and the flowers fell like white stars. Enrique said, "You can have that house, for when you bring Anjolie from Louisiana. When you marry her."

Gustave had eaten a plate of food on the porch that night, the way his own mother had at the end of a hot day when she couldn't stand being inside the two small rooms, one taken up with a stove that radiated heat, one taken up by their beds.

They used to eat their lunch in the cane field, because it was too far to walk home. They had bologna sandwiches on white bread, and his mother put seven drops of Louisiana Gold onto the pink moons of meat between the bread soggy from the heat. She put the tiny bottle back in the pocket of her work dress.

Gustave heated up a tortilla over the burner. Blue crown of flame in the dark. Black spots in a circle on the tortilla.

There were miles of groves—navel and Valencia oranges, lemons and grapefruit—around the city of Rio Seco when Enrique brought him here. The Mexicans had shown him the tortillas. When he first worked the groves, the Mexicans gave him burritos rolled tight like white pipes, hot from having lain on the truck dashboard all morning, baked by the windshield.

He ate the dry soft tortilla, tasting the burned marks. The old gas stove smelled like iron. His mother had sat beside him in the cane the day before she was stung, giving him part of her cornbread softened with cane syrup. Anjolie cried the first time she saw the blue flames and knew she didn't have to gauge firewood for cooking.

Gustave took a sip of rum from the tiny glass on the counter. Then he carried a handful of pistachios and stood by the screen, cracking the nuts, holding the shells in his palm. Enrique's boys were talking with some others, up at Enrique's wide porch.

The pistachios were green and pink and salty. Nothing else tasted like that. Gustave had refused to eat them the first time someone gave him a bag. A man grew them over in the next town.

When Victor came to stay with him for a few days last year, when Glorette was in the hospital with pneumonia, he would poke at the foods on the counter and say, "How you gon live on tortillas and nuts and coffee and beans?"

Gustave would say, "I made eighty, oui? I eat what I want. When you eighty, eat what you want. Cush-cush in the pot for your breakfast."

His grandson would pour sugar and milk on the hot mush and eat silently, his headphones buzzing as if insects were trapped inside his ears. When he was finished, he would say, "I ain't drinkin no coffee."

Gustave would say, "Oranges on the table. Eat one call it juice. Then I take you to that school, there." He threw the pistachio shells into a bowl. He had never seen the boy's father. No one had.

Until he was five, Gustave had known his own father, who was already dead by the time of the 1927 flood, shot in a bar fight in New Iberia. The men said his father had put his hand on a woman's rump and another man shot him.

He tried to imagine what had bitten his mother to make her ankle so swollen and red she couldn't leave her bed that morning, of the water. Bee or wasp—snakebite would have left marks. Spider? All the things in the cane field, hiding in the forest of cane stalks.

His own mother's ankle. The pigs feet. Ham hocks. One ham hock could flavor a huge pot of beans, she said. Salted and dried and shriveled, and then floating swollen and revived on the surface of the simmering water. She'd get every bit of flesh from the cartilage and skin and gristle.

He tried to imagine the buttocks of the woman in the bar. His father's hand on the meat. The bullet in his father's chest. His father had been twenty miles from the bayou, and no one had even known who he was. The body was kept in a morgue. A meat freezer. A man had told his mother two weeks later, but by then he'd been buried. So Gustave had to picture his father's face, frozen in a smile or shout or frown, and his hand, frozen in the shape of rounded meat, and his chest, with a small hole or large.

His own toes and tendons, when he took off the Army-issued boots and lay in the field with the others. His daughter's legs, when they grew long and thin. Her dolls. The hair ornaments and beads and makeup and lotions and nail polish like spilled jewels on the dresser.

The voices floated down the dirt road toward his door. Two of Enrique's boys stood on the wooden steps. "Unc Gustave," one said, the two words flowing into one, the name they had always called him though their father was not his blood brother.

Pig blood on Enrique's hands.

"She's here," the son said. Lafayette, the older one, his forearms marked with white dried plaster. Gustave went out onto the steps.

"Glorette?" he said. There was no one else.

Lafayette lifted his chin. "Glorette. We brought her. She—"

Gustave knew. He breathed the sharp dust raised by their feet. Dry and August. No rain. The dust went inside him.

"Someone found her. Over there by the Launderland."

He closed the old screen door behind him, the hiss of the little pump latch, and they let him go first to see her body.


SHE LAY ON the couch in Enrique's big front room. Enrique's wife, Marie-Claire, was waiting for him. She was smoothing the small hairs like lace plastered down on Glorette's forehead.

His daughter was on her back. Her mouth was open. Her eyes were closed. Her hair was a tangle like black moss on the couch cushion. Her stomach showed ribs under the bra she wore. Her skin was pale as raw pecans. She'd slept in the day and gone out in the night. She smoked the small rocks he'd seen. Like grit taken from a chicken's throat.

No blood, no marks, no cuts or bruises. Except two small black half-moons at her collarbone. Like she'd scratched herself.

Gustave touched her collarbone. The knob of bone where it had healed, after she'd broken it falling from an orange tree. He couldn't touch her hair. When she was fourteen, the flesh of her body had rearranged itself, and her eyes had grown watchful under the fur of eyebrows and eyelashes. Her hair had come out of the braids his wife made every morning, and she had coated her eyelashes with crankcase oil and painted her lips, and disappeared into her room. The fear of her beauty wound its way through his entrails. That was where he'd felt it. Inside the tubes that took food through his body.

The collarbone somehow announced her beauty, and the hollow at the base of her throat.

"Some man come up to her at the store ax again do she want to model," his wife said, back when Glorette was in school. "Say she kind of small, but can he take her picture." She would catch her lip between her teeth and hold it until it looked like a staple mark left there.

His own wife, with skin the color of an old wedding dress hanging in her mother's house, with her black hair braided high on her head in a crown, with a French grandfather from Bayou Becasse. His wife had been hidden in her own mother's house for two years, after Mr. McQuine saw her at the Seven Oaks store. Mr. McQuine had raped three girls by then. He owned Seven Oaks and all the land around it, where they worked the canefields.

That was how all the other women of Sarrat, Louisiana had come to be here, on this land Enrique had bought in California. After the flood, when the cane was planted again and the houses cleaned of water trash and dead animals, and the people had come back to work, they'd had daughters. Six girls. Mr. McQuine had stalked them in the fields and dirt roads and woods. Like a dog who'd tasted chicken blood, Enrique said.

So they sent the girls here, to California. Except Anjolie. Her mother refused to let her go. Her only child. Her father built an armoire with a lock—when Mr. McQuine's car raised dust on the road, her mother would put her inside.

Gustave went back for her, once he had this house.

Mr. McQuine had nearly smothered Claudine with his huge belly, and he'd broken Mary's wrist. Sometimes at night, even though he had never touched Anjolie, and she knew Enrique had killed him, that he'd burned in a car run off the road into a ditch, Anjolie would cry out beside Gustave and say he was crushing her.

That day, he had asked his wife if she were afraid of Glorette's beauty, and she nodded. He had asked her where she felt the fear, and she said inside the bones of her hips, where Glorette had rested so long.

When Glorette left, after the man who fathered Victor disappeared, Gustave had gone inside her bedroom, the first one back from the front. Her Barbies sat on the windowsill, their legs dangling into the air. His wife had bought the dolls for years, saying, "All the girls have them doll. Barbie and all them clothes. Got her own closet. Got 'tite hangers inside, oui."

Now he knelt beside the couch and picked up his daughter's hand. The skin was not soft. It was not hard. It felt smudged. She had broken her wrist, too, years ago, and he felt the healed bump of bone there. He had brought home from Kmart a long piece of plastic and attached a hose so that water ran in a stream. The boys called it slip-and-slide. All these children—all these grown men standing on the porch waiting for him—threw themselves down the blue furrow and screamed. The bones were so small. "Calcium collects at the site of a break," the doctor had said, his eyes avoiding Gustave's blackened hands, thick with citrus oil and dirt and rind from the navels he'd crated all day.

Marie-Claire said in French, "I know you, Gustave. I won't say it."

He nodded. She had been his wife's best friend. Her cousin. She wouldn't say, A blessing Anjolie don't see this.

But it wasn't true. Anjolie had known the whole time, ever since Glorette had not wanted to go to school or walk to Rio Seco with the others. She was too beautiful, and no one would leave her alone.

Enrique stood beside him. He could smell the cigar smoke. Gustave knew Enrique would try to kill whoever had done this. Ever since he fed him meat still smoking and half-raw on the levee, in the dark, Gustave had taken care of Enrique. Then, Enrique had taken care of Gustave.

Now Enrique said, "Let Marie-Claire sit with her," and he took Gustave's arm as if they were married and led him toward the barn.


LAFAYETTE AND REYNALDO had parked their truck under the big syca-more tree near the barn. Enrique and Gustave sat at the wooden table where they worked on engine parts. Gustave picked up a new air filter from the bench. Glorette had put one around her throat when she was small and said it looked like a queen collar she had seen in history class.

"How you bring her?" he asked now.

Lafayette was thirty-seven, two years older than Glorette. He said, "The truck."

"How you find her?"

Lafayette nodded to the third man, the one Gustave didn't recognize. He wasn't from Sarrat.

"I found her in the alley off Palm, Mr. Picard," the man said. "I'm Sidney Chabert. My papa used to work on your refrigerators and washers."

Gustave looked at the man's dark bare chest, his ribs, a name tattooed over his heart. "Who that?"

"My daughter. Sarena."

Gustave said, "Who kill Glorette?"

Sidney squatted before him, forearms on his knees, and said quietly, "Mr. Picard. I knew Glorette way back in school. I saw her around the alley before. You know. I'm sorry." He paused for balance, and said, "I work at the video store, and I was walking home, and she was in the alley. First she was—she was waiting for some dude, looked like, near a shopping cart. Then her friend came by."

"Tall one?" Gustave said. Since his daughter had left home, she had always run with a tall, dark, scar-faced woman. Friends with that one and never the other girls from Sarrat.

"Yeah," Sidney said. "They were talking in the alley. I mean, that woman was talking, and Glorette didn't say nothing. So maybe she was already—you know. When I went back out to the alley, no one was around, and Glorette was in a shopping cart."

"Who put her there?"

Sidney shook his head. "Coulda been her friend. Sisia. But I know who didn't do it. Them drug dealers didn't do it—cause they would just shot her, from a distance. That's how they do. They don't get up close and touch nobody."

Enrique had been listening. He said, "Alfonso work that alley. He got a gun. He run with them." Gustave remembered the boy—Bettina's son.

Sidney went on, "And I don't think some—customer—did it, cause he woulda left a mark. Maybe Sisia. Maybe they had a fight. But the way Glorette looked—I think she smoked too much rock and had a heart attack."

Gustave watched Sidney rise and bend over as if he couldn't breathe himself. "Chabert. From New Orleans?"

Sidney sighed. "You know what? My papa was from New Orleans. But I'm from here. Rio Seco. We're all from here."

Gustave stared at him. Not a boy. A man. It was hard to see that sometimes. "Why you ain't call the police?"

Sidney threw back his head like he was studying the stars. But these young men didn't know the stars. Then he said, "I didn't want them to disrespect her. The way they would talk about her, poke around. They wouldn't care who killed her. So I took her to Lafayette and Reynaldo. They could take her home." He folded his arms and his daughter's tattooed name was gone. "But we could all get arrested. Me for sure. Moving a body. I need to get my ass home now."

"You touch her? Earlier?"

"Mr. Picard," Sidney said, "I always looked at Glorette. I ain't gon lie. Every brotha in Rio Seco looked at her. But I never touched her. I ain't had nothin she wanted."

Then he walked from the barnyard and headed out the narrow gravel road through the groves toward the canal, where Enrique had put a gate all those years ago. The canal bridge was the only way in or out of Sarrat, and the gate was locked. Only people who lived in Sarrat had a key.

Lafayette watched him go. "He gon walk back to Rio Seco," Lafayette said. "Man, that brotha was sprung on Glorette all his life, and he ain't talked to her but three, four times, he told me."

"Sprung?" Gustave said, watching the small figure enter the tunnel of orange trees.

"Serious love," Reynaldo said behind him. "Like a disease."

Gustave drank some of the coffee from Enrique's old silver thermos. *Sprung.* That's what they called his daughter. Sprung for something that looked like nothing more than a pill of old Ajax, dried on the edge of a sink. Something that entered her throat and lungs and brain to make the world look like—like what? What had that smoke done, all those years? He tasted the coffee. Dark, roasted black every morning when Marie-Claire moved the pan over the flames. The same way his wife Anjolie had done, even the week before she died. He had smelled these beans all his life. His first memory—his mother roasting the beans and putting one in her mouth, and Gustave tasting one and nearly choking at the burnt bitterness.

Enrique poured himself a cup and they waited. He could hear Enrique's throat work.

Coffee beans and rice and sugar cane. What they had lived on in Louisiana.

Pig. Pig meat.

Gustave put his head down on his arms like a child, on the smooth oily table. The smell of wood.

The woman named Net. Her body floating down the water with trees and snakes and cows and foam.

Enrique drank the last of the coffee and set his cup down so gently that Gustave heard the tap like a child's finger on the wood. The men waited. Gustave lifted his head and said, "I come right back. I try to call her boy."

He walked unsteadily to his house. He could feel himself leaning to the left. He needed a Swisher Sweet. Then the smoke would gather tears onto his face and hold them until they dried like spiderwebs on his cheeks.

The small cigar made the sounds of tiny coals glistening. Fire. The coyotes in the river bottom laughed their eerie song, so different from the night sounds of Louisiana.

The Barbie dolls sat on the windowsill with their tiny shoes, heels pointing down like needles. He hadn't wanted to live with anyone, to marry anyone, because then there would be a body someday. Enrique had known that. Gustave was forty when he went back to Louisiana to marry Anjolie. She was nineteen then, when he brought her here.

Now Glorette's body lay inside the house. The coyotes laughed again, maybe six or seven of them. What did they smell?

Night was when he'd killed the pig. He could smell the blood. The people left on the levee were starving. Meat had floated past for days, but nobody would touch it. The big woman named Net watched the babies cry and cry until the sound was like a saw rasping in the wood she cut up for a fire, and then the cries faded while their eyes grew bigger and sunk into holes in their skulls.

Skulls didn't surface until months after the water had gone down. The memory was eighty years old, and yet at night he could smell the water, and the sickly sweetness of unwashed bodies and death, and the blood in the smoke near him and Enrique. Enrique's eyes wide and flat and dull.

The soldiers had come. They pointed their rifles at the men and herded them into their boats, told them they were headed to weak points in the levee overlooking Mr. McQuine's plantation fields. They would fill sandbags all day and into the night, and then they could come back for Red Cross beans boiled with some oil and salt. That was what they left for the Negroes. It was marked on the boxes. Everyone knew what the *N* really meant.

The soldiers stood up in the boats like tall herons, one pointing his gun at Gustave's head. "That one ten or so. Worked in the field. He can work now."

The woman named Net pulled Gustave to her, next to her son Enrique. "Seven," she said. "Only seven."

The one man left behind was old, his legs thin and shiny, the skin stretched too tight over his ankle bones. He slept without moving.

The women broke up their chairs and lit the legs on fire under the one huge pot. They waited for the men, who never came back.

The two soldiers who had stayed sat on the far end of the levee, smoking, talking to each other, their guns held loose and slanted. They'd told the women and old man not to touch the pigs, or any of the animals in the water.

Those cows and pigs and horses—Gustave knew whose they were, and so did everyone else. The men had known, before the soldiers took them away. He'd heard them talking up on the levee, with chairs and blankets and children piled around them, waiting for a barge to move them to dry ground because someone had gone past in a small pirogue and said the steamboats took only white people. The men couldn't pull out a cow still alive and bawling; they couldn't shoot a pig from the small bunch that had gathered at the far end of the levee, couldn't do

the boucherie right there and feed all the people because that was stealing from Mr. McQuine or any of the other men who owned every tree
and fence and horse. The soldiers would arrest them even if the animals had swum right out of their fences and would end up in the Gulf
or die on the levee because no grass was left.

But the men were gone, and then the beans had been eaten and the
people were hungry again. The two soldiers looked bored and afraid, but
they ate something from their bags. Then they slept, sitting up, their
white chins like stone in the hard moonlight off the water.

Gustave pulled the smoke deep into his lungs. The soft soft lungs that
filled with smoke, or water, or air, or nothing. The old man died that night.
When they rolled his body into a blanket and left it there near the boxes,
Gustave found a hammer. He lay with it under his arm, and the next night,
he crept down the levee to the place where the pigs had gathered, and with
the hammer, he hit the small mud-covered skull of the one close to him.
The pig was young, the size of a sack of rice, and it jerked and snuffled and
squealed and then looked into his eyes. Black seeds. He hit and hit until
the skull melted into the mud and the snuffling stopped and the other
pigs screamed, but he dragged the small pig behind him into the shelter
of the weeds. He ran back to the levee camp and shook the huge shoulder
of Antoinette.

Her apron had once been white and was now gray and brown and
even red with blood, where Enrique had a nosebleed from crying for
too long. She was not soft. Her shoulder was hard like the pig's ham,
the top of the leg.

Gustave said, "I seen your knife. I got a pig."

Crouched in the weeds beside him, she slit the pig's belly, and the
entrails steamed until she threw them into the swaying water. Oil slicks
washed past like islands of rainbow. Branches and roof shingles and
sometimes a body, floating facedown, brought to the surface by the air
trapped under the shirt, like pillows sewn under the cloth. Only the back
and shoulders and thighs showed. Dress or coat stretched tight.

Gustave watched the ribs. Net wrenched the knife into the side meat.
"Them soldiers come back, they smell smoke. Hurry."

She chopped at the soft flesh and he held up the hams that were not ham yet. Ham was pink and feathery and salty. This meat was slippery, and somehow he could see through the thin parts to the bone.

Net cradled more bloody meat in her apron and headed up the levee to the embers she had never let die since the boat had dropped them there, on the narrow rise of land that looked like a long road. Gustave had tried to walk it once when the soldiers first left, but when he looked back and couldn't see any of the people, Net's tignon like a puff of smoke rising from her head, the old man's white handkerchief laid on his forehead, he stopped. Ahead was nothing, only the levee thin and green, drowned trees on one side, and brown water sliding past near his feet.

He washed his face now, in his kitchen, and leaned over the sink. Then he got out the piece of paper from the top drawer. The ten numbers. He dialed carefully, his finger barely fitting inside the circle, the metal pinching his skin. The cricket trill of ringing. Then a voice. "Hey."

Gustave said, "Hello. Victor. This your grandpère."

Then the voice said, "Gotcha. If you gettin this message, you ain't gettin me. Leave me the digits."


HE WALKED BACK toward Enrique's house. The men were still at the table, waiting for him, their cigarettes red embers in the dark.

Was his grandson sleeping? Hungry? Where was he? In a car? Wearing his headphones? If he woke up and his mother wasn't there, it wouldn't be the first time.

Inside the house, Marie-Claire had tied something around Glorette's jaw. Her mouth was closed now. "No purse? Nothing?" he asked, and Marie-Claire shook her head.

Gustave didn't even know where she lived. No address, no license on his daughter. He looked at her bare toes, her cracked heels. She'd walked enough miles, as if she lived in another time. The men had gathered around Lafayette's truck now. They had to go get her son.

Sidney Chabert might know where he was.

THEY SAW HIM walking along the road that led back into Rio Seco. Dark back gleaming with sweat. Gustave was sitting in the truckbed, on a crate, his back to the cab. He said to Reynaldo, "Where his shirt?"

Reynaldo said, "Back here. He wrapped her up in it, when he was carrying her."

When Lafayette's truck came upon Sidney, he stopped and stared straight ahead, as if at a rabbit. He was afraid they didn't believe his story. He was afraid they were going to kill him. Rio Seco people knew Sarrat was another world. Some of them maybe knew how Enrique and Gustave had gotten here, about the man Enrique had killed in Louisiana, from the stories Sarrat daughters had told to Rio Seco fools who thought the girls were country and pretty and light-skinned and dim-witted.

"Where she live now?" Gustave called hoarsely to Sidney.

"Jacaranda Gardens," Sidney said.

"Show me where," Gustave said. "I want my grandson."

Sidney climbed into the truck bed and Gustave threw him his shirt.

They were silent while the truck moved along the asphalt road toward the city. Only two miles. All the Sarrat children walked to school in Rio Seco along this road, and walked home, for years. Lafayette and Reynaldo had married Sarrat girls, but they lived in the city now. Only a few people were left in the ten bungalows along Gustave's street.

"You ever touch a dead body?" Sidney asked.

Gustave listened to the tires popping over fallen palm fronds. "Oui," he said. "Only one time. I was seven, me, and Enrique was three. Flood of 1927 come. Take my maman body and our house, and I never see her again. We stay on the levee. High ground. About a hundred people, wait for days for a boat. Them soldier come and take the men, say they have to work the crevasse. Where the water run into the farm. They point the gun for the men get in the boat, say, Time to work, nigger."

Sidney was silent.

"No food. We wait for the food, or the boat. One baby die, and then an old man. I touch him. We wrap him in a blanket, and the baby. We can't bury. Water everywhere. They sit right next to us."

Enrique's head leaned against the glass of the cab window. His hair was flattened and gray. His son turned the wheel, and the truck moved onto Palm Avenue, the main street, past the packinghouse where they delivered the citrus, and then into the business district, where markets and dry cleaners and taco places had darkened windows.

Sidney said, "What you all gonna do with Glorette?"

Gustave didn't answer. He wanted to see the alley. Back in Louisiana, they call it *allee*. A lane of oak trees that led to Seven Oaks, the white home with black shutters.

"Tell Lafayette where you find her," he said, and Sidney said Spanish words to Lafayette through the cab window.

"El Ojo de Agua."

"What that say?" Gustave asked.

"The Eye of Water," Sidney said. "I don't know what it means. What they named the taqueria. Must be something from Mexico."

No shopping cart in the alley behind the taco place. The truck idled at the mouth of the dirt lane, the chainlink fence, the closed doors of buildings, the dumpster. Sidney said, "I took the cart to Sundown Liquor because I knew they'd be there."

His daughter's body had floated in the cart, like a metal pirogue canoe, down the dusty alley. His mother's body, floated from her bed to the Gulf. His father's body, buried before anyone knew who he was. His daughter, lying on the couch with Marie-Claire humming beside her, as if she were only napping. His wife Anjolie, dead of a diabetic coma, lying in the cemetery at the edge of the orange groves. She'd never told anyone about her headaches, her dizziness, her fainting.

Sidney had done the right thing. The empty alley—no police would care, and the men who drove around the alleys to look for Glorette would find other women—maybe her friend Sisia. Only that woman, and Victor, would know she was gone.

Enrique said, "No place to die." His eyes were red and muddy when he looked at Gustave. Enrique said to Sidney, "You find her here? You ain't play with us? You ain't touch her?"

Sidney said, "I ain't lying. I found her right there." He pointed to a spot near some weeds, at the fence. "Her son came into the video store last month. Said they didn't even have a TV at his place, but he had to watch some history movie at his friend's house. I asked if he was okay, and he said you gave him a cell in case of emergency."

"I call. Nobody there."

Gustave looked up at the palms, electric in the moonlight. Sidney stared up, too. He said, "You know why I took her? Cause I saw rats running across the phone wires, and I couldn't hang with that. I just took her."

Gustave said, "You did right. You take me to where she live. I tell her boy she call me, and I come and get her, and she die at home. On the couch. She just give out."

Enrique nodded. "Her heart just stop on her." He threw his cigar butt into the dirt. He said, "Then I take care the rest, me."

Gustave knew what he meant.

They would build a coffin for Glorette, and dig the hole in the old cemetery where no one but Sarrat people came. Victor would say goodbye to her. The only church would be their words, the way it had been on the levee. Then Victor would sleep in her room.

Sidney took them down the next street to the apartment building. The stucco walls were gray. The wrought-iron railings were black. The windows were shuttered with old sheets and broken shades. The word *Picard* was written in pen on the mail slot for number sixteen.

Gustave climbed the pebbled stairs slowly. The railing felt rough and pitted, as if someone had cooked on the iron. But he smelled no food here.

The door felt hollow when he knocked. He called softly, "Victor. Victor." But no one answered.

He pushed, and the door gave way. The lock had been broken many times. In the living room, a futon lay in the corner near the heating vent. A glass-topped table and two chairs sat near the window. The Formica counter held nothing but Shasta cola and a plain paper bag. Inside were empty cornhusks streaked with orange grease. Tamales.

The bedroom door was closed. He went inside quietly. What if Victor had a gun?

But his grandson was asleep. His ears were covered with headphones, and his arms were gripped tightly around something on his chest, under the blanket. Sharp corners. Maybe CD cases. A pile of books lay close to his head. The cell phone must be under his pillow, or his back, Gustave thought, and he sat down on the carpet.

A bowl beside him on the floor, a lone dried noodle like a worm trying to crawl up the side. Carpet with strands tangled and dirty like more worms. He would take Victor to his house, and Victor would hate it, and hate the oranges, and the beans. He would want hamburgers, and Gustave would buy them. He wouldn't say what he said last time. "I make my meat in fall, when Lanier bring me some pig for that freezer. We buy a whole pig. Not no piece of pink sponge in some plastic. Enrique and me have to have some good meat."

On the levee, Net had carried the meat to her fire, laid it on a pan there, and when her baby woke, she'd tied the baby to her breast, inside her shirt, to keep her quiet. But the soldiers smelled the smoke. The fat rising in the black. They came with their guns and said, "Where you get that meat? That a knife?" Net went toward them with the knife and they shot her. She fell into the water and went under, and only her broad back showed when she surfaced downstream and floated away.

The other women screamed and screamed and the soldiers pushed at the people surging toward them. They didn't shoot again. Gustave pulled the half-burned meat from the fire and squatted near Enrique. He tore pieces from the ham and pushed them into Enrique's mouth, shielding him from the people. Enrique pulled at his hands, and he saw the blood glistening on his knuckles.

Victor's shoes, under the covers, made lumps like bread loaves. Gustave cupped his palms over his eyebrows, moving the loose skin there back and forth like he always had when he waited, on the levee, in the barracks, in the cane fields.

His grandson slept like the dead.

Seventeen. Never had a job. Half-grown. That was what the soldiers called the boys on the levee. "Take the grown ones. They don't want to come, you get them half-grown niggers. They got small hands but they got two. Shovel take two hands."

He didn't want to frighten the boy. Something like pink seashells lay on the floor near the mattress. Gustave leaned down to touch them. When had he gone to the ocean? No—these were hulls of pistachios. A small bag, like you'd get at the liquor store. He held the shells in his palm. He could hear the engine of Lafayette's truck outside. He could see the palm fronds up close from this second-floor window. Dates like small gold worlds, way too high for anyone to pick.

# NIGHTBIRDS

ENRIQUE WORKED THE irrigation on the Valencia grove until midnight. Gustave got tired around eleven, and Enrique drove him home. Then he took the truck back to the grove to check the gopher traps. 109 yesterday. The gophers were chewing through PVC pipe like it was hollow peppermint stick. In August, the trees would wither in a few days without water.

He stood in the kitchen drinking one last cup of coffee when he heard his son's truck. The tools bouncing loose in the metal bed like always on the gravel road.

He went to the front window. Lafayette was carrying a woman up the lawn.

A thin woman. Her head lolling back like an actress in some movie, but then Lafayette moved his arm up and the head nestled back against his chest. Her hair fell over his arm like a black waterfall.

Glorette.

Enrique saw her only a few times a year, when Gustave had him drive to whatever apartment she'd landed in—each place a dim cave where her son would look up from his bed on the floor. What they called it—some Japanese word. They went if the boy was sick or needed money.

Her hair was always in a twist on top of her head. *Chignon*, the women used to call it back in Louisiana. So high it was a complicated structure. But tonight the hair was loose over Lafayette's arm, swaying against his leg.

Dead.

They came up the slope, Reynaldo just behind. Like they were killers. Her feet in high heels, dangling.


THEY PUT HER on Marie-Claire's couch. Pale green. Enrique never sat on her couch. He was always dirty from the groves. He sat on the porch to drink his coffee, and left his boots in the wooden orange crate she put on the side of the house for him. Then he went straight to the bedroom to change.

Glorette lay with her feet splayed, her mouth open. The first thing he thought—*Marie-Claire come out here, she see a body on that couch.*

"Quo faire?" he said to his sons.

Lafayette held out his hands, palms up, like he didn't know whether he should wash them, like he didn't know how his hands had done that.

Done what?

Reynaldo kept rubbing his thick eyebrows like he always did when he was confused, when he was waiting for his older brother to talk first, to see if there was anything he needed to refute or deny or explain.

"Man, I ain't never touched a dead body before," Lafayette said, quiet.

Reynaldo said, "Me neither," which he didn't need to say, because he did nothing without his brother.

Then Enrique smelled urine. Like when he'd killed the German. His heart felt a hot bloom—a dried plum fattening up in hot water.

He looked down at her face. The most beautiful woman he'd ever seen, even more beautiful than her mother, who'd been famous in Louisiana when they were young. Her mother Anjolie was Marie-Claire's distant cousin. Gustave had gone back to Louisiana to get her, taken her from the house where she'd been locked up in an armoire to protect her until Enrique killed—

Killed the third one.

His sons looked up.

SHE'D BEEN JUST one of the children running in and out of the house, where Marie-Claire always had food. His daughter Fantine, and Glorette—racing the boys in the groves, the soles of their bare feet like pink shrimp. Then Fantine refusing to hoe the weeds out of the irrigation ditches, hiding in trees and behind hedges to read, always reading, grown paler and thin and narrow-eyed and hateful. Glorette's face suddenly shaped like a pansy, with that same symmetrical shape but her cheekbones gleaming. Skin gold as a mothwing. Men following her everywhere.

One day, when he was a boy and he'd been taken to New Orleans to help an old man deliver sacks of oysters, they'd walked out of the restaurant on Royal Street. Djokic, the old man, had told him to wait outside a doorway. Niggers couldn't shop in the French Quarter. But a boy could wait near the window, if he was on an errand with a white man. The sun shone on the glittering stones inside. One made into a dragonfly. Emerald wings, ruby eyes, gold thorax. And a dragonfly lighted on the wooden ledge of the window, facing its twin. Dragonflies were everywhere that spring, hovering while his aunt washed clothes in her yard. But this one didn't move for a long time, waiting for the other, until Djokic came out slamming the door.

Glorette's forehead was darker gold now. Her eyes were closed, her mouth open. She had dust on her elbows.

He felt the hotness and blood moving velvet soft because his brain was already considering the pieces. Place to place like roof corner to low tree branch—the first strand of a spiderweb—random threads at first. The complicated puzzle and planning. The smell was already deepening in the heat.

He lifted up her hand—thin and small as a child, but with long fingers held curved and graceful even in death. Fantine had always been jealous of Glorette's effortless beauty, the way she moved. No blood under her arm, near her ribs. She wore a black bra like runners on TV, and tight pants, and her stomach was unmarked. Her feet dirty. Her high heels worn down—miles of walking—and brown with dust. A pink scar—perfect circle—that must have been a cigarette burn on one ankle. He moved her head just for a moment, to see her neck, but he didn't want to touch her hair. No blood. She hadn't been shot. Not even with a small-caliber bullet. She hadn't been cut.

He looked outside. Gustave's house was just down the gravel road. Gustave was walking slowly up the lawn with Lafayette and Reynaldo. And now he saw a man sitting in the truckbed, head in his hands. Shirtless, dark-skinned, looking away from the house.

If he was the one, he wouldn't be sitting in the truck. Because even though no one knew how many men Enrique had killed, everyone knew about Mr. McQuine.

Glorette worked the alleys. She was probably found there or in some dirty apartment. And now it was the terrible exhilaration of the puzzle that made him wide awake, already seeing the apartment stairs and wrought-iron railings, the place where he would watch. He felt as if he were thirty again. The complicated pieces of tracking, and how he'd find the man, or figure out if it was the young man in the truck.

He turned to see his wife in the doorway. He was ashamed of the quickening inside his chest and throat and behind his eyes. He hadn't even thought of her. Just of Gustave and how his face would look coming into the room, seeing his only child. And he'd forgotten the grandson.

"YOU BRING ME a body? Like we in Louisiana?" she whispered, wrapping her arms around herself like she was cold, even though the heat hadn't broken yet for the night. "That Glorette?"

She moved toward the couch and touched the loose hair on the forehead. "You bring her here?"

Enrique said, "Them two." What he always called his sons. The shorthand of being married.

She bent over the couch, her spine like a rope of tiny boudin sausage showing through the nightdress. She was shaking.

But when Gustave came inside, Enrique couldn't look at his face. The face he had seen more than any other his whole life. Not mother. Not wife. Not children. Only Gustave, since he was four and Gustave seven. Every single day except when Enrique was in Germany, and when he'd first come here to California after the war, alone.

Gustave touched her shoulder, and her forehead. Like he and Marie-Claire were baptizing her. The sweat under his white t-shirt made darker maps at his back. When he raised up, his face was like a mask. Enrique was relieved. They had both learned how to keep their faces that way since they were small, since they were orphelin on the riverbank and they knew the rest of their lives, people would use crying—even the stretched-out mouth of wanting to cry, of considering tears—as weakness. Reason to beat them with a stick.

*'Tite mulee*, Gustave used to whisper to him, in whatever shack or camp they lay, shivering in their clothes. *We just baby mule. Mule don't cry. Mule kick. Or bite.*

HE WENT TO the kitchen to wash his hands.

Two new boxes of cereal on the counter. That meant his grandsons were asleep in the back bedroom. Lafayette's wife always brought two boxes because it was expensive and the boys ate it dry out of bowls, like little dogs. An old man pirate cartoon. Cap'n Crunch.

That damn cartoon his grandson had drawn. The box with the knife and dripping blood.

His granddaughter staring at the man on the TV, saying, "Serial means a row?"

Enrique didn't see the face of the German he'd killed until he turned him over. The helmet covered the face—ice crystals on the eyebrows. But he smelled it, sometimes, the smell of sweat that froze and then melted and froze again. The smell of shit from the woods, and cheese. The German had cheese in his pocket, probably stolen from a farmhouse nearby.

It was the forest outside a village in France. Why couldn't he remember the name? The Germans were as scattered as the Americans after the firefight. For each farmhouse, Enrique didn't know who was watching—for a lone man moving through the trees. So he'd taken days to circle back. The snow piled like soapsuds on the pine branches. Sodden gray under his boots.

Even though Enrique hadn't eaten in almost two days, he didn't touch the cheese. Milky and ripe from the pocket, from the body. White. White. The snow and the cheese and the eyebrows and the teeth, when the lips curled back after the body lay in the snow and he turned it over. The blood on his knife already freezing.

*Would killed me, him. Called me nigger first.* That's what he told Gustave, when he got back. Gustave nodded.

But he knew that wasn't true. Maybe the German would have pretended not to see him. Let him walk past, in the forest, to keep trying to find his company. Maybe the German would never call someone nigger. Maybe he would have thought Enrique was Mexican, like some of the other soldiers thought.

He was the only man Enrique regretted killing, sixty years later.

He heard his wife walk down the hallway. Was she looking for a winding sheet? This was 2000. No one used a winding sheet. You took a body to the mortuary. But he and Gustave would bury Glorette here, on his land. The orange groves, the small chapel, the cemetery between his land and Ramon Archuleta's grove.

His land because he'd killed Atwater. Who said he'd never sell to a nigger.

He had shot at countless others in France, but their bodies lay tangled in the distance, and no one knew whose bullets had killed them, or whose grenades. But four men he had killed with his hands. The only one that sent a wash of guilt along his back—like a hand passed along his shoulderblades—was the German. Because his teeth were so small, his gums so pink and new, and his throat unshaven—Enrique knew he was a boy. He might have scared the boy off, and gone past him.

The other three men had to die. The boy from New Orleans would have shot him. Enrique knew he had a gun inside the shirt. Mr. McQuine would have murdered Marie-Claire or another girl.

Atwater never threatened him. Not his body.

Every time he saw the nights he'd killed them—dark blue of past midnight, and trees black each time—he remembered that there was no other way. Different birds but night sounds.

Now he was seventy-six years old, and he would have to take care of whoever had killed Glorette.

A row. No other way to put it, because he was planning every detail.


"WHAT THE HELL are you drawing?" his daughter-in-law Clarette said to Reynaldo Jr. last week. Enrique was watching TV with his grandsons. He liked to see the backs of the boys' heads, the small skulls through hair. He tried to imagine which one might work the groves.

Reynaldo Jr. said, "This band Green Jelly—they got a song called 'Cereal Killer.' Everybody's drawing what they think it looks like." He'd sketched a long knife through the blue coat of the old man pirate, and red blood dripping from the cereal box.

Danae said, "Like that man—he picked up boys and killed them and threw them on the freeway." On the television was a white man with glasses and fat cheeks like uncooked biscuit.

His daughter-in-law said, "I told you not to listen to that. Serial means in a row. Like a series," she said. "A guy who kills several people in the same way. Nobody evil like that coming all the way out here. Now stop being in grown folks' business."

"But Cap'n Crunch could be a good cereal killer name," the boy said softly. "Like, a dude that crunches the bones after they're dead. That would be funny."

"Don't joke about that," she said. She was in her uniform. She was a guard at the youth prison in Chino. "Not funny." She put a bag with other clothes on the table. She had to work Saturdays, and the kids stayed with Marie-Claire. He always got dirty in the groves, and Marie-Claire made him change.

"Alfonso said when he was in Chino he knew a serial killer."

"He met a lot of people he didn't like."

"Alfonso didn't say he didn't like him. He just said he was a serial killer. He calls Chino, like, the Club. He always says, When I was in the Club…"

"Alfonso's an idiot," Clarette said.

Rey Jr. said, "There's a boy from Ireland in my class. He says eejit instead of idiot."

"You need to close that mouth before you get in trouble."

"I can't chew with my mouth closed."

"You better try."

HE HAD KILLED the first two quickly, without thought. Water and knife. He had planned the other two. Fire and poison.

That was not a row.

Gustave came into the kitchen and said, "She ain't had none to steal. Why they kill her?" He washed his face at the sink and then said, "They taken Chabert son to the barn."

They drove down the dirt road. At the wooden tables near the open barn door, his sons waited. The shirtless man was Sidney Chabert. Same age as Lafayette. His arms gone soft, his navel a deep darker hole in his belly when he squatted in front of Gustave to apologize, to say he hadn't done it. Then he walked away.

Maybe he had. He had the look of love, and years of sadness around his eyebrows. One of those downturn-mouth, down-slant-eyes young men.

Could be him. He'd never had her.

*You act like God before,* his wife had said. Maybe Chabert's son had acted like God.

Enrique had the .45 in the dash drawer. He had the rifle in the truck-bed, in the toolbox.

But they picked Chabert up on the road outside the gate, because Gustave needed him to point out the apartment. He wanted his grandson.

*  *  *

THE ALLEY WAS a narrow dusty lane, almost like a tunnel in places from the pepper trees and bushes. Enrique drove past slowly. This wasn't like hunting McQuine, where he'd known every place the man drank. It wasn't like Atwater, where he had months to think while Atwater taunted him.

No shopping cart. No one walking. Glorette's tall friend—with the ruined face—was nowhere. He'd have to find her, too. Unless whoever had killed Glorette had come back for her.

The apartment was Jacaranda Gardens, but only three palm trees stood dusty in the courtyard. No garden. Gustave brought her son down the apartment stairs. The boy with hair in those little twists. Sticking up from his head like when Lafayette's boy drew pictures of the sun with rays coming out.

Victor. He climbed into the truckbed and sat with his back against the cab. A bag at his feet. Gustave had told him nothing yet. Enrique could tell. Enrique said to him, "You know Sidney?"

"Some dude work at the video store?"

"He ever with your maman?"

Victor frowned. "No. Why? She at the hospital again?"

Gustave said, "She get sick, and he call us. We take her home."

Victor said, "How sick?"

"She bad off. She okay when she leave you tonight?"

"I wasn't home. I was checking out registration for city college."

Enrique said, "Where Alfonso?"

Victor squinted up at him and said, "How would I know?"

Enrique knew he couldn't press the boy, that they needed to get back to Sarrat, but the alley was only two blocks away, and men still walking, and Alfonso had to have seen something. He rode with the boy who sold drugs at the Launderland on the corner.

"He your cousin," Enrique said.

Victor leaned his head back against the cab's window and looked up at the sky. "Sorry, Uncle Enrique. Even in the complicated arcane way we identify family, he's not really my cousin. Alfonso's pops and Clarette are brother and sister, so that makes them related to Lafayette and Reynaldo. But my moms? Nope. And whoever the motherfucker was responsible for my genetics—he definitely isn't hanging around here for Alfonso to identify as someone who might want to buy rock. So let's just go."

He spoke like a professor, someone just visiting with them. Getting a ride to a dinner.

"I'ma find that knucklehead," Reynaldo said, getting in the truckbed.

Victor shrugged and closed his eyes against the streetlight above him.

VICTOR DIDN'T CRY. He didn't kneel down and hug his mother, or touch her. He slid down onto the floor and sat with his back to the couch, her ribs just behind his head, and with his forearms on his knees, rested there with his eyes closed.

Marie-Claire must have washed the smell from Glorette. Somehow Glorette smelled like his wife. She was lying stiff, half on her side, her legs covered with a blanket.

"You hungry?" Marie-Claire said to Victor. He didn't open his eyes or his mouth.

Enrique looked at Victor's shoes, the fat white ladder of the laces. It was as if the boy had sat there a hundred times, while his mother slept oblivious on a couch just behind him, maybe in the morning before school, just after he'd tied his shoes.

He was orphelin now. No mother, never a father. *Mo tou soule*, Enrique wanted to say to him. *You seventeen. I was orphelin when I turn four, me. Gustave seven. We tou soule. No one. Seventeen—that year I kill the first one.*

Victor's hands and arms were unmarked. No cane scars. No fingers missing. But when he turned his wrist, Enrique saw words written in ink all over his palm.

Gustave whispered to Victor, "She okay when we go. She must just get tire. Her heart."

Enrique stood up, and Gustave moved, too. But Victor said without opening his eyes, "Can you just chill for a minute, Grandpère?"

Gustave sat in the wing chair facing the couch. Marie-Claire met Enrique's eyes. The kitchen.

When he stood at the sink to pour one more cup of coffee, she put her hand on his and pushed it to the old white-enameled drainboard. She kept her voice down. "You can't leave her here."

"Can't take her nowhere else. They find her in a basket."

She looked at his face. He glanced out the window at the eight small grove houses he'd cleaned and painted all those years ago, before he went to get her and the other girls. "You think we gon bury her here? Up there by her maman? We can't just bury her. We all get arrested. Probably ten law we break. Move a body, don't call police. You move a car after you hit somebody, they take you in."

He said, "All that done now. The first one move the body, him, and they bring her here. Can't put her back, no." He looked at his wife's bare heels, the edge of dry skin, in her slippers.

He said, "You call police, they find something in the barn. They find Bettina house full of dirt, take her boys away. They find Alfonso, he have a gun, sure."

Marie-Claire washed her hands at the sink and put water on her neck and her shoulders, wetting the edge of her nightdress. Then she said, "You ain't God."

"Non. C'est vrai I ain't God." *And I ain't the other,* he thought. *Mo tou soule.* What he'd chanted to himself when he walked miles through the snow and trees in France. When he walked miles along the Mississippi after he'd pushed the New Orleans man into the river. *Mo tou soule. Me, I'm all alone.*

Except when he was with Gustave. Gustave didn't go to war; Gustave worked the sugarcane and orange groves back in Louisiana. Something with his heart. Something they heard.

"You act like God before," she said. Her nostrils widened, the only sign she was angry. Her lips always curved the same—she didn't even know how much breath she needed when she wanted to fight, but it had always been easy for him to see. "Back then."

59

She meant back when he killed McQuine. She didn't know about the others.

McQuine had raped three girls. He said Marie-Claire was next—told Enrique that, smiling, his fat straining at the white shirt under his tie, scalp pink where his hair was combed back in furrows.

"God say eye for eye. He don't do that, but they say he say it. I ain't God. I do what Gustave want."

She looked down the hallway, and then Gustave came to the kitchen. Marie-Claire poured him a small white cup of coffee. He held it for a moment and then said in French, "All they do, cut her up. He ain't need to see that. His maman cut up."

Enrique waited. He felt in his pocket for the pack of Swisher Sweets, but it was empty.

Gustave drank the rest of the coffee. He said, "I take the boy home."

Back in the front room, Victor's head had sunk onto his knees, and his arms covered the back of his neck. Gustave whispered to him, lifted him up by the elbow, and took him across the street. He would sleep in the bed that used to be his mother's.

Then Marie-Claire knelt beside the couch and said, "You go get Archuleta."

"Ramon?"

She shook her head. "The other one."

"You think Archuleta do this?" Enrique looked at the two tiny half-moon cuts on Glorette's collarbone.

She twisted her neck and frowned up at him, her face lifted like a sunflower planted in the wrong place. "The uncle. The priest."

He nodded. "I get him in the morning."

"You find him now," she said, voice low and vicious. "She die without a blessing. In this heat—we have to make the vigil tomorrow, and bury after that." She faced him, her arms folded in that shelf below her breasts. "You ain't God. Just sometime you think so."

"The priest retire now." Then he said, "Mais oui, you right. I get him."

\* \* \*

HIS SONS HAD gone down to the barn to drink beer and wait. He didn't want them to ride back to Palm Avenue. If they found out one of the men in the alley had killed her, Reynaldo would try and beat him to death right there. If it was over drugs, if one of the Navigator boys was angry with Glorette, Alfonso was the one with the gun. He had to know who'd done it.

They'd turned on the floodlights that hung from the ramada. Beto had helped him build the ramada—wooden structure like a scaffold, and every year a new palm-frond roof. He'd been born up the river, in the Cahuilla village along the bluffs of the river north of here. His father and uncles had dug most of the canals that brought the water to the groves. After they died or were chased off the land and ended up back in the desert, Beto worked day labor in the groves or trimmed trees in the winter. He slept in camps he made along the river, in places he'd known since he was a child.

Under the ramada, they worked on the trucks and tractors in the summer, cleaned guns and sharpened tools on the wooden tables.

The fringes of palm fronds glowed silver. "We need the coffin," Enrique told Lafayette. "Bury tomorrow night."

"What? You crazy?" Reynaldo said. "You can't be buryin people without—"

Lafayette interrupted him. "Without what? Sidney's right, man. You gon call *Law & Order Rio Seco*? Find out how many fools done been with her tonight?"

But Reynaldo didn't back down. He paced in the dirt, his boots lifting dust that hung in the light. "Cause if they find out she died from smokin some bad rock, ain't nobody killed her. Then ain't no need for us to hunt no hardhead."

Enrique said, "She don't put herself in a basket, no."

"Why not?" Reynaldo said. "How you know she ain't tired and climbed in there to take a nap?"

Lafayette shook his head. "In them heels? You can't get in no basket. Sidney said look like somebody put her in there."

"Sidney might be the fool need to get got himself." Reynaldo still pacing.

Enrique reached into his shirt pocket for Swisher Sweets. But he'd smoked the last cigarillo while walking the irrigation. He said, "You measure the wood, and I go get the priest."

"Oh, cause you want to do it yourself, right?" Lafayette fixed him with a stare like his mother's.

"Your maman tell me get the priest."

"That's all—just bury her, and it's all cool. Nothin else."

"Can't bury with no coffin. You and Reynaldo know how to cut the wood, make it nice. You work on all them house."

"Build a damn coffin in the barn," Reynaldo grumbled. "Like *Twilight Zone*."

But then Lafayette said, "You remember we watched that thing on TV where they were up in the mountains, and they just put the body up on a shelf? Vultures and shit, man. And the Indians used to leave bodies up in trees, cause the ground was frozen. They couldn't bury nobody til it thawed."

Reynaldo said, "Ain't frozen here. So damn hot and dry the ground like a brick. You can't dig no hole tomorrow."

Enrique said without thinking, "I done it before."

Reynaldo cocked his head.

Enrique threw the empty cigar packet into the barrel by the door. "Bury a dog, me, before you was born. Up on that hill. In August."

"A dog."

"Oui. A dog."

He'd buried Atwater in August. Near the stone houses.

Lafayette looked at his father. "You ain't never let us have a dog. Cause of coyotes." He ran his tongue over his teeth and sat at the wooden table. "You tryin to find out who did it. And we up here with the body."

"You bring her here," Enrique said to his son.

Lafayette shook his head. "Bettina was right. You act like this a kingdom."

*Act like he a king and this his damn kingdom,* she shouted when Enrique told her she had to move out of her grove house. *Ain't no fuckin king.*

Lafayette stared right into Enrique's eyes. Near forty. His cheeks heavier than Enrique's would ever be, because he ate meat all the time. Chicken and pig. Hamburgers after his football games, when he was young. Meat and football and beer. His arms still muscled, twice the size of his father's. "What if the cops show up out here?"

Enrique kept his voice the same as always. He felt like he was talk-ing to Beto, all those years ago. A body. "Who tell where we put her? She need to be bury up there by her maman. Police don't care. They call her—"

She was a whore. They would say a different word. They wouldn't know Fantine had confessed to Marie-Claire one night that Glorette had fallen in love, and the love was like pure rum lit up—purple flames when you threw it into a campfire down by the river. Marie-Claire had told him in the dark of their bedroom, "Fantine say she never feel like that. She cry and cry, they been drinkin down there with them boy, and no one ever love her like that. Cause Glorette look like she do. And this musician— play the flute and the drum—he a grown man. Twenty-two. He done left her behind. And Glorette havin a baby."

"I guess you right," Reynaldo said, finally. He walked over to the far end of the barn, past the old harrows and a few smudge pots. Wood was stacked on shelves against the wall. Douglas fir and pine, from when they'd had to saw boards to replace the wood floors in two of the grove houses and lay a new floor for Marie-Claire's kitchen ten years ago.

Reynaldo turned and said, "No human involved. I heard some cops say it. We were at Sundown and they talked about some Mexican guy got run over. No papers. They called it NHI. No big deal."


LA REINA AVENUE ran along Archuleta's grove, then his, and then crossed the arroyo and headed into the city. The only way to get out to his place. A thousand times he'd driven this road.

He turned onto Palm Avenue, the four-lane that cut through Rio Seco, and worked his way back toward the alley. Two Mexican women sat hunched at a bus stop and stood when they saw the truck. Their hair was dyed the dark red of pomegranate husk, and one was missing teeth on the left side. They wore sports bras, like Glorette, and tiny skirts.

He drove very slowly past the Launderland. The blue Navigator was parked in one of the five spaces before the front door. A Mexican woman carried out two baskets of laundry—clean and folded, one piled atop the other like a tower that reached above her face. She put them in the back seat of a little Corolla and drove away.

When he circled around again, Jazen was standing, arms folded, leaning agains the door, staring at Enrique stone-faced. He was going to fat, his huge white t-shirt with a dark shadow at the waist where his belly touched the cloth; he had always been loud, bully voice constant when Enrique saw him with Alfonso at the liquor store or anywhere else, the kind of boy who never worried his loudness would scare away his food or bring someone to where he hid. Because he always had Alfonso to watch, from the passenger seat.

But not now. Jazen was alone. He kept his eyes cool, chin high, and Enrique knew he must have called for a replacement. Alfonso was hiding somewhere. After a few more minutes, a slight dark boy, maybe sixteen, slid out from the other side of the parking lot and got into the Navigator. Jazen tilted his head at Enrique, and they drove away.

He didn't follow them. Jazen wouldn't have killed Glorette—she bought drugs from him. Alfonso wouldn't have shot his cousin. But he must be hiding because he knew who'd touched her.

The women probably walked the same route every night, but who knew where the men took them if they got into a car. He could have killed her in a car and then put her in the shopping cart. The alley was still empty. The man could be cruising around, still looking for another one, or wondering where the body went.

His watch said 1:16. Archuleta.

There were three cars in the parking lot at Sundown Liquor. Two old Japanese cars—Corolla and a Honda—with rough-looking men in their fifties drinking paper-bag beer. They were talking to each other out the open windows. They both glanced up at him and then went back to saying something about the Raiders. The other vehicle was a brown van parked in the far corner, with a woman sitting in the passenger seat, looking out the window so he could see only the back of her head. She wore a red scarf with tails hanging soft on her wide square neck.

Archuleta sat in his special chair at the counter. He'd bought Sundown Liquor twenty years ago; he lost his left leg to diabetes about ten years ago, and the stump ended halfway up a thigh massive as sewer pipe. He was about fifty now, with his belly and chest huge behind the Cuban-style white shirt, his beard going gray. Enrique knew he had a shotgun under the counter.

"You out late," he said to Enrique. But his eyes were on the man over at the cold cases.

"Water all them tree," Enrique said, knowing Archuleta knew he was lying. "See I'm out them cigar."

Archuleta reached into the case before him and got out a pack of Swisher Sweets. He glanced at the other man again, and Enrique moved his own eyes. Dark skin, square black goatee like a new paintbrush on his chin, and slanted eyes. He brought two cold bottles of malt liquor to the counter and lifted his chin at Enrique. "You done, Pops?"

Archuleta swept the cigars to the side and rang up the bottles. He didn't speak. The man gave him a twenty, and Archuleta put the change on the scarred black Formica counter. "Hot like fuckin Vegas out here," the man said, holding a bottle in each hand like bowling pins. "But no lights and no goddamn money."

Archuleta said, "Three hour drive get you back to Vegas."

The man said, "What, you don't want my money? Come on, now. This New York money."

"California sweat on it now," Archuleta said, and rang up the cigars for Enrique.

The woman appeared just outside the glass door. The headscarf, her arms folded. The man held both bottles up and she snatched the door open. "We goin back to Vegas tonight or next year? Tired a this country-ass place. Country-ass bitches. I rather head back to New York."

The man said, "You don't pick the place." He went sideways out the door and it closed. Her mouth moved with no sound and he prodded her in the back with the butt of one bottle, toward the van.

Archuleta said, "You're never here this late."

Lafayette and Reynaldo usually got him the cigars before they came home. He looked out into the parking lot, where the van was pulling out fast, tires slipping for a second on the sand tracked in from the alley. His sons usually sat under the pepper tree at the side of the lot, toward the back. The battered folding chairs were empty.

"Sidney Chabert come in here tonight?" Enrique took the penny nail from his pocket and slit the plastic on the Swisher Sweets.

Archuleta frowned and said, "You makin a joke?"

"Why?"

"He don't like to come in if I'm workin. Cause of the leg."

"What?" Enrique put the cigarillo in his mouth, tasted the paper.

"He burnt up my leg. Workin at the hospital. They all give him a hard time about it. But he came in here about half an hour ago and bought a Corona. Looked me in the eye and told me get him a lime out the case."

So Chabert was feeling good. Enrique nodded. "Your uncle retire now. The priest."

Archuleta nodded. "Him and my dad go fishing down at Ensenada once a month."

"Where he live?"

Archuleta raised his brows. "My uncle? In one of those senior apartments where they clean and cook. But he always wants my mom to bring him enchiladas and shrimp. He's eighty-four."

Enrique looked out the window again, at the entrance to the alley. "You got his address?"

"What the hell, Mr. Antoine? He's asleep. Late to be knockin on an old man's door."

"You call him in the morning? Tell him come to Sarrat soon as he can."

"Everyone okay?"

"My wife. She need to see him. She got some with her heart."

Archuleta wrote something on a piece of paper. Blue letters. He handed it to Enrique.

"I ain't got my glasses."

Archuleta shrugged and said, "I'll call him in the morning."

Enrique said, "You see Alfonso?"

Archuleta shook his head. "Happy not to see those little fools," he said. Suddenly Enrique remembered his grandson saying *eejit*. The way the Irish boy said idiot. "Happy when they don't play that music in the parking lot for an hour." He bit his big pink lips and said, "You know what? The drums hurt my leg. So damn loud it bumps up against my bone and hurts." He patted his thigh.

THE NARROW STREETS were crowded with apartment buildings where she'd lived, each one set longways like boxcars with black railings along the sides. He parked across the street from this last one and smoked one cigarillo. No one came in or out of the cement courtyard—the windows were all closed tight and the swamp coolers humming hard. But someone lit a cigarette, and then another. Two embers like animal eyes. Spaced on the balcony.

It was nearly 2 am. He couldn't knock on the door of a senior retirement complex now. Marie-Claire knew that.

What did she want?

He moved the truck to the space under a pepper tree near the mouth of the alley. The brown van drove slowly down the dirt path, the top nearly scraping the low-hanging branches of the wild tobacco tree that arched over the fence. The woman's arm hung out the window. But she was arguing with the driver—her face turned away.

The dust twisted and settled, and he lit one more cigarillo. Then Enrique heard the rattle of a shopping cart. Two blocks away? The wheels grated across asphalt, and then the rattle changed in the dirt of the alley.

Sidney. He pushed the cart toward the wild tobacco tree and stood there. Shoulders shaking. Crying. Then he scraped leaves and dirt into a pile near the fence. Trying to cover something near the wild tobacco tree.

Beto had told him the first night, "We can smoke this." The leaves bitter and harsh.

Enrique pulled the .45 from the dash drawer. He aimed it out the open window.

Drive-by. That's what Lafayette called it. Alfonso and Jazen riding past shooting at people they didn't even have to look in the eye.

He got out and put the .45 in the waistband of his workpants. He crossed the street. Sidney had one hand on the cart handle and one holding the balled-up shirt like a blue cabbage.

"That the cart?"

Sidney's face was smeared with wet. One drop on his bare chest. "Yeah. I left it behind the Sundown dumpster but that seemed wrong. Nowhere to put it. I can't leave it here because it probably has my DNA or something." He held up the shirt. "And this, too. I put it on a dead person." He looked up at the sky like he was trying to hold in the water from his eyes.

"What you bury?"

"Vomit."

Enrique looked at the pile of dirt. "Why you sick?"

"Cause she was dead!"

"You sick cause you kill her." Enrique saw a glitter on the last knuckle of the smallest finger of Sidney's left hand. A tiny flower ring. Glorette's. "You the one."

Sidney threw the shirt in the cart. "You know what? Just fuckin pop me! Yeah. Go head. My life ain't worth shit right now anyway. Insurance for my kid if you pop me."

"How you know I got a gun?"

"What—you gonna strangle me? Shit." He threw out his arms so his chest gleamed. "Go head. Cap me. Pop me. Whatever."

Enrique felt the 45 handle hard against his skin. He couldn't have her so he killed her. Crying. The one burnt them bodies in the hospital.

Sidney walked toward him. "Do it."

Enrique turned away from the eyes blurred and huge with tears. The name in green letters on his chest. A daughter. Sidney wasn't going anywhere. He must not have a car. The shopping cart glinted in the streetlight. He had to live close by.

Maybe he'd feel so guilty he'd go home and kill himself. Then Enrique wouldn't have to do it.

When he turned, a pepper branch stroked his face like hair and he flung it out of the way. He got back into the cab without looking to see where Sidney went, or whether he stayed there by the cart.


EVERY TIME HE left the Westside, and the city behind, the freeway underpasses and exhaust and trash in the vacant lots, every time he steered the truck onto La Reina Road, he paused to smell the water.

The scent of warm silver running down the canal. His water and Archuleta's.

He drove slowly through the Washington navels through his gate. His daughter-in-law's car parked in the yard now. He unscrewed the hose and lay it silently in the truckbed. He didn't want to see his wife, or Glorette, or anyone else.

He needed to look for Alfonso at the box houses. And there would be an extra hose at the shed. Enrique had to soak the ground at the cemetery. It had been over a hundred for ten days. It would be 112 tomorrow.

The brilliant white sheets wrapped around her body. The two dirty flowered sheets he and Beto had wound around Atwater, once he was dead. Before they buried him and built the rock-walled shed in a square above his body and then poured a cement floor.

Enrique had kept tools and spare engine parts and orange crates there for years, just beside the stone houses where the Italians used to make boxes with the labels of La Reina, a beautiful olive-skinned woman with a crown of black braids, holding an orange in her hand as if it were that round thing a queen held when she sat on her throne.

It was where Bettina had been living for the past six months, ever since Enrique told her she had to move from the house next door to Gustave. She kept trash in the yard, and Enrique had seen raccoons, ants, and two coyotes in her yard. Her house was filthy, her boys sleeping all day and not going to school, and truant officers or social workers would come onto his place. Just like they had in the seventies when her mother

Claudine started drinking. He couldn't have police come down that gravel road again. Never.

Bettina had shouted, "Like this a fuckin kingdom and you the king."

The three boxmakers' houses had been built back in 1900, at the eastern edge of the navel acreage. He parked in the clearing. On the cement slab of the open shed, someone had parked a white golf cart with the name Webster painted on the side.

It was 3 am now, and the blue-green light of the TV filled the small window like swaying ocean water. One trashcan by the front door had a white plastic bag spilling out chicken bones scattered by animals, and the other was full of crushed beer cans. Her two young boys recycled—they brought him the cans, and he gave them ten or fifteen dollars, because she never bought them shoes.

He banged on the door. He could see her sleeping on the couch. She rose slowly, her shoulders huge and pink as hams in the black tank top. "What?" she said, her voice thick.

"Alfonso here?" he said.

"No. I ain't seen him for two, three days. What he do?"

"That for you to know," Enrique said, peering past her. No man on the couch with her. Only one other room in the house, where the boys slept. "You the maman."

"He grown," she said, half-closing the door.

He put his hand against it and pushed. "You golf now?"

She peered out at the golf cart on the cement slab. "I ain't seen that, neither." She shrugged. "Maybe Alfonso hang out with Tiger Woods."

He let her close the door. He walked over to the shed. The faucet dry.

The four walls built from hundreds of stones Enrique and Beto had pulled from alongside the Santa Ana River for nearly a year. They had piled up the stones in the eucalyptus windbreak while they decided how to kill Atwater.

He uncoiled the dusty black hose. Bettina never watered anything. He and Beto had walked back and forth from the river to the trees, and then, when the body was wrapped in two sheets—that's all Atwater deserved, two old sheets with faded flowers—they had to soak the ground. It was August back then, too. August 8, 1959. No hose. Just them filling buckets of water from the irrigation pumps and walking back and forth to pour it slowly into the shallow hole they'd scratched. Wet the soil and dig some more, all night.

Beto was Indian. He'd been born up the river, in the Cahuilla village along the bluffs of the river north of here. His father and uncles had dug most of the canals that brought the water to the groves. After they died or were chased off the land and ended up back in the desert, Beto worked day labor in the groves or sharpened tools in the late summer. He slept in camps he made along the river, in places he'd known since he was a child.

After they poured this cement slab, Beto left for a year. When he came back, it was different. He said, "You know he was wrong, but you're wrong, too."

Enrique bent to look inside the golf cart. It was parked over Atwater's body, which would be bones now, five feet down. In the ignition was a tiny key.

THE CEMETERY AND old adobe chapel were up on the rise between his grove and Archuleta's. Enrique took the coiled hoses from the truckbed and attached them to the one at the faucet near the chapel. Back when the land was divided and the trees planted, the chapel was built and blessed by Archuletas, the only ones who lived along the river until Northcutt.

But no one had come for a Mass here since Anjolie died five years ago. Then the last priest retired, and Archuleta's uncle had been sent to tell them he could visit the chapel and cemetery only if they requested at the diocese, because there weren't enough priests to go around.

"No young men want to give up everything," Father Archuleta said, cheerfully, his round brown face smooth as a loquat seed, his soft hands like grubs when he took Enrique's fingers in his. "Not anymore."

When the four hoses were attached, he chose the rectangle of earth five feet from Anjolie's grave. The headstone read *Anjolie Marie Picard. Beloved Wife & Mother.*

Enrique remembered her hiding in the wooden armoire from Mr. McQuine.

71

He laid the trickle of water in the center of where they would bury Glorette. The drops slid out and remained whole on the hard ground for long moments. Like mercury. Then they disappeared. The drip had to be perfect or the water would run away.

All those years in Louisiana, on the oyster boats, hauling in the load scraped up from the bottom with the tongs, sorting through with the cudgel and cracking the oysters apart, he had to keep throwing water from the deck.

When he worked the canefields for Mr. McQuine, storms filled every ditch. He and Gustave had to open gates to Bayou Sarrat to keep the young cane from drowning.

But here—he paid for the water, moved it around carefully like molten money, and even in winter, the rain was hardly ever enough.

He needed picks and shovels.

THE TOOLSHED WAS in the eucalyptus windbreak near the river. A narrow dirt road ran from the chapel to the acreage along the Santa Ana River. A mockingbird called from the trees, just like years ago. There was always one male here, and one in the pecan trees behind Gustave's house. They always started after midnight.

Back when he and Beto were digging, two mockingbirds fought over their territory by singing, each song more elaborate and frenzied than the next. When he stopped to rest, his hands bloody from carrying the rocks, Enrique could hear the patterns in the songs. The same sounds over and over.

AFTER THEY LET him out, when the war was over, he'd walked from Camp Anza to the river, and then spent his two leave days studying the orange groves that grew on the east side. The other soldiers had gone to Los Angeles. He'd told them to drop him off at the edge of Rio Seco.

The Santa Ana was so shallow and clear that he waded across it, kept on through the sandy earth past the river, the willows that smelled medicinal, and came to the eucalyptus windbreak all along the citrus. The oranges were bigger than the satsumas he'd worked in Louisiana. There was no fence. He wandered, then slept in a camp by a hollow downed cottonwood.

Beto came in the morning, holding a knife by his leg. Enrique put up his hands.

They talked all day, in the heat. Beto worked during harvest in Northcutt's groves. When Northcutt hired Enrique, he commented on his name, asked if he was born in Mexico, and Enrique shook his head. "America," he said.

He learned to eat burritos for breakfast with the other grove workers in the small shotgun houses. After five years, Northcutt decided to retire back in Massachusetts, and he hired Atwater, who'd come to him for a job after they fought together in Italy. Atwater would manage the place until he could sell it.

Atwater emptied the grove houses and said he had to clean out the Mexican dirt.

"The barn. You boys can sleep there til I decide what to do with this place. I might paint them grove houses and call some people I know in El Dorado. Arkansas got good workers. Not like Mexicans. And niggers—not so many niggers here. That's why I like it. I think I'm gonna stay here so I ain't gotta see so many niggers. We got pine lumber in El Dorado. I like these here trees you ain't gotta fell."

It was winter. Every night Atwater sat up on the porch of Northcutt's white house and drank beer. He'd call Beto and Enrique up to work on his truck, and words spooled out of his mouth with steam.

"Yeah, I'd sell to a Mexican before I'd sell to a nigger. Maybe the right Mexican. Cause a Mexican, maybe he used to live here before all them wars. Least he got some kinda claim on the place even if he's so lazy he'd barely grow enough oranges to feed all his relatives. But that's better than a nigger. A nigger got no claim at all. Shoulda sent ever last one of them back to Africa soon's it was done. They got no claim here. Rather run a place into the ground than work it. Seen it happen over and over in Arkansas—let a nigger work a place and they run it down so nobody ever want to live there again. Wouldn't be enough to clean it. Have to burn the damn house down."

He threw another beer can into the barrel he kept off the porch.

"Beto, you claim you're a Indian. Then you wouldn't want no place like this, right? Cause a Indian like to move around. Go from pow-wow to pow-wow."

In the riverbed, Beto had shown Enrique the straight stems of arrow-root where his father had taught him to make arrow shafts. Wild tobacco. Gourd for making soap. Jimsonweed—that made men crazy.

"We could get him to drink it—make him see visions and maybe knock him out, but he might shoot us. He got that 45. He might think we're ghosts."

IT WAS 4 am. For the first time in seventy-two years—since the moments after the soldiers shot his mother and Gustave caught him by the face, fingers hooked behind Enrique's ears, and pulled him down to hide—he didn't want to sit with Gustave.

His mother's body floating down the swollen Mississippi River, her back to the sky, her blouse rising with air inside like a blister. The baby tucked inside her front, drowning underneath her.

She was buried nowhere. She could have ended on a snag in the river's edge, with all the wood and broken houses and other dead animals—horses and cows and pigs. He hadn't been able to think of that for years. Not until he was in a forest in France, sitting next to the body of the German, which would freeze and then disappear under snow. How quickly would the German rot in spring before someone found him?

Had his mother decomposed with the other animals, until their flesh was soft enough to be eaten by the fish and birds?

Had she and the baby floated down the center of the river for miles, all the way to the Gulf of Mexico, and sunk to the bottom where pirates and treasure lay? The treasure and bones his aunt told him about, from Lafitte?

The birds were finished. Enrique smelled the damp earth from where he'd irrigated earlier. *Not a love song*, his own daughter Fantine had told Glorette, when they were small, sitting in this truck cab with him one night when they'd come out to get tools. *He's not telling the other birds he loves them. He's telling them this is his territory and they better not come in. That's what my science teacher said. You should have come to class.*

*I couldn't,* Glorette said softly. *I couldn't go in there.* And his daughter cocked her head and frowned at Glorette.

*What does that mean? You couldn't? You couldn't walk into class and sit next to me like you were supposed to? Because you think you're too fine?*

Glorette got out of the truck then, in the dark, and ran into the trees. He knew immediately that someone was bothering Glorette in the science class.

When Fantine said she was going away to the east for college, and Marie-Claire cried, Fantine said, *Resistance is futile, maman.* Enrique could barely understand what his own daughter said half the time, but she said that clearly, and explained it, and it was close enough to French that Enrique knew it meant there was no need to fight.

The eucalyptus trunks glowed in the faint moonlight. They shed bark all year, smooth and white. The trees from Australia. Not here. This was his forest now. He came here alone to sleep in the truck, think about the cypress swamp back in Louisiana, the plash of water when animals leapt from the trees into the bayou ahead of his boat.

The frozen forest in France, where he'd walked for five days trying to find his company. Each step on the ice like a gunshot, and he was afraid the German snipers would hear him. Crawling instead so it would be quieter. The branches heavy with snow that muted all sound. The birds gone away after the firefight? Dead from the cold? Flown to Louisiana like all the birds he'd shot in the ricefields and roasted over winter fires with Gustave?

He put his head back on the seat. The air was still warm—maybe 70—and the wind that never stopped here in California moved the leaves like he was underwater.

Animal feet in the dried foxtails. He didn't want to see his wife's face. He'd left her a body. He slept sitting up here. Like his mother's aunt said the slave woman who was his ancestor slept—sitting up in a chair, near the fire, watching to make sure no one stole her daughter in the night.

Glorette was dead. Fantine would be here in the morning.

Fantine had yelled at him once when she was in high school, thought she was the smartest human ever born, and he made her hoe the milk-weed from the irrigation furrows to keep them clear. "This is a fiefdom! We're all peasants and serfs and you're some lord, right?"

Enrique said, "Me—just a farmer. Don't nobody fief, oui?"


THE HEAT WOKE him, sun burning the side of his face and the sound of saws snarling from the barn.

But he'd heard the snapping of dry bark—someone was walking in the eucalyptus grove toward the truck. He got out the .45. Never. He'd killed them all by hand. His head was filled with syrupy light and heat. The smell of menthol all around.

Someone coming. The same path Beto had always come, up from the river. Beto walking toward him every day back then, after he'd gone to wash in the river he'd known as a child. Beto telling him they could have just made Atwater sick with the oleander branches, trimmed to skewers threaded through two rabbits. Roasted them in a fire here, brought the meat to Atwater, and he ate it for two days. Jimsonweed boiled into a liquid added to his beer.

Beto wanted him sick. A joke. But Enrique wanted him dead, after he signed over the land.

Two scorpions he'd caught under a rock. Kept in a jelly jar.

They like to get down in the foot of the bed where it's warm. That's what you said. *We ain't had no scorpion in Louisiana. Have moccasin snake. But you can see snake come. You can't see this when you get in the sheets.*

The sound approached so slowly. Hesitant. A ghost. A hunter.

The shade was swarming with heat. Near eleven.

How the hell had he slept that long? Marie-Claire must think he'd gone out to find Archuleta and got killed.

He was an old man.

He pointed the gun toward the sound. Wheels snapping the bark.

Alfonso sitting in the golf cart. Grinning young fool. Tattoos on his collarbone and his skull. He'd killed Glorette. He worked for the other boy. His job was to ride. He'd killed Glorette because the fat boy had told him to.

"I ain't wakin up like that no more, Uncle Enrique. I left my gun in JZ's ride. I ain't up for that now. I'm tired. I'm ready to be out. So if you gon get me, go on. Then you have another body. However many you got."

His grandmother, Claudine—the first one raped by Mr. McQuine. She must have told him what Enrique did.

The boy wasn't afraid. He wasn't. His eyes were light green as mulberry leaves. Suddenly the clearing was filled with color. Eucalyptus trunks gleaming fresh new skin, like washed bone. The heat bore down on the leaves, and the reflection of the golf-cart taillights was like cherry Kool-Aid splashed across them. His own daughter said that was Glorette's favorite— the dark red drink she poured into the old jam jars.

Alfonso kept his hand on the gearshift of the cart. "I went by the barn. Lafayette puttin a cross on the coffin. He nailed decorations on the cross. Like metal flowers. Reynaldo went up there start on the—"

He paused. "Start diggin. So you ain't gotta do it."

The sound of the saw—growling through the trees—had stopped. A pickaxe in the barn?

"Gustave waitin for you. He sittin on the porch. He look bad. Axed me did you show up by Glorette's place last night and get hurt."

Enrique swallowed the little saliva left in his mouth. His teeth dry and huge behind his lips.

"And that old man up there at the house. The priest."

"He bless the body?"

"I seen his car parked at your yard. You can't miss that old Buick Regal. I ain't went inside. I see Glorette almost every night. I don't want to see her now. Like that."

Enrique slid the gun off the windowframe. The dash drawer hung open like a jaw. He put the gun inside. He found the bandanna and wiped his face. "How she get like that?"

Alfonso didn't answer. Then he said, "You know, I slept out here a couple times. In the trees."

"You?"

Alfonso nodded. "I seen you come out here sometimes. I used to sit out here at night. When I first got out the club. It was so much damn noise all the time in there. And my moms don't never shut up. Jazen always got the sounds on in the Navigator. So I came out here just to chill. I had me a Mexican blanket I got at the swap meet. I used to sleep right there."

"I find that blanket, me. I throw it away."

"Yeah. You thought some homeless dude broke in, huh? But I was out here about two weeks before you saw it. You used to park right here and chill, too. I heard you snorin."

There was no need to pretend he'd been watching the fences, like he used to, when homeless men might steal oranges to sell on the street.

"Make you tired, huh?"

"What?"

"They always think you the one."

"The one."

"The one gotta take care the problem."

Enrique looked into the sickle-shaped leaves. "No problem out here."

"No problem back there neither."

"What you mean. Back there?"

"In the alley. What happened in the alley. Ain't no need to take care of it. Problem gone." Alfonso got out of the cart and picked up a few rocks in the dried wild oats.

When his grandsons sat at the kitchen table doing their math homework they said, "Problem solved!"

"Problem solve?" Enrique said, looking at the boy's tattooed skull. Green letters.

Alfonso was quiet. "No." He threw a rock over the fence into the riverbed. He'd been able to throw a football or baseball farther than anyone at the high school. Then he started riding with that boy near the Launderland.

"Problem took off. Ain't solved for nobody else," he said. "But I ain't solved it, if that's what you mean. I ain't you."

What was he supposed to say? Only one and not four? Alfonso had shot someone in the alley, when he got sent to prison. Shot him in the leg.

"I ain't killed nobody close up and shit," Alfonso said softly. "I liked to shoot them rats when Lafayette showed me. But I ain't up for aimin at nobody like I had to. And I ain't up for touchin nobody neither."

Claudine must have told Bettina, or Alfonso, that he'd bashed in McQuine's skull with the piece of wood before he lit the car on fire. That he'd looked into McQuine's face.

Enrique found the packet of Swisher Sweets on the seat beside him. He waited to hear if there was more. If he knew more.

"What you think you up for?" he said.

Alfonso threw another rock. Then he walked back to the cart and leaned against it. "I just wanted to play football. I just wanted to hit people and have em get up and then I hit em again. All day. I like to hit em in the chest and knock em all the way back. I like to hit em sideways. But I needed that cash. If my moms wasn't so crazy—"

Enrique got out of the truck, his legs stiff. The eucalyptus seed pods were brown buttons underfoot. He touched the roof of the cart.

"They got ghost, man. The problems. You ain't gotta do nothin."

"Ghost."

"They gone."

"Mean you make em ghost."

Alfonso shook his head. "I ain't you."

"How you know they gone?"

"I seen em go."

Then he said, "I got this for you." He nodded at the cart. "Rich white kid gave it to me. He owed somebody. His dad got it for the mail. Their house is up in Hillcrest, man, so high up the fuckin driveway is half a mile. Webster used to ride the cart down the hill for the mail."

He patted the steering wheel. "So you can ride down here real quiet and don't have to raise dust or use up much gas. If you just checkin shit out. By yourself. Or if you just forgot one little thing—like a shovel or something. You ain't gotta take the truck. You and Gustave, man. You can style."

Then he turned and walked into the trees, the back of his head shining in the light, the stubble of his hair glistening with sweat, and underneath the letters Enrique couldn't read.

# ALFONSO

IF HE HADN'T had to pee before midnight, by the end of the hottest damn week in August, he wouldn't have seen the woman who called herself Fly down the alley yelling at Sisia and Glorette.

A rat ran across the phone wire above his head just when he stepped behind the dumpster at the back doorway of Los Tres Cochinitos. He ducked, but the rat leapt into the branches of the tree across the alley, and he could smell the rotting fruit on the ground in someone's back yard. Nectarines. Damn—the rat was leaving Los Tres for dessert.

When he first started with Jazen, he had to figure out this part of the Westside. Block after block of apartment buildings between downtown and the freeway to LA. Then the long strip of business along Palm Avenue, which ran for ten miles through Rio Seco. But this alley was like a long dirt road with its own traffic. Old wooden houses on one side, with mostly Mexican families now, fruit trees like the nectarine that leaned over the fences. On the other side, all the back doors—video store, nail salon, El Ojo where two women made the best tamales, and Los Tres Cochinitos—The Three Little Pigs. Their food wasn't as good, but the cartoon pigs on the sign were comedy.

Why the hell would Fly come here? The van her old man drove had New York license plates. They came to the Launderland yesterday, washing clothes, and Alfonso heard her say, "LA one more fuckin hour drive. And your punk-ass van wanna break down here. Country-ass place."

It was about eleven. He usually tried to wait until midnight to pee the first time, but it was over a hundred again today—and he'd already drunk two Cokes trying to keep awake while Jazen talked and talked about Angie, the girl who braided his hair. She didn't want to get with him. Never. Not even when he said she could be the one. The only reason JZ wanted her was because she still said no.

Alfonso zipped up his jeans and turned back to the alley and another rat skittered across the wire. This one was huge—must be pregnant—slow. Almost fell, rolling off and holding on upside down like an acrobat in the circus.

The nine was in the car with Jazen. But you couldn't shoot here in the city anyway.

He had shot the fool from LA in the ankle last year. Dropped him from a block away.

The first time Jazen came up to him at school, when they were juniors, Jazen said, "You one a them Sarrat niggas, live out in the groves, right?"

Alfonso already knew it was best to just look at someone. Don't say shit.

"I heard you a good shot. You on the football team?"

Alfonso had lifted his chin.

Lafayette and Reynaldo had taught him to shoot the summer when he was twelve. Sarrat was all orange groves, and palm trees near the riverbottom with wild grapevines covering the trunks. You saw Chia Pets on TV—these were monster Chia Pets, Alfonso used to think when he was little. The rats kept eating the tomatoes and red peppers in Lafayette's mama's garden, and chewing on the oranges in the grove.

Lafayette and Reynaldo had been watching Alfonso practice on gophers in the irrigation furrows and rabbits in the riverbed. Drought year, and their pops Enrique was pissed about the poor orange crop. Lafayette's mama held out her hands for the cottontails Alfonso carried in his belt, the way Lafayette showed him. "You a good shot, you," she said, smiling, and gave him the hindquarters after she fried the rabbit.

"Taste like chicken," Reynaldo joked across the table.

"Taste like rabbit," she said, squinting outside at the heat hanging heavy on the trees.

The next week Lafayette handed Alfonso the old .22 rifle and told him, "Them rats, they gon fly, and you better hit em in the air."

Lafayette lit the base of the palm tree on fire, and when the flames reached the tangled vines, the rats leapt out as if diving into an invisible ocean. They sprang into the air. Then they dangled for a second. Like Kobe. Hang time. Alfonso sighted them through the wire shaped like a diamond and pulled the trigger. He killed twelve rats in twenty minutes and Reynaldo said, "He got it. He a natural shot."

Alfonso looked down the alley. The streetlight at the next corner, Hyacinth, shone on the wires coming from behind each business to the poles across the dirt, along the chainlink fences that hid the backyards. Wires glowing like liquid mercury, like when he broke the thermometer to see the squirmy drops and his moms beat the shit out of him.

They walked into the alley from Hyacinth. Tall black silhouette with high heels. Shorter thin silhouette with red sandals and her hair like a cloud piled on top of her head. Sisia and Glorette.

The brown van pulled around the corner. Fly. She parked behind El Ojo de Agua and Alfonso heard her yelling at Glorette. "I told you, bitch," she said, her voice so strange it was like she spoke another language. Chess and the fools who hung out at Sundown Liquor said her voice sounded like Spike Lee, and they laughed forever. She had come up on Jazen and Alfonso her very first night, when the brown van was a lot less dusty. She was about twenty-five, short, with powerful thighs in her black Lycra shorts and her stomach poking out like bread under the sports bra. Old dude in the driver seat. Pimp. There was a white girl around last week, and the pimp kept messing with her. She was from Palm Springs, she'd told JZ in the liquor store. Alfonso had seen New York corner her in the alley, push her toward the van. But she twisted loose and ran. The pimp went after her, and she actually threw a rock at him. JZ and Tiquan thought that was hilarious.

But now it was just Fly trying to work the alley, running off two Mexican women yesterday. The pimp was around, even if you couldn't see him. Alfonso knew he was always watching from some parking lot.

Her deal was the van, tricked out with a stereo and satin sheets and drinks. She was pissed that hardly anybody went for it. Maybe that shit worked in New York. She had ashy dark brown skin and her hair was short, straightened and shiny with waves the first week she got here. But she must not have known where to get it done. By now the waves were all fucked up with lint and dust, and her hairline was rough.

She'd been yelling at Sisia and Glorette for about three weeks. Now it was like she was bored, and chasing them in the alley.

Sisia had laughed at her the night before, in the parking lot of the Launderland. "Get you a hose and wash down the van and you same time. Dusty here in Cali."

"You old out here in the alley."

Jazen and Alfonso had laughed. The women sounded like insane female rappers.

"Don't nobody want to get in no van. Dirty sheets and lice all up in there."

"Shut up. You so old and ugly they close they eyes. Say, back that azz up so I ain't gotta see that face."

Sisia spat on the van's hood. She said, "I get mines." She had a face like a pitted cast-iron frying pan and a body like a black Barbie. Fly was right. But the men still stopped Sisia and Glorette. New York was working for money. Sisia and Glorette were half strawberry. They'd take rock most of the time. And nobody wanted to get in the van cause they thought the pimp would rip them off. They just wanted head in the alley, in their own cars. They were used to the system.

Fly hated Glorette. Alfonso could tell. She hated Glorette's face.

Alfonso only paid attention to his own mother's face until he was about four. His moms Bettina was big and pink and freckled, with thin brown hair she always wore in a scrunchie and bangs that stuck out like antennae after she sweated. The other women in Sarrat—Fantine, Cerise, Clarette—they were vague and beige and never around. But Glorette—her skin was gold as the fake coins they gave out at Chuck E. Cheese. Her hair hung down to her waist when she washed it and sat on the porch to let it dry. She looked like she was wearing makeup even when she wasn't.

His mother drew on her eyebrows, and the first time he saw her without them, he was scared shitless.

The woman called herself Fly yelled, "I told you bitches, you played out." Even the way she said *bitches* was New York. Sisia yelled something back. But Glorette just stood there, looking up at the sky like she was so bored. She didn't even recognize. She was so beautiful that the same men would always want her. Chess, Sidney, a couple different white dudes who came every week, and guys cruising down Palm who just saw her face and stopped.

Fly rolled her van right up behind the women now and hollered, "You two old and played out. You played out. Move long now, move long with yo yellow country ass."

That was for Glorette.

Alfonso heard Glorette laughing when he headed back to the Navigator, and the van sped past him in a rush of dust.


IF HE HADN'T had to go home on that Wednesday in May and give his mother some money for the twins so she could buy school pictures, he and Jazen wouldn't have seen Victor walking down La Reina Road away from Sarrat, and they wouldn't have picked him up, and he wouldn't have started rolling with them now and then, and Victor wouldn't have gotten Alfonso thinking about all those SAT words. The analogies. The damn analogies stuck inside his head like a bad song. Bad lyrics. Like when his mother played "Heaven Must Be Missing an Angel." That Tavares shit that stayed behind your forehead all night.

Then every night when Alfonso saw Glorette, he kept wondering if Victor had taught her any of the words, whether she thought about the analogies when she lit up the pipe every night.

Victor was carrying a big book. He got in the back and said to Alfonso, "Test is next Saturday. I been studying for two months. So many words rolling around in my head it's like the lotto machine—I never know what word shows up."

"Like what?"

"Magnanimous. It's magnanimous that JZ stopped the ride for me, cause it's hot as hell out here and I had a stride ahead."

"Like generous?"

"Like generous with—something else. Generous with whip cream and shit."

They all started laughing, and then JZ turned the stereo down a little. The speakers were bumping next to Alfonso's leg. Chamillionaire. JZ said, "Where your moms stay now?"

"The Villas."

Glorette moved every three months. Sometimes she lived with Sisia. Whoever wasn't being evicted. You could keep a place about three months without paying. So if Victor was staying with her, and walking out to Sarrat to hang with his grandpère, and studying for this SAT test, he—

"Oh, shit," Alfonso said. "You right. Magnanimous, anonymous, magnificent—all that shit you have to hear when you in English class."

"Or watchin CNN."

"I ain't doin neither."

"You lucky."

But Victor looked out the window, and when Alfonso glanced back at him, his twists all sculpted so they looked messy—the way poindexters hung out back at Linda Vista High—he could tell V didn't think Fonso was lucky at all. Thought he was a fool.


IF HE HADN'T been such a good shot, and he hadn't been so cut from playing football and working out, Jazen wouldn't have pressed him. It wasn't like you had an interview and shit. Jazen just kept pressing him, kept saying, "You the one, nigga, I need your time." One day Jazen came by the parking lot after school and said, "You want to roll? I gotta make a run to Rialto."

Alfonso rode shotgun and knew something must be in the dash. Mostly he was just big. Football big. Guns showing in the t-shirt. Keep the arm out the window so they could see.

And J gave him a hundred dollar bill.

After that he showed up once a week or so, and then Alfonso had seen the pickup place and couldn't really say *Naw, man, I ain't up for it, I got practice.* And then one night in January they got stopped, and the cops took pictures of him and JZ up against the brick wall with shirts off and arms up, and he was a known associate.

Riding with Jazen was like riding with some grumpy old man. Like Bernie Mac, only nothing was funny. All he did was complain. Sitting with Moms was like sitting with some nightmare doll that wouldn't shut up. She could talk about shoes or Glorette or the twins or BET or Jada Pinkett Smith or the weather.

But Victor was hilarious. He had always been hilarious. Like a cross between a comedian and a professor. He knew so many words and so many songs and so much shit that everything he said worked. Jazen had hated Victor since he met him. Back when JZ first showed up at Linda Vista as a freshman, when his moms moved back from New Orleans. They were all in freshman football together, and then Victor quit because he hated the coaches, and JZ quit because he hated practice, and Alfonso was the star at strong safety until he ended up at Juvenile Hall after patrol pulled them over the second time and found the gun.

It wasn't Alfonso's gun, but he was a known associate.


IF VICTOR HADN'T been so funny, and Jazen hadn't been so bored, they wouldn't have picked him up after school a few times in the first week of June. "Loquacious."

"The fuck that mean?"

"Somebody who talks a lot."

"My mama."

Victor laughed. "Yeah. I was out there cause my moms told me Grand-père was sick and I had to hang with him, and I kept trying to study and your moms was all up on everybody's porch all the time." Then he made his voice cautious. He stopped smiling. Scared of us, Alfonso thought. "I mean, she just—"

"Shit, nigga, she crazy. My moms is fuckin crazy. She just drink that Hennessy and talk. Every minute she ain't asleep. Why you think I try not to be out there?"

If his own moms didn't talk so fuckin much, she wouldn't have driven every human out of the house. Even the twins tried to stay in the groves most of the day. Tavares and Tenerife. Named for the band, and some city her cousin Fantine told her about. Canary Islands.

Alfonso had turned eighteen, and now his mother was talking yang about he was the man of the house. That was bullshit. She had the twins with some fool from San Bernardino named Tommy and he was doing five years for little shit. Driving the twins without car seats, got a ticket for that and for speeding, and then the tickets went to warrant, and then he got pulled over for expired tags, and then they found out he didn't pay child support. Tommy was man of the house.

His father Alphonse was man of *his* house. He lived in Rialto in a shitty studio apartment. They hadn't let him back in Sarrat for ten years, since he brought the cops down there to the orange groves when he was running from some deal. Enrique had told his father he could never come back. Enrique didn't want cops there. Which is how they all knew Enrique had done some shady shit in his own past, way back when he bought the land.

Sarrat was ten houses in the orange groves, and his moms would wander up to anybody's porch so all those words he imagined like gallons of fucking alphabet soup could come rolling out of her mouth.

"You goin out to Sarrat, or you headin to The Villas?" Jazen asked Victor. "Villas."

The Navigator headed away from school. Jazen said, "Y'all some country-ass niggas. Out there in the trees and shit."

Alfonso always had to think ten seconds before answering Jazen. All day long. It was tiring. You never knew whether Jazen wanted to argue or laugh or just talk and talk. "We ain't in the trees now." Was that enough to remind JZ of why he wanted Alfonso to ride shotgun? It wasn't a shotgun in the glove compartment.

Gloves. Who in the hell gon have gloves in there now?

"The whole book fulla words?" Alfonso said.

Victor opened to a page and said, "You got analogies. A whole section. They give you two words and you figure out the relationship, like this: Debater: laryngitis. So you go, a debater needs to talk, and laryngitis means he can't. You got five choices: Pedestrian: lameness. Actor: applause. Doctor: diagnosis. Swimmer: wet. And writer: paper."

Jazen said, "Pedestrian: lameness. If lameness mean the motherfucker can't walk. Cause if the motherfucker just lame, then it could be player: lameness."

Everybody was laughing when they turned onto Palm, near the 7-Eleven and the Launderland. Victor said, "Ligneous: wood."

Alfonso said, "You gotta know science to do the English part? Damn."

Victor said, "Cellular: microbe. Nautical: water. Igneous: rock. Osseous: bone. Fossilized: plant."

Jazen said, "Shit."

Alfonso said, "Osso Buco. Some dude was cookin that on the food channel when I was at my moms' the other day. So that had bones and shit. Nautical is, like, boats. They always got boats in them ads for Nautica. How long you get for each one?"

"Not very long," Victor said. "Igneous is a kind of rock, and sedimentary I remember is the one with layers, like sand. Igneous was the other kind." He turned the page. "It's D. Osseous. Bone."

"Give me another one," Jazen said, pulling into the 7-Eleven. The Villas were two blocks away, down Hyacinth, one of the narrow side streets where all the complexes got named for flowers. Jacaranda Gardens, Jessamine Villas, Hyacinth Court. Like SAT words.

Victor hadn't even looked up from the book. He read, "Lullaby: barcarole. Choices are birth: marriage. Night: morning. Cradle: gondola. Song: poem. And carol: sonneteer."

"The *fuck*?" Jazen said, hands on the wheel. "You gotta know Spanish, too?"

Alfonso looked at the hundreds of pieces of darkened gum on the sparkling cement in front of the 7-Eleven. Black moons. The sun was going down. Victor's moms Glorette would be out here soon, with Sisia. Victor wasn't paying attention. He was murmuring to himself. Christmas carol. Sonnet was a poem, right? What the hell was a barcarole? A gondola was a boat. In Venice. "It's C. Cradle: gondola." Victor looked up. "So barcarole must be a song about water. Lullaby and cradle." He blinked at the face watching them through the 7-Eleven window. Mr. Patel. With his arms folded, frowning at the music bumping from the speakers.

Jazen got the three lines on his forehead. He was pissed. Bored. He lifted his chin and Victor opened the door, and Alfonso watched him hike the backpack up on his shoulder when he headed fast across the alley and down toward the Villas.

That was Friday night.

Alfonso heard shooting around one in the morning. Then the Blue Bird circled over the apartments, and patrol went racing over there.

He heard what happened Monday. Sisia had taken two fools back to Glorette's apartment for some extra money, and the fools got in a fight and one shot up the place. Patrol took Victor, too, cause he was in the bedroom asleep. With the book, Alfonso thought. Probably had that book under his fuckin pillow. Victor was still seventeen, so they took him to the Hall and no one showed up to get him for three days. The SAT had been Saturday morning. Eight am.


IF HE HADN'T seen Victor tonight at 7-Eleven, he wouldn't have the analogies stuck in his head again. "Hey, man," Alfonso said. Victor was buying pistachios and coffee. "You drinkin coffee? It's August, man, fuckin 106 today."

Victor poured hazelnut creamer into the coffee. "I got registration for city college tomorrow. I'm still thinkin about my schedule and I got a lotta reading tonight."

Alfonso got another Coke. "What you reading?"

"James Baldwin." Victor held up his pistachios. Pink. "These damn things keep me alive, man. Salt and coffee. You know what Baldwin said? Anyone who has ever struggled with poverty knows how extremely expensive it is to be poor."

Alfonso looked at the nuts. What was he supposed to say—*I saw your moms in the alley earlier and she had a bag of ramen? She said ten for a dollar, over at Rite Aid, and you go through them motherfuckers.*

"Yeah," Victor said. "City college. Like thirteenth grade."

Alfonso had seen Victor's eyes the week after he'd missed the SAT. Small and pink-rimmed like he'd cried in secret for days. The last test he could take before applying to USC or UCLA. He said the fucking words wouldn't leave his head. They were all floating around there like moths that come out the cupboard if you buy some flour with worms in it and then they hatch. "What you takin?"

"Psych, English lit, world religions, and world music."

"Damn," Alfonso said. He remembered the quad, the old brick buildings, the big jacaranda trees.

He'd checked out the football team, junior year, back when the coach was recruiting him. One of the players took him around and when Alfonso said, "You gotta take English class, right?" the quarterback said, "I speak that language fluently already, my brotha."

"Where you stay now?" Alfonso said. "You need a ride?"

Then Victor grinned and shook his head. "See? Where do you *live* is a standard construction. Because most white people *live* somewhere. But we always say where do you *stay*. Because historically we're used to being there just for a brief time, Fonso. A minute. I stay in Jacaranda right now. With my moms."

Alfonso laughed, and then Victor said, "You still live with your moms?"

Alfonso looked out at the traffic on Palm. "I stay in the damn Navigator most the time. I hate bein at my moms', and I'm startin to hate ridin with JZ."

"For real?" Victor frowned.

Alfonso nodded. "Yeah."

Victor lifted his chin toward Jacaranda Gardens. "Save your money, dude, and let's get a place. But not down there. By the college."

Alfonso laughed again. "Save my money. Man, my moms get all my cash." Then he stopped.

"And my moms gives all her cash to you," Victor said softly.

She gave it to JZ. Or somebody bought rock and handed her the little pebble instead of a twenty. "I'ma come down there with you tomorrow," Alfonso said. "Check in with Coach Ken."

"If you ain't just talking shit, meet me up there at the quad at nine, man," Victor said, and held out his hand.

IF HE HADN'T taken the first hundred, he wouldn't be ridin right now. What the youngsters like Tiquan didn't know was how hard it was just to listen to people talk all day and night. They thought his job was the easiest—ride in the Navigator most of the night, then chill at his mother's house during the day. But that meant watching every minute for who might try to run up on Jazen. Like last year when the LA fool showed up to stay with his cousin in The Riviera and wanted Launderland and the whole alley because he thought Rio Seco was country and Jazen would just back down. He came up on the Navigator with a .45 one night, talking about city mouse, country mouse, and he'd be back tomorrow.

All night Jazen talked about it while Angie redid his braids, and Alfonso wished he would shut up so he could see the way the scenario would play out. How would the fool approach? He could take out an animal fifty feet away that had frozen and crouched in what it thought was camouflage. Wild grapevines under the cottonwoods. Oleander bushes with their nasty poisonous leaves.

Uncle Lafayette said that was how his own father had killed the man who tried to take the orange groves and the land away. Back in 1950-something. Oleander and scorpions. Said he overheard some Indian dude tell his moms the story one night. Dude was drunk. But he said he and Enrique buried the white man under cement and he'd left a sign. A round black stone with a white eyespot in the south corner.

Alfonso had seen the stone, on the old rockwall shed near his mother's house.

Enrique had killed like five guys. He was an old man who just watched everything. His eyes moved first, then his head, when he checked you out. They said he could still shoot gophers in the dark, he was that good. But Enrique said, "Never shoot nobody, me."

He'd killed them. With his hands. Bullet or no, they were dead.

That was all the story anyone cared about. TV, movies, books. Victor had told him that once. What you learn from Russian novels and American movies is that there's only one story—how somebody had to kill somebody else, and did they get caught or not. He said the world was only about punishment. And sex.

The LA fool came up the alley from Jessamine, walking toward the Navigator where it was parked behind Sundown Liquor while JZ was talking to Chess in the parking lot under the pepper trees. Chess bought rock for Glorette every Friday night. It was a trip.

The LA fool had his right hand in his coat pocket. Alfonso leaned both hands out the car window and shot him in the ankle from nearly a block away. He went down like his bones turned to jello. The ankle bone. Must have hurt like a motherfucker. JZ stayed cool. He got in the car and drove away slow.

What Tiquan and the youngsters didn't know was his mother woke Alfonso up after he'd only slept maybe three hours, so she could talk about his father, and about the man she was seeing now who sold bootleg DVDs and was always trying to get Alfonso to carry some in the car, like the Navigator was a little Mexican pushcart with mainly paletas inside but also ears of boiled corn and cotton candy dangling from the sides. With those little silver bells so you could hear the man coming from blocks away. The Navigator had woofers and Lil Wayne.

Alfonso just wanted to save up enough money to get his own apartment. A big ass bed and headphones in his ears with that ocean-wave shit playing, and sleep all day. Pull down the shades and turn off the cell. Nobody talking. Twenty hours of sleep.

IF HE HADN'T had to pee again after midnight, and hadn't wanted to talk to one more damn person, he wouldn't have been in that part of the alley when the one called herself Fly started messing with Glorette again. Jazen was calling girls in front of Launderland. Only a little product in the third dryer from the left.

No bathrooms in Launderland or the 7-Eleven, and unless you bought something in the taqueria, no bathroom, and even then the two Mexican ladies looked at Alfonso like he was crazy if he went in there more than twice in one night, and it could be fools from Siete Street Locos in there, and even though Alfonso wasn't Westside Loc Mafia, Jazen claimed them when it was useful, and Siete would shoot anybody black now anyway. They called it snail hunting.

Or he could go to Angie's apartment in The Riviera, four blocks away. But there were always girls there, and he was tired of talking.

Alfonso had no choice after midnight. He'd been drinking Coke, laughing to himself about how Coke had come from cocaine and Georgia and, what, they had put the powder in the soda back then? and it was a leaf from down in Colombia and some dude had to plant it and water it and pick it—just like sugar cane when he was in Louisiana, and that was a stalk—and then somebody had to, what, dry it? Wait—there was a paste and then powder, and that was Victor made Alfonso think all this anyway, the analogies and the sentence completions. Dirt, mud, earth, sand, powder.

Alley dirt like powder. People walking and driving all the time, so the bathroom situation wasn't working. Crackheads looking for JZ or heading to Launderland. Men looking for Sisia and Glorette and the other strawberries. Mexicans coming out the back door after they ate at Los Tres or the taqueria because someone who looked like la migra came in the front. The Mexicans who worked there, dumping wash water or trash or taking a smoke break.

He passed the open back door of the nail salon. The two Vietnamese women were playing cards with a man. That chemical smell rushed out and made his eyes water.

The only place to go was the space between the shed and the wild tobacco trees. The back of somebody's yard, and they'd cut the chainlink fence and put in a metal shed, and there was a gap along the side. A little cave under the bushes. He felt bad for a minute, for whoever lived there, but he had no choice. He wasn't buying another taco, and he didn't want to go another block to the video store or Sundown Liquor. The old dudes were always in the parking lot there—Chess and Lafayette and Reynaldo played dominoes under the pepper tree in the back, and they'd yang and yang about why he was riding with JZ.

*Punk ass. Knucklehead. You gon do time. Just wait. Somebody gon get killed.*

He slid himself along the metal wall. It was hot as a griddle after pancakes. Still smelled new. He peed on the dried weeds at the base of the shed. Then he heard the wheels of a shopping cart. He stood still against the hot metal.

Glorette. She kept a shopping cart sometimes. She had the ramen in a plastic bag. Ten for a dollar.

She had stopped to smoke. She must not want to share with Sisia this time. He heard the hiss of the match and the sucking in of her breath. He looked out carefully. He hardly ever saw crackheads smoke. The rock glowed like a tiny star inside the pipe. An old air freshener tube. Somebody else made them with a blowtorch and sold them.

She dropped it on the dirt. The smallest sound. Then he heard Fly. "I told you."

She had come up behind Glorette. The van was nowhere. Fly had walked. Maybe the old dude had taken the van and left her.

Fly was saying something to Glorette. About her hair. How it was a weave. She grabbed Glorette's bun and jerked her head back, and then all the hair fell out the bun and over Fly's arm. Like black seaweed.

Glorette didn't say anything. Her face was turned up to the sky. What was she lookin at? What was he supposed to do? Head out there and punch Fly for being a crazy bitch? The nine was in the car. What if her pimp came rolling down the alley in the van?

Shit. Fly was still pulling the hair back and Glorette's neck was bent like a giraffe. Her legs so thin, buckling under her like a giraffe. Gazelle. Antelope. Doe. Shit. Victor's words. That was Victor's moms.

Fly was bent over the shopping cart. Doing something. She was still talking, but it was too low for Alfonso to hear. He closed his eyes. He didn't want to see any weird shit. Was she stealing the ramen? That would be fucked up. Then he didn't hear her anymore.

He waited for Glorette to walk past the shed. Walk away. But she didn't. He heard another rat, on the roof of the shed. Whispering clawed toes. Right over his head.

Alfonso looked back out at the alley. Glorette was on her knees. But not all the way to her knees. Her hair was tied to the handle of the cart. Her head was jerked back so far she was staring at the night sky and her mouth was wide open.

She wasn't moving.

He edged out from the shed wall, the metal corner burning up. Glorette's bottom teeth white like a little bracelet lying in her mouth. No breath. Nothing. Noise all around—music bumping from an apartment window, dogs down the block, helicopter a few miles away—but having a person this near and total silence made him so scared he felt one more drop of pee slide out. Victor's moms. Her ramen like books stacked in the bag. She came to his moms' yard once when he was little and showed him how if you stood in the right place, the full moon would light up the palm fronds like some god plugged in the tree.

Shit. Alfonso pulled his head back in and then he heard Sisia hollering, "Glorette! What the hell you doin? You was supposed to meet me at twelve. I been waitin all this time!"

She came down the alley. Her high heels crunching in the sandy dirt. "What you trippin on, girl? Why you down here like this? Where he go?" She sounded pissed. "See, you had to have that one. I told you I wanted him, cause he wasn't so bad, and you start laughing and say he want you. You had to take him. He wasn't lookin right in the head. Anybody go with some bitch like New York there got a problem."

So the pimp had tried to get both of them? Or another dude? But that was Fly, just now. No one else.

Alfonso steadied himself against the metal wall. A new wasp nest above him. Sweat ran down his back into his waistband. If he came out now, Sisia might think he did this, that he went off on Glorette. For what? For product?

Because JZ told him to. He was the killer. Anybody would believe that. He did what JZ needed him to do. They'd think Glorette had stolen some product. They'd tell Victor, *Dude, Alfonso was right there, man. Cold-blooded. I never knew he was such a cold motherfucker.*

"No. No. Glorette." Sisia was slapping her face. Alfonso moved his head slowly. One eye around the corner. The ridged tin burning his cheek. Sisia had untied Glorette's hair. All that hair. She was picking her up. The body so thin. Like a movie. And she put Glorette inside the shopping cart and sat down in the dirt and cried.

He kept his face against the wall. After a while Sisia got up and left. He heard only her heels in the dirt again. Not the cart.

She couldn't call patrol either. She couldn't say what had happened. They might think she was the one. They'd take her in.

Alfonso slid down to a squat and waited. Two more rats crossed the wires to the nectarine tree and he could hear them in the dry leaves. A few trucks and cars with systems went by on Palm, a block away—bass and drum like heartbeats when you weren't in the car right next to the speakers.

He waited for a long time for quiet. Complete quiet. It came, and he couldn't even hear crickets. No heartbeat. Nothing.

He edged out of the space where his own pee had dried long ago. He didn't want to look at Glorette. She was dead. No blood. Fly hadn't had a knife—he'd have heard. When Fly tied her hair back like that, maybe she broke Glorette's neck. He was frozen, a few feet from the cart, and a breeze came up and rustled the plastic bag. Victor's dinner. Then Alfonso felt his face filling with tears—how did his cheeks and mouth and everything feel big and salty? He hated that, when he was a baby and his mother had laughed. The plastic moved soft, sounded like glitter thrown in the air.

Alfonso ran toward the corner where the nail salon was closed now, and just when he reached the sidewalk Chess came around and almost knocked him down. "Hey, youngblood, you need to chill," Chess said. "You ain't playin football now. Why you in such a damn hurry? You jack somebody?" He started laughing. "Lookin all suspect. You just get some in the alley?"

Alfonso backed off. Chess used to be a baller, back in the day. He had bow legs in his sweats. Chess held up his hands and Alfonso headed across the street. The Navigator was gone. Don't go down the alley, he thought. Don't go that way. But he heard Chess say, "That Sidney fool ass up there?" and he made himself walk slowly down Jacaranda.

He didn't run. At Jacaranda Gardens, Victor's apartment window was dark. He stood in front of the door marked with a million dark fingerprints from people banging on the gray paint, and then he was afraid Chess had followed him, so he moved down the walkway, holding on to the wrought-iron railing, past all the window coolers that growled and growled, and knocked on Angie's door.

She was braiding a girl's hair in front of the TV and he said, "Can I sleep in the back? Just for a while?"

She raised her eyebrows. "Where your bighead partner?"

He said, "I don't know. I ain't seen him for awhile. Please?" He thought he would faint. Like a girl. She nodded.

HE DIDN'T WAKE until near three the next day. Angie had stuffed a towel under the door so it had stayed quiet. He opened the door and smelled burning hair. Angie was flat-ironing someone. "I didn't say nothin to nobody, Fonso," she said, pulling the hair toward her like sparkling black threads. "I figured you needed to rest. You looked like you had a fever."

The hair. It made him nearly throw up, and he ran to the bathroom and washed his face. The smell of lotion and shampoo and hair. Alfonso went out to the front room and said, "I'm cool. But thanks."

She nodded.

Little kids played in the courtyard. Someone barbecued on a little Weber between Angie's door and Victor's. Victor's door was closed. The blinds dangled and shivered in the wind from the AC.

He walked down the hot sidewalk. It was too far to walk home. To Sarrat. He walked the other way, to the city college. He was supposed to meet Victor. The quad was deserted. Victor must have found his moms. The sun was blazing. He found a pay phone. A fucking pay phone. He'd left his cell in the Navigator. Jazen said, "Who the fuck this?"

"Me," Alfonso said.

And Jazen was silent. For a long time. He finally said, "I don't know what the hell happened in the alley, but Chess put the word out he gon kill you. You better get gone for a few days, man. On y'all farm out there in the trees."

HE STAYED IN Sarrat four days, listening to his mother's voice like a radio you couldn't turn off. That first night he came out and walked in the orange groves, when he knew Enrique was looking for him on the Westside. He knew his mother lied about where he was. In the morning, he got the golf cart out of the shed where he'd hidden it, after the stupid white kid gave it to him in payment. He'd heard saws in the barn. He knew the old man was hunting. But after he talked to Enrique, Alfonso slept with his little brothers in one bed, their breath ketchup-hot and red. He knew he'd have to go back to Jazen in three more days, because his mother would be out of cash by then, and the bootleg brother wasn't coming around.

If Jazen hadn't already gotten Tiquan to ride with him for the day, and Tiquan hadn't insisted on staying in the backseat that night since he was a youngster and thought this was his chance, and if Chess hadn't been drunk enough by eleven that he stood there in the parking lot of Sundown Liquor and waited for them to drive past and then shouted at Alfonso, "She just fuckin disappeared? Like the Rapture? No, young-blood!" If he hadn't lifted his hand with his index finger like a gun so that Alfonso would know he was going to come sooner or later, and if Tiquan wasn't a little fool and he'd just let Alfonso do what he needed to do....

Chess finished pretending to shoot him and held out his palms like "What, you don't believe me?" and Alfonso aimed just for his left hand, the pink outside edge. But Tiquan rolled down his own window and fired, too.

Alfonso's bullet went through the webbing of skin between Chess' last two fingers. Tiquan's went into his chest.

ALFONSO TOOK THE old white Toyota truck. He wasn't going back to Chino. Jazen had kept the truck in a storage yard off Palm. It was lowered like from the nineties, and when Alfonso drove it across the desert, through Arizona and New Mexico and Texas to Louisiana, to his mother's Uncle Henri who had a wooden house way out in the canefields, he kept the radio off most of the time. First he heard words—all those words, like Victor's moths. But by the second night, he just heard humming.

# BRIDGE WORK

SHE WAS THERE the first day Mike's crew started the earthquake retrofit of the Central Avenue bridge, coming out from the huge oleander bushes that lined the banks along the freeway. He'd never been up close to a horse, only seen pictures of them, but that's what her legs looked like. Big and round at the thigh, narrow and long at the calf. She had on those tight bike shorts like most of the hookers around Rio Seco.

Mike watched her make her way down the loose dirt, hidden from the freeway by one pepper tree and the huge humped oleanders. The only other people they ever saw here along the interstates were homeless, or prisoners doing cleanup with their bright orange shirts and matching plastic bags. He didn't like to look at them, since he probably knew some of the guys or their sons. "Hard to tell if it's men or women, since everybody wears ponytails," his wife Shelly would say, staring from the slow lane. "I guess it's better they pick up trash than just sit around in jail. I can't imagine being out there in this heat."

*I'm out in the heat every day,* he thought, *with Gary and Les and Jose.* Happy to be sweating even in August because Sanderson Construction had gotten the contracts for all the retrofits. Ten bridges in Rio Seco County, and this was his crew's first. They were setting up the scaffolding, clearing out remnants of someone living in the black cave of overpass. Newspapers, a box soft from someone's sweat. Coke cans and a pair of socks. Men's socks. Not hers.

She stopped at the edge of the scaffolding, and the crew all glanced down. "Twenty bucks," she said. "For whatever."

Her hair was dark blonde, the color of dried foxtails along the street, and her lips were so chapped Mike saw a trace of blood in a crack. Maybe that was why she kept her mouth closed when she talked.

"Come on," she said, nodding at Jose. "You want a guera, or what?"

Jose was surprised, Mike could tell. "You speak Spanish?"

"Sometimes," she said, her breath heaving her small breasts under the tank top. "When I need the money."

Les laughed and said, "Go for it, Jose, come on. She wants you. You're the one."

Mike watched Jose look back at the company truck parked in the sandy spot on the other side of the bridge, like he expected Danny Sanderson, the boss's son, to holler at him over the radio any minute. Les thought that was hilarious. He was constantly ragging on Jose. "You can't use the truck, you gotta take her back to the bushes," Les said. "Unless you don't want none. Too early in the morning, right, cause in Mexico you always slept late? Cause you didn't have a job."

"Shut up, man," Gary said. He hated almost every word Les said. Mike tried not to listen, especially when Les talked about women, because Mike was the only one married and Les usually added on to the end of whatever sex story he told something like, "Well, shit, I guess Mike wouldn't know, since he's been screwing the same woman since the Iron Age."

Gary was only twenty, never been married. Jose's wife was somewhere in Mexico and he'd been here ten years, and Les was divorced. Twice. That was why he didn't like women too much, except in a bar and then, Mike guessed, preferably in the dark.

"I got the same job as you now, cabrón," Jose said, and the girl moved her feet in the dirt, turning around.

"Whatever," Mike heard her mumble, and then Les said, "Hey. Can you cuss good in Spanish? English, too? Can you say whatever I tell you to?"

She shrugged, and Les climbed on down the scaffold. Jose said, "Shit," and shook his head.

Gary called, "Hey, Les, I'm not doing your work, I mean it."

Les just disappeared into the oleander behind the girl. The bushes were so big and the leaves pointed like knives, each hedge was like a line of green-splintered explosions. The county had planted those oleanders along the freeway when it was finished, when Mike was five, and he remembered the stems stuck like arrows in the steep-banked dirt when his dad drove along the black road for the first time, hauling a truckload of crated oranges to Los Angeles. His dad used to rent a house out in Sarrat from the Antoines, and Mike picked oranges after school.

They kept working on the scaffold, laying the wood planks. Didn't hear anything, didn't say anything, until Les came back through the tunnel between bushes, the top of his blond brushcut bobbing along like a furry sun. He kept his head down because he was buttoning his jeans, and when he looked up, Mike could tell Les wanted to make sure everyone saw him doing that.


"WHAT'S A GUERA?" Gary asked the next day, at dawn. Mike hadn't seen her since she came out ten minutes after Les the day before, and headed straight down the sidewalk toward the store. Maybe she'd come back after dark, he'd kept thinking while they laid out the rebar. Down Central was a church, a park, a Kentucky Fried, and a liquor store. She was too young to drink, he thought, but hell, she was too young to be asking for twenty dollars and laying down in the dirt. She couldn't be much older than his daughter Katie.

"A blondie," Jose said. "Guera means white girl."

"She's not a true blonde," Les said, with that shitty grin like he'd had yesterday, when Mike couldn't believe he'd walked off the site without even looking back at him or the truck or the sign that said *Sidewalk Closed*. "All the way down, if you know what I mean," Les said. *Shut up,*

Mike thought. *Shut the hell up. Man, it's my crew, been my crew five years, and you do too much talking, too much deciding about lunch, and way less work than anybody else.* Les was forty, five years older than Mike, and he got away with a lot because of his size and the way he could charm the secretaries and even the guys at the yard with his stories. Mostly the crew just wanted him to shut up because every story got old at dawn on a site, especially under a bridge.

There were crews working all over California, Mike figured, after all the quakes in the last ten years. He'd be smelling the pee and wet dirt and exhaust, climbing up and down the scaffolding as they built it, remembering bunk beds. A line of stuck traffic bumped and screeched behind them early on, but by ten, the street was pretty quiet. That's when she came down the hill, scuffling and concentrating until she got to the bottom of the scaffold.

Same shorts, same black tank top, same ankle-high black boots. Katie'd had some of those boots two years ago, thrown them away by now. She and Shelly had gone to the mall all the time before Katie left for college in San Francisco. The girl looked up at Jose again. "You don't like gueras, huh?"

Jose glanced at Mike, then at Les, who motioned his head toward the bushes. Then, what the hell, Les looked at Mike. *You wanna play?* Mike thought. He said real quiet, "We got a whole lotta work to do today. If we don't start getting this rebar in, somebody's gonna steal it."

The girl laid her head back so far on her neck she looked like a broken Barbie doll. Except she was healthier. Those Barbies Katie and even Shelly played with always gave Mike the creeps. Shelly had kept about twenty of them in Katie's room, sitting with their legs bent on a shelf, spooky eyes and those boobs like road cones.

"Hey," the girl said, and something sounded torn in her throat. "Twenty bucks. Whatever you need today. Twenty bucks."

Her mouth was still half closed, her words mumbled and all wet like she was going to cry. Mike couldn't look at her. He walked along the wood away from her voice, toward the pile of material stacked inside the chainlink area near the truck.

He heard Les laughing, heard him say something in Spanish, and Mike knew from the sound that Jose had climbed down the scaffold.

HE WAS THINKING sex hadn't been her job very long. Mike knew women who'd worked like that for years. They looked different. Like Glorette, this woman from Sarrat he'd had a serious crush on during freshman year of high school. It was when they'd lived out in the orange groves and Mike hung out with the other kids at the river, drinking beer after they'd finished picking for the weekend. But his father had three dogs—hunting dogs—and he kept arguing with the grove owner. A man named Enrique. His mother never remembered to keep the dogs in the house, and first they caught gophers and squirrels in the trees. But then they got bloodthirsty, and Mike understood the word. They kept getting out at night and bringing back bodies to the yard— raccoons and skunks and rabbits. They drew the coyotes closer and closer til one night Glorette's mother screamed because a whole pack of coyotes was in her yard, red eyes and all, waiting for Mike's dad's dogs to come out.

His father loved the dogs more than anything else. He moved the furniture out of the little white house the next day. Glorette kissed Mike on the cheek. Her lips smelled like root-beer lipgloss.

Shelly said Glorette had been roaming the streets for years, ever since she got on drugs. One night, Mike had driven from up in the hills to downtown, and he'd passed two women on a corner. Glorette. She was sideways, not looking at cars. But he could see smudges of darkness on her arms. And she stood—like they stood when they worked.

This girl was just there, in the oleander. There were homeless camps in other parts of the city, in the riverbottom and downtown. Why was she living near this bridge?

Mike looked up at the thin wire spikes lining the shelf under the freeway, where the cars were whining over his head, thumping over one crack over and over all day. When his dad used to stop the truck right here, Mike would see the pigeons sitting under the trestles, their shit piled frosty white all along the cement. Except in schoolbooks, it was the closest he ever saw to snow.

He and Shelly drove under here now and then if they came down from the hills and went to the movie theater in the mall. But he figured it had been five years since he'd been to the mall. Katie was a junior at San Francisco State, and Shelly went to the mall with her friends.

Back when they'd just gotten married, homeless guys were already living under this bridge. Two or three men he could make out by their cardboard houses in the shadow, lit cigarettes looking like animal eyes in the dark when Mike idled the truck. Shelly would say, "Damn, can you imagine? Not me, baby. I can't."

She never had to imagine it because of him. She'd had him since she was twenty.

*I got nothing to say,* he thought, not when Jose came back after about an hour with no wrinkled clothes or marks on him, just a frown so deep between his thick eyebrows it looked like somebody'd run a jackhammer into his skin. Not for the rest of the day, when Les wouldn't shut up but kept asking what they did, did she blow him or did Mexicans only like missionary, cause it took them back to their fucked-up Mexican past with all the nuns and priests. It just went on and on until Jose took a swing at Les down by the truck around three, and it was over a hundred degrees out there in the sand but dank and wet under the bridge.

Mike saw Les pull his head back like a turtle to avoid the fist. He knew Jose didn't want to land it, and then Les laughed, and Jose cussed him out in a string of Spanish.

"Call it a full day," Mike shouted, and Jose started for his car, an old Nova he'd parked up the street near the church.

When Mike got home and took a long shower, Shelly was gone. He could see she'd been to another church rummage sale, because there was more junk in the living room. That was the only thing he hated after all these years, the vases and doilies and clothes and plates that looked like other people, smelled like other people, made his house look like someone else's, someone who couldn't throw anything away. Shelly'd left a note saying she was at a movie with her friend Cerise, and he must've fallen asleep. When they got back, he heard their voices in the kitchen sweet and high as breaking glass.

THE OLEANDER BUSHES were like black VW Bugs out there in the dawn when they started. Gary had to ask. "Do you think she's okay in there?"

Les laughed. "Hell, yeah. She's gotten forty bucks in two days."

"You really touched her?" Gary kept on while he unloaded the rebar. After all these years, the wrinkled iron still felt like giant antennae in Mike's hands, because that was how he first saw them, when he was Gary's age.

"Hell, yeah, she blew me. That's what I gave her twenty bucks for. It wasn't worth twenty, cause she didn't hardly know what she was doing," Les said, drinking his 7-Eleven coffee. "But I got off anyway."

"I can't believe you did that," Gary said, his mouth curling up. "What if she's got AIDS?"

"Yeah, pendejo, you can get AIDS from a sore and her spit." Jose shook his head.

"How am I gonna have a sore on my dick?" Les threw his empty cup into the truckbed. Twenty or thirty paper cups. "I don't use it for a hammer. Shit. If her spit had AIDS, then she swallowed it. And some of me." He headed toward the scaffold behind Mike. *Man, I'm tired of hearing it,* Mike thought.

But Gary was right behind them. "And what if you got it? AIDS?" Gary climbed up, tools clanking, and Mike turned to see Les' boot heel fly past Gary's face. Then they stood on the narrow planks. Mike dropped the rebar so they would think about work, goddamnit. "You coulda gave it to her," Gary said.

The cars flew overhead like clouds they couldn't see, clouds full of cement that scraped along the asphalt and sometimes hit that one pothole with a thunk like a single huge heartbeat. Mike remembered when his wife had the ultrasound pictures with Katie, and her heart was about as big as a speck of rice, but the sound on the machine was loud. *Boom, boom, boom.* Scared the shit out of him.

Les yelled, "I don't have AIDS! And if she doesn't want it, she shouldn't let guys stick their dicks anywhere, okay? Hey, asshole, I'm doin my job. She's doin hers. Why don't you do yours?"

They worked for a long time with nobody talking. The rebar would look like a long low jail cell when they were done, Mike thought. *Then we'll cover the whole thing with concrete, so all you see when you drive is a smooth face where no one could sleep or light a cigarette and watch you roll past in your car.*

Like before, she didn't come out until the traffic thinned. Was she waking up just now, after a long night? he wondered, hearing her boots in the sand just as he put down the solder gun. Doing what? Did she take her twenty and buy fried chicken and sit in the park all day? Sleep in the church? Did she get high? Give the money to someone else? He doubted there was a man back in the oleander, because Les would've said something about it. Jose hadn't said a damn thing all morning, and when she mumbled, "You know the deal by now," singling out Gary's face under the hardhat, Jose walked the other way down the scaffold, twirling his body past Mike where he checked the solder.

"He's a virgin," Les said right away, not even looking down at the girl or shoving his hardhat up on his forehead. "He's savin himself for somebody. Somebody who'll probably lie to him anyway. Ain't the first time, won't be the last."

Nice foul mood. Les smelled like the alcohol already seeping from his pores and wafting in a steam cloud around him. Mike didn't know what the hell to do, didn't even want to look down at her, and Gary's whole face and neck were like fire in the dim orange light coming through the safety screen. He came over and whispered, "I can't just drop the money on the ground. That would be rude."

"I guess," Mike said, and picked up the solder gun. Gary inched his way down the ladder and handed her a bill, and Mike saw her reach out and grab his wrist, whisper something to him. Then she turned and walked down the street the way she always did, her black shorts dusted gold, her ass too big for California.

That's what Jose said, laughing nervous. "Man, she's got a Mexican ass. Two watermelons. But you cabrónes don't like that here. You like them starving. Like two tortillas." He laughed his head off while he headed back toward the truck, and Mike saw Les and Gary both watching him.

"Get to it," Mike said, moving down a section. *We'll be here for a month*, he thought, *and I'm not watching this shit every day. I know she won't look at me.*

*Shelly's ass was medium-sized when we were in high school. Two what? Two grapefruit? Hell, I don't know. Two...two sacks of flour now?* After Katie, and the two babies that didn't make it past the ultrasound. She'd heard their hearts. That made it harder. But she had Katie. *Shelly's ass is fine with me. I never looked good, like Chess or Lafayette, back when we were on the football team. I'm not a ballplayer. Not a player of any kind. Just a foreman.*

*Katie's butt was so little when I tried to hold her after they came home from the hospital. She kept sliding down my chest, hollering, and Shelly kept taking her away.* "Men can't hold babies right. It's okay, Mike, it's my job. Not yours."

It never was his job to hold her, or touch her. And her butt now—probably the same size her mama's was, when she was eighteen, and some fool probably touching it when he can, while they're standing in the hall at the dorm, when they're walking across the campus. *Hopefully he isn't an asshole, and hopefully they go to class—costs something like five hundred bucks an hour.*

"Come on, guys, move it," Mike said, and he soldered the next section.

HE DIDN'T KNOW why he drove under the bridge on Sunday. Shelly was at church. Mike told himself he was checking to make sure nobody had ripped off any of the materials, but he knew they wouldn't be stealing in the daytime and if the stuff was gone, he couldn't do anything about it until tomorrow.

But when he cruised past slowly, looking up at the scaffolding like empty bookshelves from a distance, he saw Gary coming out of the oleanders. His face red as a burn under his slicked-back hair. Gary looked up and saw the truck, and instead of looking guilty or grinning, he started crying.

"Shit," Mike said, and opened the door. Gary got in. He nodded his head toward the church parking lot, where he must have been parked. "What the hell you doing?" Mike finally said.

"She told me Les said, 'Get on your back,' but then he did what he said." Gary held his knees like stickshifts.

Mike had to picture it, even if he didn't want to. Les didn't want her on her knees in front of him—even that was too kind. He made her open her mouth while she lay there. Her head on the dirt.

"Yeah," Mike said. "And you?"

He took a big-chest breath. "I wanted to give her another twenty. I told her she should go away, because I don't like seeing her around."

"You know her?"

He shook his head. "No. I just don't want to hear Les no more. I can't stand it."

Mike looked at Gary's stubby red fingers. "You sure you didn't get in trouble?"

He looked right at Mike. "Hey, I'm not getting AIDS, okay? Rubbers break. I didn't touch her. And Jose didn't neither. He told me. He just gave her ten bucks and told her get something to eat. He said he doesn't need anything like that."

Gary got out and walked over to his new Dodge pickup. Mike thought, *Yeah, Gary can buy a truck and still give money away. He's only twenty.*

She had to be about eighteen, too, like Katie. On Monday, he waited for her.

Les hadn't shown up to work. Hangover hell, Mike knew. Les liked being late, making a big deal of what he'd done on the weekend, how much he was hurting today. Because otherwise, he wouldn't have anything to say.

So it was quiet when she walked out of the bushes, and Mike went down to meet her before she could mumble her usual. Jose and Gary were quiet, and he could hear the crows in the pepper trees, and the rebar Gary dropped on the concrete ringing like a bell.

"What?" she said, and Mike nodded his head toward where she'd come from.

He followed her through the dusty leaves, and it wasn't far to the little clearing in the bank. The traffic was a roar like wind that never stopped. The girl turned and said, "Your boss isn't here today, so you want your turn, right?"

Mike felt coffee coming up his throat. "Les isn't the foreman. I am. I don't want a turn."

She sat back on the ground and swung her knees open and closed, moving like something he'd seen before, but he couldn't remember what it was. He was staring, after all. "What?" she said again.

What—like what do you want? What—like what's wrong? What—like she thought he'd said something?

He could smell her. Cigarettes and hot sauce from the trash nearby. She had as much stuff collected as Shelly's kitchen, stocked for earthquakes, floods, riots. Thinking of Shelly made the coffee rise up again. The girl lifted her arm and then he smelled sickly sweet, like she'd put on perfume. Her hair hadn't been washed. It had ridges and grooves, like when white guys comb through Brylcreem.

"What?" she said, louder, her eyes the same dusty green as the oleander leaves. "I been with a black guy before."

"Yeah? I haven't." He didn't want to ask her why she was here, where she came from, who—none of it. She didn't owe him a damn thing until he dropped the twenty. Mike didn't owe her a damn thing and he wanted to keep it that way. "I don't want you hanging around my crew, okay?" he said, watching her knees. "I think you should move on."

"You do? You think I should mosey on down the road? The yellow brick road?"

She sounded sharper, even with her mouth still mumbly, and he said, "You go to high school?"

"I did."

He wanted to know if she knew Katie. But he couldn't ask that. "Where?"

"Palm Springs." Her knees were like two wrinkled tan faces knocking together and swaying away.

This all sounded stupid, but he said, "You graduate?"

"Last year."

If she'd lived here, maybe she would have known Katie. Probably not. But her eyes, the eyebrows like fingers pointing at each other, the shorts bunched up around her thighs like tiny black tires ringing her skin.

Then the girl grinned for the first time. "What? You can't fuck someone without a diploma?"

Her teeth were gone, most on the top and only two he could see left on the bottom, like tiny headstones far from each other. "What happened to your mouth?"

"A guy knocked em out. He said I didn't need them any more. They just get in the way."

He wanted to throw up at the raw red dents left in her gums. "When?" Had Les punched her, here by the bridge?

"Last week when I was down there on Palm Avenue. I had just got here. Palm Springs was done." She swung her knees one more time, then rubbed at her brows so the tiny hairs drooped down like ferns. "Guy from New York did it. He caught me in this alley. Then he—you know. He said he'd try me out."

Mike rubbed his hands over his head, already sweating.

"I had already gotten away from him one time. Cause him and his girlfriend have this van, and she does guys in there, and he said I had to work for him. I said, Hell fuckin no. And he said no independent contractors out here—he said all this shit about White girl thinks she too good for me, like that. And he punched me out."

He looked away from her face.

"Then I was sitting there trying to stop the bleeding and his girlfriend comes up and tells me to go. She said her man might fuck me up but she'd kill me. Said she killed some other chick the night before."

Mike couldn't help it—he remembered Katie lost a tooth playing soccer, and Shelly put it in milk and they raced down to the dentist. The tooth floating in a sippy cup.

She said, "So—what? You don't want anything or what? You think I can't do a black guy?"

He swallowed again and made his voice hard. "I think you can tell I want you to leave before my worker comes back," he said. "I'm the foreman, okay? I don't want to call anyone."

She nodded, serious all of a sudden. "I wouldn't let him come back anyway. That one dude? He's psychotic. I feel sorry for you. I saw him twice. You have to see him every day." She stood up and turned her back to Mike, and he saw prints of leaves on her back, dusty blades on her tank-top. "I was going anyway. You were the last one to hit up. There's plenty of bridges, right? Plenty of assholes."

He couldn't say anything. He turned around, walked up the chalky path through the oleander and past the lone pepper tree. The pink berries Shelly used to collect when they were really poor, living in a studio apartment near the arroyo. Shelly put pepper berries and old bougainvilla flowers and rose petals in a big bowl and said it was potpourri. Like from a department store. Mike smelled the berries when he stepped on them and headed up the bank toward the bridge, where Jose and Gary were pounding away even though he wasn't there.

# WHAT IT WAS

BECAUSE IT WASN'T nobody else, okay? You gon ask me that question, straight up, now that you thirteen, and you haven't looked around all your life? Who you saw?

Lafayette. Fine brother. Played football when we went to school. Uh-huh. Left Cerise cause she workin and he ain't. Like she jumpin for joy about that situation. Like she ain't scramblin. Tryin to keep up with her boys. You seen her when we were at Rite Aid. She drives all the way to Pomona for work. Yeah, you walked away when we started talking.

They hung out at the basketball court. At the park. Same as we did. Me and your daddy. We didn't go to the movies. Ain't had no car or money half the time.

Didn't call it dating. You sound like some old lady.

People just said, You mess with Chess now? And you said yeah or no. They would say to him, Is that *you*, brother? And he would say, Hell yeah.

That's me. Then you just hung out. House party sometimes. Or the park.

Then he wanted Glorette. Like all of them. He said that was his true love.

Nobody said it was Louisiana or Alabama. Now you need to close your mouth, cause you edgin over to rude and I ain't readin that map now. Not while I'm drivin your behind to another birthday party where I gotta hear you talk about how our party is you go shoppin with your daddy and then I take you out for étouffée. Creola's where my mama always took me for my birthday, and if you don't like it you can make yourself some eggs.

No, I ain't stayin. Sonia bring you home when she get Trinette.

Cause by the time they hit that piñata it feel like they crackin my skull.

Cause it's August, okay? What does that mean?

Right. Means it's hot as hell, and you know I do that one late return every year for Ezekiel Baptist. That's about two hundred pages Reverend Hines gave me last week.

Here. Take the present.

What? When you buy instant chai? Thanks, baby. Go.


WHAT DO YOU mean, Give up? Why did we give up?

What? Why did I give up on him? Like it's my fault he—

No. I ain't doin this now. Wait til we get on the freeway, please, before you start the game show.

Yeah, I heard you. Trinette's daddy was there. And—

So Sonia gave him some cake? I know what he did. He probably got to the rink late, stood around with Darnell and Nacho and them, watched y'all untie your skates, said y'all were gettin too big and he could hardly stand lookin at you, and then Sonia gave him some cake and pizza and they talked for a couple minutes and then y'all did presents.

Why wouldn't I be right? You think this is a movie?

So Sonia supposed to scream at him about the past and throw cake in his face, right in front of Trinette?

And he would move back in with Sonia and be a daddy like you see on TV? Turn into Damon Wayans or some shit like that?

Yeah, I cussed.

Don't even think about it.

Cause that's half of Trinette. And I ain't sayin a damn thing more, so you can turn up your Walkman and turn your face out the window.

WHEN I SEE y'all walkin around, it's like seein me and Sonia and Glorette and Sisia in some crazy funhouse mirror.

What you mean, where? Everywhere. The funhouse is every street. Every walkway in the damn mall. *That Seventies Show.* Girls have Afro puffs and those puckery shirts we used to wear. But the belly. We didn't show ourselves like that.

Yeah, you seen Chaka Khan, on that first Rufus album. Those big bellbottom jeans and a little t-shirt. Okay. Her stomach flat and her navel look like it's laughin.

Yeah. Y'all can call em flares.

I looked like Nona Hendryx. Patti Labelle's runnin buddy. No, you ain't gon find no album cover with her. Not unless you look through all the albums your daddy took with him.

Eight years ago.

Navel string. You know what? The old ladies on Jacaranda Street, when I was so little, used to tell my mother and the others, "Bring the navel string home from that dang hospital so we can bury it by the porch. Else you gon lose your child."

They lost most of us anyway.

But you girls. No, you ain't gettin left here by yourself. I'll wait for you. No, I ain't goin into Payless. Not today. Cause my feet hurt. I ain't lookin at shoes today. Mall benches hard as sittin on a curb.

We had little babydoll shirts, too. But we didn't have the bra strap danglin out in a special color. Belly rollin over the jeans, the diamond hangin on a chain out the navel, pubic hair practically showin. That blonde girl—I can see her hipbones way above her jeans. Like she went and sewed rocks under her skin.

We used to see those ads for Wate-On in Ebony. So you could get your womanly curves and the brothers would want you. But we didn't have no trouble with them wantin us.

YOU GOT DARNELL, the brother you see with the landscaping truck. Three girls. He ain't run away. But it's somethin about him. He likes that truck, likes his house, likes comin home and Brenda makes gumbo and he drink a beer and sit on his porch. Cause that's what he does.

Esther ain't had nobody since Killer Joe. Cause she do hair all day, got ten people in the house, and all her kids. You see her across the street sittin on the porch at night. Glad to be alone for a few minutes before somebody want somethin.

I know you see them. I see them. I'm sittin on the porch with you, okay? You. All your clothes clean, and your hair braided, and your homework done, and my pile of 1040s sittin there waitin for me when you take your narrow behind off to bed.

That's enough questions.

No.

You ain't watchin *Law & Order*. Then I gotta hear why I ain't hooked up with that fine brother work for NYPD. Cause he don't exist, okay? And if he did exist, he sure wouldn't live on this street. Wrong side of the whole continent, okay?

Plus I'm too old.

Don't even go there. Thirty-five and you think it's a miracle I can still walk.

No.

You ain't grown. Go.


SONIA. YOU TIRED?

How's Trinette?

Yeah. I know it's late. What you mean, What I want?

I know you still waitin on that dryer to finish. Don't play like you done.

Remember when we used to say, What it is?

You forgot? Lafayette and Chess and Sidney come up and say, What it is? When they were tryin to rap to us. What it is, girl? All cool. And we used to say, What it is, what it ain't, what it never will be.

Okay. Trinette twelve now, right? She asked you about JT yet? Why y'all ain't together?

I heard. He came to the party and made his appearance.

Melisse gon ask me why I ain't married somebody responsible. Somebody stayed around. Why I had to mess with somebody like Chess.

Yeah. Even gotta talk about his name. "How did he get a stupid nickname like that? Didn't guys back then ever call each other by regular names?" Uh-huh. After I told her not to disrespect anyone grown like that, she gon get mad about her own name! Told her for the hundredth time she called for her grandmère and she gon say she got a old-fashion name and everybody make fun of it. Told her that's disrespect too and sent her butt to her room.

Yeah, again. What, Trinette turn into an angel this week?

See? I don't take away TV cause we don't have cable anyway and according to Melisse, Ain't nothin on.

Yeah, I'm tired. I'm still workin on the returns for Ezekiel Baptist. Reverend Hines eighty now. I been doin all his taxes for ten years.

Look, all I'm sayin is your time gon come. Trinette ain't jammed you up, she will. Then you get to say what I did. Damn. Melisse gon tell me she can't believe wasn't nobody like Theo from the *Cosby Show* around. She saw *Tribute to the Cosbys* on TV last week and now she think we just in the wrong place. We should be livin in New York. In a brownstone. She like to say brownstone. Says stucco a foolish word anyway. Italian word and here we are in California. Her teacher said she's got a huge vocabulary and she wants her to study for the SAT real early. College prep.

Well, yeah. Why Theo didn't come on vacation over here to Rio Seco? Coulda shown him the Westside. Coulda taken him to Oscar's for ribs.

Girl, he probably didn't eat pork.

WHAT YOU MEAN did I play chess?

They call me that cause when I was on the court I got everybody movin just where I wanted em to and then I made my move and took the rock to the hole.

That all you called for?

Go on to bed, now. Your mama probably think you talkin to some fool.

CAUSE THEY ALWAYS want something.

Even when they say they don't.

Put on your seatbelt or your mama gon kill me with her eyes.

Why you gon ask me that, Melisse? Your mama told me you ain't allowed to go out with no fools til you fifteen. Got two years to figure it out your own self. Why you gon ask me?

Melisse. This ain't my job. My job for you to pick out them clothes for school. Summer last too long for you. You got too much time to be thinking if you askin all these questions.

You asked your mama?

What she say?

What you mean, She say what she said. You gettin a mouth?

Cause they always want somethin. Look, you want clothes right now. And your mama know every August I buy the clothes before you start school.

Watch your mouth. You ain't half grown, okay?

Look, it's too goddamn hot in this parking lot to argue. Cause we didn't have nothin back then. And we was playin ball or whatever, playin three on three, and then the girls come around and want to hang out. And everything costs money.

I'm talking about, Buy me a ice cream from the truck. Give me a ride. You don't think gas cost money? And everybody ain't had a car, so we had to borrow a homey's ride, and he gon want five dollars for gas. And then she gon say, Why you ain't got me nothin for Christmas? And you just hung with her on the court three, four times. You want somethin and she want somethin and you think what you want free but it ain't.

No free lunch? Your teacher say that? Ain't nobody wanted lunch.


SONIA. I HEARD Glorette got herself killed last night. The alley behind that taqueria. She was still workin Palm Avenue. Girl, she still looked so good, and I swear, I would see her walkin and think, How she gon live her life like that, doin all them drugs, and her hair halfway down her back and her legs like Tyra Banks?

Yeah, it was a lotta exercise. Sonia, you too cold.

But we all the same age. She used to sit in front of me in math class.

I used to think I would meet somebody, sittin at the mall waitin on the girls or in New Hong Kong at lunch when I was takin a break from returns.

Not Melisse and Trinette, but shoot, those older girls, they pass by with everything hangin out and their hair perfect. And thongs. At the top of the jeans. The boys have those little-girl twists like we did when we were in diapers. Pants hangin down past sweats hangin down past gym shorts hangin down past boxers.

Melisse say she don't know how the boys can stand wearin all them piles of clothes to school. And the girls half-naked—they got goosebumps like—like chickens. When my mama used to pluck them in the back yard.

That ain't dating. I don't know why she calls it that.

Well, they're twelve. Melisse say plenty twelve-year-olds already goin to the movies, out to eat.

I'm hip. Chess never took me out to eat until we were married.

Shut up.

Well, yeah, after that I cooked. So did you. These girls probably go out more at twelve than we did at twenty.

Cause Chess always say nothin free. I wonder what he told Melisse. I wonder did she ask him. I can't believe Glorette's gone. Chess say she just vanished off the face of the earth. He said he know who killed her, and I hung up. I ain't in that. I don't even want to hear that. You remember she met that musician? Whatever he called his fool self. He just up and left her when she got pregnant.

She fell in love and she never was the same. I ain't telling Melisse about her. Not about love or whatever else Glorette thought she was doin.

Sonia. She said they would never settle for what we settled for. How am I supposed to tell her?

Wait—that Trinette's voice? She still up? Alright then. Later.


SONIA.

Sonia.

Why he had to stand out there? Sonia. Why? He knew them kids was dealin around the Launderland and Sundown Liquor. He knew they been fightin. He used to always tell me, Bullet got no name on it—meant for whoever in the way.

Sonia. Why he have to buy Camels? Midnight and he gon stand out there like it's some goddamn movie from the old days. Foxy Brown. He *knew*, Sonia. Girl, what I'm supposed to tell Melisse? Oh, my God. Dear God.

You comin now? What about Trinette?
Sonia. Sonia.


SONIA. SHE MAD at me. At *me*. Keep askin me why I had to be with him.

Why. Why I had to have her with him.

She mad at *me*. Like it's my fault he's dead.

I heard them kids. Talkin about *He got gotted.* That's how they call it. And Melisse in her room screamin at me, Why you had to be with him?

Because it wasn't nothin but him.


HOW YOU GON look at me like that?

Like that.

Like you want me to die, too. Right now, on the way to Target. You think I want to be goin to Target to buy you a black dress? You think I want to stay up all night makin pound cakes for your grandmère? Your daddy's mama can't make enough food for all them people, and it ain't nobody else to help her.

I ain't Glorette, okay? I ain't plannin to die. I ain't doin nothin for me to die. Yeah—I eat fries and I got blood pressure. But I ain't in the streets. Her son Victor—he lost both his parents now. You got me.

I loved your daddy. Every day. Didn't have nothin to do with what you thinkin.

I heard you. I always hear you. Just cause I don't say nothin don't mean I didn't hear you.

SONIA.

Now she ain't said nothin to me for days. Since the service. All them people, and she ain't said nothin about none of em. Ain't asked me about a single one. Ain't made fun of their names, ain't talked about the funky clothes or how old we all look.

Nothin.


NOW THAT YOU in the front seat I can't help but hear you. Drivin all over God's creation for you. Practice and shoppin. What you gon put on his grave? I used to put a slice a ham and a beer on my papa's grave.

Big Hunk bars and a basketball? You know what? I think that's perfect.

Melisse.

Don't cry.

Melisse. If I hadn't met him, you wouldn't be you.

Yeah, I know that's junior high biology. But it's true. Your eyes, your fingers, all that.

Well, yeah, you got my thighs. Way of the world, baby.

Melisse. Come on.

Okay. Must be better if you talkin cellulite. See, we didn't even have that word. We just said must be jelly cause jam don't shake like that. And back then, with your daddy and them, that was a compliment.

Yeah, I know you find that hard to believe.

Where's practice? Isn't it at the school gym? Why didn't you tell me?

Yeah, I washed your socks. Don't I always?

\*   \*   \*

YEAH, YOU SMELL fries. You think I never have to drive during work? I eat in the car on my lunch hour so I can get my prescription or whatever you need at the store.

Why you care what I eat? I know what you eat. Whatever they got at school.

Sometimes Mickey D all I have time for. Drive thru.

Well goddamnit, I know it ain't good for me.

I know it's got too many calories, and I know where they go.

You know what? Close your mouth for a while. Til we get off the damn freeway.

We ain't off yet.

Let me tell you what you told me this month. You said, Mama, look at *People* magazine. Check this out. Foxy Brown got a necklace and some dog tags all covered with diamonds. Worth $250,000.

You said, Mama, Tyrese top lip longer than his bottom lip. What that tell you about a person?

You said, It says here the shortest celebrity marriage on record was eight hours.

I ain't seen you get all mad about that.

Because I heard you. I always hear you, even when you think I don't.

I heard you, but when you keep askin me Why you pick him? Why weren't you smarter? And I said Wasn't no pickin, really, back then. Things just happened. And you got all smartass and said, Excellent. Good plan, Mama. And my mama woulda slapped the pink off your lips.

Yeah.

You ain't heard Aunt Felonise and them talk? You ain't listened. You hear them at Christmas, every year, talking bout Xbox and GameBoy, start with Girl, back in 1946 we sure didn't get nothin but a orange and a scarf. Maybe two hard candies.

Cause oranges why they all came here. California. Oranges. They left Louisiana and came to stay with my aunt in her big old house cause of some man. Then they all worked the groves out there.

Yeah. Now he's buried with his people. And you here. With the ones you got left.

SONIA.

Sonia. She gon ask me, Why couldn't you pick somebody like that guy who came to our school to talk about college loans? He was nice.

Probably from LA.

I don't know how I feel. It ain't like I thought he would ever touch me again. Ain't like he looked they way he used to. But I remember crazy things—how can I still remember exactly how he smelled—that old Drakkar Noir. What his shirt felt like? When we danced?

I know. On my cheek. They don't even dance like that. Never will. No Isley Brothers.

Well, yeah, I heard the new song, but it ain't like the old ones. Not like ours.

Melisse roll her eyes when I change the station to Art Laboe Killer Oldies. She say I should be ashamed to listen to somethin with the word old in it. Then I go into her bedroom and she's sleep, and I smell perfume on her sheets where it rubbed off—that new glittery body spray all the girls wear? And I can see sparkles on her pillow. Make me cry right then. She don't know. All the times we talk, right, and she don't know.

Sonia. Girl. We didn't know.

I didn't.

Hold up—my dryer's done, too. Them damn socks. She's got practice twice a week, but look like them socks tangle up into a knot every night.

Alright then. Tomorrow night.

What did you say? You're crazy. I tried to tell her Chess used to say, What it is, baby? And we'd say back to them boys, What it ain't. What it *was*.

# RED RIBBON DAY

THE PHONE RANG just after Felonise had hung up the white clothes in the backyard. It was Friday, late August, and the clothes swayed in the California wind that blew hot and soft from the moment the sun came up out here in the orange groves outside Rio Seco. The dishtowels, the sheets from the fold-out couch where Teeter had spent the night when his brother had a concert, and the white socks her daughter Cerise called Peds. The ones Felonise liked to wear at night around the house. Could wash them after one night. Cleaner than slippers.

Back in Louisiana, Mama used to say Least keep the feet clean. All that dirt from the canefields, but least don't put dirty feet in my sheets.

*Only once a week I got to wash white clothes,* Felonise was thinking when she moved toward the phone. *Not like the old days when me and Marie-Claire and Claudine first come out here to the orange groves and we all had to share one washer.*

She opened the back door and reached for the cordless phone her daughter had bought from Target. "Hello?"

"I'm calling about Lafayette Reynaldo Martin."

"My grandson?"

The woman hesitated and said, "Hold on, please."

During the scratchy time when the receiver was jostled on the desk and the school women's voices murmured like distant puppies in a yard, she hoped he wasn't hurt. Too hot to be in school. Seemed like school in August was wrong—they supposed to play in summer. But so many kids now, Cerise said they made the school year-round schedule. The boys would be off in October.

Stove clock said 11:03. They had probably called Cerise, but she was at work and couldn't hear the cell phone in her purse. Last year Teeter had fallen off the bars and the school had called Cerise but said she didn't answer. Cerise had come over that night, crying until her eyes were red and swollen as peach pits.

"I was in the bathroom, maman," she'd moaned. "The only five minutes all damn morning I didn't have that damn phone with me."

"He only have a sprain wrist, now. Nothing he gon remember."

Cerise had turned up her face to Felonise and said, "Maman, they remember. The ones at the office. The teacher. You don't know. They think, Oh, another little black kid and his mama's some crackhead like Glorette who doesn't even care enough to show up when we call."

"Don't say that about Glorette."

"I'm sorry. But every time I see her on Palm or in Rite Aid, and she's high out her mind, I always think she makes it harder for me. They think we're all like her. You know the kids say Crack Ho! Like it's a joke. All the time."

While Felonise held the phone and heard the women's voices getting closer, a black blur fell past her laundry and made a soft thump on the concrete patio.

"Mrs. Martin?" A different voice.

"Yes."

"Your name is on the list to call for Lafayette, in case it's necessary that he be picked up." Another pause, but Felonise didn't hear her grandson's voice. "Are you a caregiver?"

"His grandmother." Felonise waited. "He get hurt there at school?" She saw white—wrist bone poking out white from his skin, tooth in his palm.

"No. He was in a fight, and he's been suspended from school for the rest of the day. I've called his mother, his father, and his babysitter. There's no answer."

She didn't like this woman's tone. Lafayette wasn't no damn orphan. "His mama workin, and sometime she ain't hear that little phone. His daddy work carpenter, and he never hear nothin. And Esther might be at the doctor. So yeah, I come and get him."

"Well, we'll expect you soon," the woman said. Had to add that.

*Like I was fool enough to come tomorrow.* So Felonise added, "You tell him I'm on my way."

THE CROW LAY dead on the patio beside the washline. Another baby. Furry with baby feathers, puffed out like a piece of black boa from some old costume, the small black feet curled like ink writing. Felonise pushed it onto the dustpan with her broom. She walked over to the trashcan, and when she opened the lid, the two finches from yesterday lay there on top, stiff and dry.

West Nile virus, Cerise had told her. She'd read it in the paper. That's where she worked—at the *Rio Seco Register*, in the customer service place out near Pomona.

Felonise set the baby crow beside the finches. West Nile—something in the air, or in the blood, that came all the way from Africa to Southern California. Inside the birds and mosquitoes. Her yard had been nearly silent this August, no crows and jays and mockingbirds fighting over every scrap of bread and bit of old rice she threw out for them.

She closed her gate. Eight small white houses lined up along the gravel road, and the barn across the clearing. She smoothed the stray hairs back into her bun. She would ask Enrique for a ride to the school downtown. Cerise and Lafayette had moved downtown when they had Lafayette Jr., because Cerise said the school was good, and the neighborhood had good home values. But last year Lafayette had left her, moved in with his brother back here in the groves. He'd apologized formally, in her kitchen at Christmas.

"I couldn't hang," he said. "Gotta be perfect to live like that, Miss Felonise. Every minute. She got the boys in basketball and tutoring and piano. Lafie want to play piano like his cousin. But I'm tired when I get home from work."

"My daughter tired, too," she told him. "She call it the second shift. Say that her job, too, raise them two boy. She ain't get to rest and play domino with her friends."

ENRIQUE'S TRUCK WAS parked near the barn. Even after thirty-five years, whenever she saw the barn, where they stored the picked oranges and crates and machinery, she thought briefly of Raoul. Her husband. He'd worked only two seasons here in California. A flicker in her brain, like the news that appeared in the corner of the TV screen. He'd gone back to Louisiana to the town where they'd been born to help his uncle with the sugarcane harvest. He was twenty-five. Raoul had been driving a tractor loaded too high with cane. The foreman made him go out after two days of rain, even though Raoul told him it wasn't safe. *California nigger don't come back for vacation and tell people what to do,* the foreman said. In the rain, the wheels had slipped into a ditch and the tractor overturned onto Raoul.

Enrique was unloading boxes of fertilizer. Felonise said, "You give me a ride up there to that school? Cerise and Lafayette at work."

They headed up the long gravel road between the Washington navel trees. The dust was heavy on the trees—no rain since spring. The green fruit was almond sized. "Which one sick?" Enrique said, his hand on the gearshift. The veins were ridged high like yarn under his skin.

"Nobody sick," she answered. The truck waited at the blacktop road. Down that street was the elementary school Cerise and all the other kids from the groves had gone to. Agua Dulce. Mexican, black and white kids from the small communities scattered in the trees. When they turned onto the road toward downtown, she said, "'Tite Lafie get in a fight."

Enrique nodded. "Like his daddy."

Felonise shook her head. "No. Not like his daddy. Fight back then, don't mean nothin. Now they can't fight. Can't bring a chapstick. Can't jump off no swing." The truck went over the canal bridge. "I gotta take him home."

Enrique turned onto Palm Avenue, the big four-lane street that went through the whole city. To the west was the boarding house where they'd first stayed when they came to California. To the east was downtown, with old Victorian houses, Spanish-style bank buildings, the restaurants and stores. "Off Tenth Street?" he asked, and she nodded. "Why he can't walk?" Enrique said, and Felonise was startled.

"You know," she said. "Boogie man. Cerise and them see boogie man everywhere. Them kids can't walk."

She had told Cerise and the other girls only once about Mr. McQuine. The real boogie man, back in Louisiana. Not about the taste of his skin. But that Enrique had killed him.

Enrique's hand pulled the gearshift again—the knuckles like rocks moving under his skin. His wife said he'd killed Mr. McQuine with a piece of wood—and Felonise lay awake some nights wondering if you could hear it. The skullbone smashed.

Felonise had never told anyone—not even Raoul or Marie-Claire, that Mr. McQuine—his wide brow sweating pale as new-boiled egg, his hands fat—had caught her once when she walked home from her aunt's. His grasp on her elbow was so hard the bones ground together. She heard the sound of her bones inside her skull. He jerked her around and then said, "Oh, you one a them blue-eyed niggers!" She had ducked her head and bitten his forearm. Sweat and motor oil in her mouth, and when she turned to run, a salt-metal taste behind her front teeth that she didn't recognize until she was in the trees.

Enrique glanced at her and said, "Too hot for school, non?" Then he turned into the residential district with two-story homes, historic plaques, hedges tall as walls. Past this was Olive Heights Elementary. He stopped the truck in the school parking lot.

Felonise said, "Go head home. I stay with him at his maman's. Wait for her."

Enrique knew her daughter. He said, "She be more upset than the boy, oui?"

Felonise nodded. "She want him happy. That's the only thing."

FELONISE HAD BEEN here a few times, waiting with Cerise at the back fence when the kids were let out. Cerise worked 6 am to 2 pm, and she always said, "We gotta be early to pick up."

"Why?"

"Cause these other moms start lining up at the back fence an hour early so they can watch the kids on the playground."

"They don't work?"

"They work *inside* the home, okay?" Cerise put on lipstick, quickly. "They're like a club. They volunteer at the school, they're here all day. Bring their kids lunch."

"Ain't no cafeteria?"

"Very funny, Maman. Their kids want something from Taco Bell or Wendy's."

"Why we gotta be early, too?"

Cerise had given her a long look. She had parked her car behind a white SUV with soccer ball bumper stickers. "So the boys can see us. See we're here. Like everybody else. So everything is exactly the same, Maman. You don't get it."

She was right. There was already a parade of mothers down this sidewalk, standing with arms crossed in that waiting pose, laughing and talking, eyes on the playground. One woman had her hands splayed like starfish on the chainlink, peering inside, and then calling out to the toddler next to her, "There she is! I see Madison! She's playing tetherball. Do you see her? See big sissie?"

She remembered sitting with Marie-Claire, having one last cup of coffee while they heard the children's voices skittering down the gravel road when they walked home from school. "There go peace and quiet," Marie-Claire used to sigh. "Here come war."

Now Felonise looked down the long line of chainlink by the playground, lit gold by the sun and vibrating a little in the wind. No children were on the playground—probably too hot for recess. School in August—foolish.

The sidewalk to the office was lined with scraggly rosebushes. Would Lafayette be inside the principal's office? She stopped for a drink at the fountain near the door, and when she looked up, a drop hanging from her lower lip, tickling just exactly like when she was a child, she was startled by a young man who said, "Wow. I never see grownups drink from there."

He must have been a teacher. He smiled, blue tie and white shirt, his jeans faded. When he held open the door for her, Felonise wiped her mouth quickly with her wrist.

"They're all convinced it's toxic," he said, grinned once more, and walked down a hallway. She heard him say, "Hey, Lafayette. How's math?"

Her grandson said cheerfully, "Okay. Numbers don't lie. Like you said last year."

Three women at the front desk looked at her with blank faces. Three clipboards were stacked on the counter near Felonise. The door to her left was marked *Principal*. It was closed. Three folding chairs were lined along the wall. In one, a red-haired boy sat staring at his backpack, which crouched between his legs like a fat black dog with tags dangling everywhere.

"Lafayette," she called softly toward the hallway.

"Excuse me," said the woman in the middle. She was white, her hair short dark wings around her forehead. Her hand rested on her phone as if it were glued there. "Are you here to pick up a child?"

"Lafayette Reynaldo," Felonise said. Add the middle name, they knew you weren't fooling.

"Grandmère!" He came down the hallway. "I was in the bathroom."

The other boy lifted his head and looked up at Lafayette. Then he said, "I need to call my mom again."

Was he the one? Lafayette didn't even glance at him. He picked up his own black backpack. "You have to sign, Grandmère," he said.

"Excuse me," the woman said again. "Ma'am, I'll need your ID so I can write down the number here."

Felonise looked at the clipboard and piece of paper. A list of names, scrawled signatures, and times.

"I *need* to call my mom again!" the red headed boy said, and Felonise heard the words sharp. That was him. The boy. This was a competition. She had arrived first.

"We called her, Cody. She said she's on her way."

"Whatever," the boy said. Felonise let herself look at him. Reddish-brown hair in shiny spikes, like a wet cat sat on his skull. She glanced away before seeing his eyes.

Cerise had told her a hundred times to always bring ID with her, because the school wouldn't let the boys out unless she had it. "What other old lady gon show up to steal em?" Felonise had said, and her daughter said sternly, "Just bring it, Maman."

She lay on the counter the California ID she'd had to get five years ago for this purpose. "This isn't a driver's license," the woman frowned.

"I ain't a driver," Felonise said, and then sealed her teeth inside her mouth. She wanted to hurt this woman. She wanted to throw the wire basket at her head. Lafayette's elbow was near hers. He was almost as tall as she was.

"Mom!" The other boy was talking into a cell phone now. "I told you to come get me now!"

The woman was looking at Felonise's wrist. The black wires and blue beads of the macramé bracelet Cerise had made for her twenty years ago, some craft project, and the wires had tightened eventually so that the bracelet never came off. The woman wrote on the lines and turned the clipboard around. Felonise signed like Raoul had taught her years ago, like he'd learned to sign when he came to California. *Just make a big loop for your first letter and then a straight line, like you in a hurry. Don't make no X here. They don't know the X here.*

"The vice-principal will have to okay this," the woman said. "Because he's suspended."

Felonise let out her breath and turned around. The other boy said, "Tell them to wash it out then, Mom! Hurry up."

He closed the little phone and held it in his hand. Then he looked up at Lafayette. His skull moved to the left, and his tongue made a lump in his cheek. He was not sorry.

His cheeks had light freckles like crushed cornflakes. There was a trace of blood on his lip, a torn spot. A keyhole. She grabbed Lafayette's hand. A tiny torn spot between his knuckles. Raw pink.

"You apologize?" she said to Lafayette, and the entire office became quiet.

"We both apologized," he said impatiently. He was not afraid. His chin was lifted.

"What he apologize for?" she said.

The boy's hand tightened on his phone.

Lafayette said, "He called me a bunch of names."

"What you call him, you?" she said to the boy. His hair glistened.

The principal's door opened. The man put out his hand immediately to Felonise. "Hi," he said. "I'm Mr. Nonebeck, the new vice principal. I'm responsible for discipline."

She put her hand in his for a moment. He was tall, with brown hair and glasses and one of those faces like every newsman on television.

Felonise folded her arms. She said, "What this boy call names?"

"Ma'am, you can't speak to him." Mr. Nonebeck moved easily between her and the red-haired boy. Felonise felt Lafayette against her shoulder. The space between the counter and the door was crowded, and the wind blew sharply outside, rattling the windowshades. "We'll be setting up a meeting for you with the principal and Cody's mother and me."

Felonise said, "Set up a appointment, me? To talk to a boy?" She looked at his throat. "He call some names. I like to know what names."

"You must be his guardian," he said, his voice still very easy.

"No!" Lafayette shouted now. "That's my grandma. My mom and dad are at work. They'll come in tomorrow."

In that minute, the women breathing behind her, their phones and computers and wire baskets around them, the edge of the counter at her back, she understood what Cerise had been trying to tell her for six years. Since kindergarten.

*Raised by his grandmother. So sad, these days. No responsibility. No mother, no father, just a legal guardian.*

"What names?" she said, making her voice low and deadly, the voice she used when she wanted Cerise to be afraid, back when she was a child. This man was a child. He couldn't be more than thirty-five.

"I heard the n-word in our earlier discussion," the vice-principal said, voice not nervous at all. "But as I said, this is something we'll—"

"'The n-word'?" Felonise said. She took a deep breath and felt her own chest fill with air, felt her breasts inside her bra puff up, like a bird's. "You just say nigger. Don't nobody call out *n-word* on no playground. They talk about nigger."

She said the word the way she had heard it a thousand times. Loud, on the sidewalk, at the edge of the road, in her own mother's kitchen.

"They say nigger." She said it again, because she knew it made their hearts clutch for a moment. Like a motor with a stick pulled in.

Lafayette said, "Actually, he called me a wigger."

The boy Cody looked away, at the posters on the wall.

"A what?" Felonise said. Her grandson was moving toward the door, pulling her gently. How had he done that? He had taken all the air from the room, it was swirling around him now. He had some kind of power, because then he laughed. "A wigger. Whatever."

He rolled his eyes and pushed open the door, and the blinds flapped in the wind. Felonise followed his backpack outside. A picture of a mountain embroidered on it.

"How did you get here?"

"Your grandpère."

He nodded. The wind sent leaves across the sidewalk and through the chainlink like confetti. "I like the wind," he said. "Mom hates it. She says it makes driving home really hard."

Felonise nodded. "All that dust kick up. She probably get the message now. She worried."

He grinned, but then he dropped his head. "She's totally freaked out."

Felonise thought of her daughter speeding down the freeway, having gotten the messages and not knowing Felonise was already here. She told him, "You wait."

She walked back toward the office. Another woman was struggling to open the door in the wind—carrying bags, her hair damp and streaked, the smell of chemicals wafting behind. She glanced back at Felonise's face and frowned. Then the wind pulled the door closed behind her.

*My eyes*, Felonise thought. *She look at my eyes.* The window was open. She heard the secretary behind the counter. "Would a woman that age really wear contacts? Seriously. It just looks weird."

The younger woman said, "Everyone wears contacts now."

White people never learned. The vice-principal said, "They were really distinctive, that's true. Very blue."

Then the secretary said, "Cody, honey, your mom's here."

The mother said, "I was at the salon. Hey, you guys didn't eat all the doughnuts I brought this morning."

Felonise pulled the door open and stood in the threshold. She said, "Excuse me. Call my daughter back on her phone and tell her I came for Lafayette. So she don't worry."

Mr. Nonebeck began to smile and nod, and Felonise held up her hand. She looked at the damp-haired woman. She said, "Discipline come from the Bible. From disciple."

She let the door close behind her so hard the plastic slats danced.


THEY CROSSED THE street. It was only six blocks to Cerise's house. In this part of downtown, the houses were small and pretty, wood-frame with porches and trim around the windows.

"He kept sayin, *You got served. You got served.* Every time I missed a basket."

"Uh-huh."

"He wouldn't shut up. Every day he kept sayin, *You ain't down. You ain't down for shit.* He cusses all the time, and none of the playground supervisors ever hear."

"You bet not be cussin."

"I don't! They keep asking me to play ball. The first week of school, they were all like, *Get him, get him,* cause they thought I had skills."

"Skills?"

"Yeah. They were like, *What you play, what you play?* And I said piano. Then every day Cody'd be like, *You a waste, man, if I looked like you I'd fuck up every nigga on the playground.*"

"Lafayette Reynaldo." Eucalytpus leaves swirled around their feet like brown and silver fish.

"It's not like how you said it." He stopped to adjust his backpack again, and took out a small plastic package with dinosaurs dancing. Fruit snacks. The jelly-like things they ate all day, he and his brother. Felonise smelled the sharp scent of juice. "They'll be like, *Hey, my niggas.*"

"Talkin to you?"

"Everybody." The fruit shapes were gone. A glistening sludge showed on his teeth, and he shrugged.

"It wasn't like, all the stuff he said. He just wouldn't shut up. Every day. He was like, *You ain't a true nigga. You a wigger.*"

"Wigger."

"A white boy wants to be black."

She paused at the next corner. The round curb, the specked cement, the wind in her nose. All the women in the office. "You sure black this mornin."

They walked for two more blocks, and she could see her daughter's yard, the wrought-iron trellis and gate her son-in-law had put in near the sidewalk.

Lafayette turned to her impatiently. "I don't want to go home. I want to go to your house. Did you cook yet?"

"Long way to my house. I ain't cook yet." She paused, looking at the sidewalk under the tunnel of old oak trees.

But she was secretly happy. When they'd walked back to Palm Avenue, she waited a few more minutes, the faded bougainvillea blossoms near their feet, and then said, "Why you hit him then?"

Lafayette looked across the street at the Wendy's. "Cause it was just like, every day, *I know you play.* So today I played, and then he was like, *Why play the piano? Nobody plays the piano,* and I'm like, *Alicia Keys,* and he said, *So you a bitch now?* Then I had to hit him."

The cars went past in rushes of hot air. Lafayette said, "There he is. Cody and his mom. At Wendy's."

The truck was so tall Felonise could see its metal guts underneath. The red-haired boy was staring at them. His mother spoke to the woman working the drive-through window, and then Cody's mouth opened. She looked up from her lap—she must have been getting the money—and focused on Felonise.

She puffed up her hair with her fingers, almost like that old way, the beehive, Felonise remembered. In the sun, it was striped. White-blonde and honey-brown, and underneath, black as oil. Beautiful as strange pulled taffy.

Their mouths moved behind the glass. Lafayette said, "He always eats Wendy's. I hate their fries."

Then the truck moved forward, and stopped at the corner for the signal. Lafayette had just pushed the WALK button. The woman peered out her open window. "So wait, Cody, you can't go back to school today? You're gonna miss Red Ribbons?"

Felonise saw Lafayette roll his eyes.

"Because of him?" The words floated from the open window. "That kid?" Her hand dangled outside the window. Her fingernails were long and pink.

Felonise looked at Lafayette, but he was laughing now. He wasn't afraid. She said, "She want talk to me, better make an appointment," just as the woman turned left and sped off down the avenue.

Felonise tried to remember what Cerise said, when she tried to explain it to Big Lafayette. "Look," she'd shouted once, when the boys had been to visit all weekend and hadn't done something they were supposed to do for Jump Rope for Heart Health. "Look! These women are killing me because I don't sign up for anything, and Lafie's in the gifted classes with their kids, okay? Serious. If you don't give a shit, fine, but I do. They remember everything. I get *one time* not to show up at the office right when they call. The perfect mommies, they leave yoga class right when the cell rings. Or if they're late, the office staff knows them and they're in there joking around when they show up, talking about they had to pick up the paper plates for the teacher luncheon and look what centerpieces they got at the craft store."

They were coming up on the last big intersection of downtown, where they would cross under the freeway bridge. Glorette was walking up Palm Avenue. Felonise saw her in the distance. Thin arms, tall hair. "I'm not her," Cerise always said. "Glorette. But they don't know."

The Greyhound bus station was down this street, where Felonise and Marie-Claire and the others had come all those years ago to stay in Batiste's boarding house. To get away from Mr. McQuine. His skin like hardened Crisco. His blood on her teeth.

"Grandmère," Lafayette said. "The light's green. You okay? You hot?"

"No. This just a baby walk, not how we use to walk in Louisiana."

"So when he called me a bitch some spit got on my cheek. He was all up in my face."

Felonise waited. He was silent, breathing hard. "That when you hit him?"

"Daddy told me to hit him back if he got me first. Mama doesn't know he said that." Lafayette kicked a pile of gold dates off the sidewalk. "I felt spit on my cheek and I remembered Mr. Nonebeck said you could get arrested for spittin on people. Cause of AIDS. It's like assault or somethin."

Felonise reached for his hand at the crosswalk and then remembered. He was eleven years old now. She held her arms loosely at her sides until the chirping sound began, the sound that meant walk. The first time she'd heard it, the electronic *tweet-tweet-tweet* had startled her because she'd never heard a bird like that, and it sounded so loud and close to her hair.

She couldn't tell him. If spitting was assault, half of Louisiana would be in prison. She had left Sarrat when she was sixteen. Raoul said he didn't want no other girl, and he came out to California when she turned eighteen, and they got married. Felonise never went back to Louisiana until he was dead.

Mr. McQuine's nephew, Mr. Daniel, had told Raoul to go out on the tractor. Ditches all full of rainwater, earth like flour paste between the canerows. They told her Raoul said no, and Mr. Daniel said, *California nigger don't tell people what he do and don't. Get up there.*

She had taken Cerise. Was she three? What had her daughter remembered from that few months, when they'd buried Raoul in a closed casket because so little was left of him? It was 1968. Had Cerise remembered how when they went to the store at the crossroads they had to wait in back for Miss Joan to hand them the rice and sugar and coffee they needed to cook for the wake? Miss Joan said, "Think this California? That what put your man wrong." And Miss Joan's husband, Mr. McQuine's nephew, spit snuff in a brown stream onto Cerise's foot, on her new funeral shoes.

"MAMAN? MAMAN?" SHE imagined her daughter's voice, frantic on the answering machine at home. "Maman? I just got the message from the school on my cell. Did you go get him? Damn. I'm on my way."

ANOTHER CROW LAY dead in the vacant lot. Recently dead—his feathers still had the glossy purple and gold sheen of movement and flight and disdain. A huge flock of crows lived in the pecan grove at the other side of Enrique's property. The birds had been there for decades, according to the old Mexican men who lived in the next grove. In fall, when pecans were heavy in the trees, the raucous cries and fighting were usually so loud that Felonise closed her windows. But this year, the sky was quiet.

West Nile virus. AIDS. Spitting and mosquitoes.

She looked at her grandson's cheek. A smear of dust like a caterpillar on his cheek—was that from him wiping off the spit? She wet her thumb and erased it. *Now my spit and that boy spit mix up.*

"Why you didn't spit back at him?" she said.

Lafayette laughed. "Grandmère!" he said. "You know how hot it is on the playground at recess? And it's all windy today." He moved his backpack on his shoulders. It was so heavy he had a red mark along his neck, she saw. "Plus, he didn't spit on purpose. He's just goofy. He gets scum at the corner of his mouth all the time cause he has so much saliva in there."

"Saliva."

Lafayette laughed again. "Yeah. Saliva has acids to help the stomach break down our food. We had that in science class. We masticate our food and then it goes down our esophagus with the help of saliva. It's pretty gross."

Felonise couldn't help but smile. "Uh-huh." But how was that different from her telling Cerise to chew her food, not just swallow it? Everyone said the same things, over and over, forever.

Wigger.

They passed through the arroyo, where the tumbleweeds rolled down the canyon.

"Like big old Chia Pets!" Lafayette said, in the wind.

"From the devil!" she said back.

"What you want to masticate when we get to my house?" she said, as they started down the narrow blacktop road toward the groves. He lifted his head higher, to see the orange trees like a dense forest before then.

"Whatever."

When they walked down the gravel road, the wind softened suddenly, in the tunnel of dark trees. Lafayette crunched into the nearest irrigation furrow and picked up two dried navel oranges, black and hard, fallen from last year. He threw them down the road. "Who's here?" he shouted toward her, and then caught up. "Are my uncles here?"

"Nobody here but me and your grandpère," she said. "Everybody workin." She pointed down to the barn. "You can go down there." She took his shoulder and turned him toward her. His eyes clear and golden as weak tea. "Don't say nothin to your grandpère bout no names. Tell him you fight some boy for a ball. I mean it. You hear?"

He nodded and pulled away. "I know," he said, impatiently. "I know."

ONE FINCH HUNG upside-down in the bedraggled sunflowers. As soon as she got inside, the phone rang.

"Maman! This is why you need a cell phone!"

"No. They call me here and I went got him."

"But I was going crazy!"

"Uh-huh." *Cell phone ain't stop that.* Where had her daughter gotten this nervousness about everything, this wire Felonise imagined strung between her braids and down her neck, twitching and coiled and different-colored as the wires inside this transparent phone?

"Grandpère give you guys a ride?"

"Uh-huh," Felonise said.

"I thought you would take him home, so I tried there, but—"

"Cerise. He want come here. He's fine."

Her daughter was silent. There was the sound of a woman laughing in the background. The other customer service operators.

"What happened? According to him?"

Felonise looked out her window at the white wash, the other finches gathered at the feeder she'd filled this morning. Yellow finches with their shivery chirp. "Some white boy call him names. Lafie hit him."

"That's gonna go on his record." Her daughter sighed into the phone—a baby wind. "The secretary called me. She said Mr. Nonebeck is gonna call me back to set up a conference tomorrow. Like I can get off before two. The other mom practically lives at the school."

"You seen this boy? Redhead. Name Cody."

"Cody Smith." She heard Cerise say something to someone else. "Hold on, Maman." Her hand made a smear of sound on the phone, and her voice disappeared as if she fell down a hole.

When she came back, she said, "Well, you need a cell, okay? Then he wouldn't have to wait so long in the office. It probably made him feel worse because he had to sit there with everybody looking at him."

"I taken him out of there and the other boy still waitin."

"What?"

"The mama was gettin her hair done. She got that all-color hair. It's pretty. Just don't look like hair."

"She came while you were in the office?"

"Oui. And she got a big truck. She pass us while we walk home."

"You were walking? Oh my God, Maman. Why did you walk? Grandpa Enrique didn't drive you?" Cerise's voice rose higher.

Felonise dished out leftover rice and chicken for two. "Lafie want to walk."

"Great."

Felonise heard it. They had seen Lafayette walking with an old lady. Walking, like—what did he call it? Losers. Like losers. Losers walk.

Her daughter said, "I have to go, my break's over. I'll call you later."

The few birds at the feeder struggled against the wind and fell away. Cody. She remembered when Lafayette first started at the school and Cerise told her that she'd overheard the mothers at the back gate saying, "I can't believe someone would name their kids Lexus and Chanel. Oh my God." Cerise did the imitation perfectly. She heard these voices every day. "And I was thinking, Dakota, Cody, Cheyenne—you name your kids after what, places you've never seen?"

Lafayette came running up from the barn into the yard. The birds scattered up to the branches of the pomegranate tree. *What a strange fruit*, she'd thought, when she first saw it here. In Louisiana, fall meant waiting for sugarcane—sweet sticks to chew and suck. The pomegranate seeds had been so beautiful that when she put a handful in her mouth and bit down, the sourness way behind her back teeth made her cry at first, and Enrique had laughed.

"Think she got some candy out here in California!" he said. Marie-Claire said, "Pomegranate come from far away, too. In the Bible they tell you. So leave her alone."

Lafayette came inside with the smell of the barn—motor oil and citrus rind. "You know what you name for?" she said, grabbing his arm.

"Some dude from France."

He went straight to the refrigerator and left a dark handprint on the door while he leaned down to see what was inside.


CERISE CALLED BACK an hour later, crying so hard that Felonise knew she must be in the bathroom or the parking lot. "Maman. He called back. Mr. Nonebeck. He was saying weird stuff like, 'There was an exchange of fluids, and so we have to take this very seriously.'"

Exchange? Felonise dried the pan, the phone tucked into her shoulder. Like kissing. Saliva.

"Lafie hit the kid so hard he was bleeding." Cerise's voice was shivering. Shivering like when she was a child and couldn't stop crying.

Felonise felt her chest fill with heat. "Don't have to hit the lip hard to make it bleed," she said. "Baby—"

"This is Lafie's permanent record! Next year when he gets to junior high the teachers will read this and think he's a little thug. These mothers will all be in the same damn PTA there, too."

The Peds were dry. Felonise stacked them on the couch. Funny little socks. Dove wings. Her daughter said, "Maman?"

"You so much smarter than me," Felonise whispered. "I didn't raise you to be so smart. You—you make yourself that way. Lafayette raise himself to be smarter than you."

"See?" Cerise was angry now, and Felonise could hear the anger evaporating the tears. Almost thirty-six and still the same. "You think it's so easy, but it's not!"

She was walking now—her breath huffed into the phone. It was 12:40. She was on lunch break. "I can't get off early today, but I'll be there by two. Damn, Teeter's still there."

"Cerise," Felonise said, the deadly voice, until her daughter stopped. "Listen to me. I know what you talk about. At that school. Enrique take us back at two. We meet you there. So you be there like always, to get Teeter. So they see all of us."

In the silence she heard the finches, the click of silverware through the holes in the phone. She breathed into the other holes. "You hear me?" she said to her daughter. "I be at that back gate."

LAFAYETTE FELL ASLEEP at one o'clock, on her couch, the shadow of the pecan tree branches waving over his face as if someone stood there with a fan. Felonise watched him. He wasn't used to walking that far. At two, she thought of Cerise coming quickly down the elevator of the building she'd said was tall and mirrored and standing where the vineyards used to be. Cerise would move quickly to her car, to the freeway, and then be stuck in traffic. She talked about it all the time.

At 2:04, she woke her grandson and made him wash his face and hands. She split a pomegranate in half, and they sucked the elusive red juice and spit the seeds like soft white rice into a bowl.

They were crowded in the front seat of Enrique's truck. Kids couldn't ride in the back now—against the law. Enrique said, "Marie-Claire say Clarette work late at the prison. Her kids come over tonight. You bring them boys, too. They all eat by us."

The truck crossed over the arroyo bridge. Enrique said, "You walk a long way today."

Lafayette nodded. He looked scared now, of what his mother would say.

Felonise put her hand on her grandson's backpack. There was no back available to pat.

Enrique looked past the boy at her. The scar at his cheek—three slanted marks like some Chinese writing the teenagers tattooed on their arms. But that was a board with three nails. Swung by a drunk white man when he was in the Army, he told her once.

He left them at the back gate.


THE SIDEWALK WAS full of women. The chainlink fence was covered with red satin bows and signs with big painted red letters.

"Red Ribbon Day," Lafayette sighed. "Just Say No to Drugs."

They walked slowly up through the mothers who were adjusting bows, little kids too small for school beside them. "The first-graders come out and do the fence with the PTA moms," Lafayette whispered to her.

Felonise leaned against a car while people passed her. The car door was hot against her backside. Cerise had said he had to wear red shirts all next week. He used to bring home Indian headdresses in November. Brown waxy crayon-shaded picture of Rosa Parks in February.

Raoul had died in December. Mr. Daniel say, *Nigger, I tell you if it's too much water. Cause niggers can't swim. But you can drive. Drove all the way from California, cause you think you too good to live here, and now you don't want work.*

"Grandmère," Lafayette whispered, nudging her with the backpack. "You can't lean on cars cause they might have an alarm. Come on."

But Felonise saw the black truck, parked right up by the back gate. Metal rungs like giant staples below the doors. To climb in? How you carry grocery up there?

The mother came out from a crowd by the fence. She motioned, and the passenger window melted down. "Cody!" she said. "Your little brother needs your help over there. I told you to put that phone away. Go help Dakota with his poster."

"Mom, I'm suspended. I can't go on the playground. That's the rules."

Felonise saw his elbow, then his face. A faint crescent moon of fat behind his chin.

The crowd shifted along the fence. A man walked down the sidewalk. The vice principal. "Let's get all the scraps and trash up off the ground now, okay?" he called, in that reasonable voice. "We're getting close to the last bell."

Lafayette bumped her with his backpack when he stepped between two parked cars. Felonise grabbed his arm. "Where you go?"

"I'm not supposed to be here either."

"You ain't here. You waitin for your mama."

"I don't want to see her!" he said, his eyes narrowed in the sun, his hand over his forehead like he was saluting.

Felonise heard Cerise's car then, the little shriek when she turned the corner—like a trapped bird, but Big Lafayette said it was a worn-out brake pad. She parked somewhere in the long line of cars, then came up the sidewalk toward them. Lafayette didn't cry. He just folded his arms, rolled his eyes, and stepped back onto the sidewalk. The boy named Cody leaned out of the truck and saw Lafayette, then pulled back his head like a snail feeling a finger.

The mother came toward Felonise now. She was carrying a black plastic trashbag, bending to pick up the tiniest scraps of red ribbon and construction paper swirling like confetti in the wind. "Oh my God, I haven't even had time to wash my hands! We've been here since lunch! But the fence looks great!" she shouted to Mr. Nonebeck, who was handing her one of the water bottles he carried in a cooler.

"Lafayette?" Cerise said behind her. "You okay, baby? Come here."

Her daughter's voice too high. The crying was caught in her throat, where it would stay. What was that hot wetness you trapped inside your... that tube where the food went down? It wasn't tears. It came up from your chest.

In the silence she knew the mother had seen Cerise and Lafayette now. She held her trashbag at her thigh, looked past Felonise, and lifted up her right hand to point. She said, "Your kid isn't supposed to be here. He—"

Felonise pulled an old handkerchief from her purse. She grabbed the mother's upraised hand. It was grimy with fence dust and sticky from tape. The pink fingernails were tipped with white like frosting. Felonise spat into her handkerchief and pushed down the fingers, and wiped the center of the woman's palm. She rubbed hard and said, "Here. Now you clean."

She didn't look up at the woman's face. She wanted to tear a little flesh from the wrist with her teeth. This kind of woman made Cerise cry. She made Cerise cry and hide in a hallway and swallow the burning that came up from her chest. She might say *welfare mama* when she told the story tonight. *Crack ho.*

Felonise folded the woman's fingers over the ball of wet cloth and looked up at the blue eyes. Saliva. A crime. Black lashes like brooms for a tiny doll. She said softly, "These ain't contacts. My grandmère get them from a wigger." She pointed at the boy hidden in the truck. "He know," she said. "That my grandson, and when you see his mama tomorrow, in that meeting, you remember me." Her own eyes burned hot—she gave the woman the look that Raoul used to say could start the back of someone's head on fire. All she ever had—that look. And her teeth.

She let the hand go, and it popped up like a handle on a slot machine.

Then she turned toward the man she knew was approaching her. He held a frosted plastic bottle and said, "Ma'am?"

Mr. McQuine's nephew only gave water once a day in the field. Sometimes he put mud in it. Felonise drank it anyway. He would say, *Don't look at me with them devil eye. Blue eye don't make you white.*

She would say, *Hat don't make you a man.*

Felonise fitted her lips back over her teeth again and walked past him to where Cerise stood, shaking her head, holding her fingers to her temples as if she'd been stung by the tiny hairs had curled there, the ones Felonise used to damp down in waves.

# MINES

THEY CAN'T SHAVE their heads every day like they wish they could, so their tattoos show through stubble. Little black hairs like iron filings stuck on magnets. Big round-head fool magnets.

The Chicano fools have gang names on the sides of their skulls. The white fools have swastikas. The Vietnamese fools have writing I can't read. And the black fools—if they're too dark, they can't have anything on their heads. Maybe on the lighter skin at their chest, or the inside of the arm.

Where I sit for morning shift at my window, I used to see my nephew in his line, heading to the library. Square-head light-skinned fool like my brother. Little dragon on his skull. Nothing in his skull. Told me it was cause he could breathe fire if he had to. *Alfonso* tattooed on his arm.

"What, he too fool remember his own name?" my father-in-law said when he saw it. "Gotta look down by his elbow to check?"

Two names on his collarbone: twins. Girls. *Egypt and Morocco*. Seventeen and he's got kids. He was in here for a year. Some LA kid got shot in the leg. Alfonso was riding in the car. They couldn't prove he did it, but there was a gun in the glove compartment. Known associate. Law says same as pulling the trigger.

Ten o'clock. They line up for shift between classes and voc ed. Dark-blue backs like fool dominoes. Shuffling boots. Fred and I stand in the doorway, hands on our belts, watching. From here, seeing all those heads with all those blue-green marks like bruises, looks like everybody got beat up big-time. Reyes and Michaels and the other officers lead their lines past the central guard station, and when the wards get closer, you can see all the other tattoos. Names over their eyebrows, teardrops on their cheeks, words on their necks, letters on their fingers.

One Chicano kid has *Perdóname mi abuelita* in fancy cursive on the back of his neck. *Sorry my little grandma.* I bet that makes her feel much better.

When my nephew used to shuffle by, he would grin and say softly, "Hey, Auntie Clarette."

I always wanted to slap that dragon off the side of his stupid skull.

Fred says, "How's your fine friend Tika? The one with green eyes?"

I roll my brown eyes. "Contacts, okay?"

I didn't tell him I saw Tika last night, at Lincoln Elementary. "How can you work at the youth prison? All those young brothers incarcerated by the system?" That's what Tika said to me at Back-to-School Night. "Doesn't it hurt you to be there?"

"Y'all went to college together, right?" Fred says.

"Mmm-hmm." Except she's teaching African-American studies there now, and I married Reynaldo. He quit football at city college and started plastering with his brother.

"Rey went with y'all, too, didn't he? Played ball til he blew out his knee?"

The wind's been steady for three days now, hot August wind blowing all the tumbleweeds across the empty fields out here, piling them up against the chainlink until it looks like hundreds of heads to me. Big-ass naturals from the seventies, when I squint and look toward the east. Two wards come around the building and I'm up. "Where you going?"

The Chicano kid grins. "TB test."

"Pass."

He flashes it, and I see the nurses' signature. The blister on his fore-arm looks like a quarter somebody slid under the skin. Whole place has TB so bad we gotta get tested every week. My forearm dotted with marks like I'm a junkie.

I lift up my chin. I feel like a guy when I do it, but it's easier than talk-ing sometimes. I don't want to open my mouth. "Go ahead," Fred calls out to them.

"Like you got up and looked."

Fred lifts his eyebrows at me. "Okay, Miss Thang."

It's like a piece of hot link burning in my throat. "Shut the fuck up, Fred." That's what Michaels and Reyes always say to him. I hear it come out like that, and I close my eyes. When I get home now and the kids start their homework, I have to stand at the sink and wash my hands and change my mouth. My spit, everything. Not a prayer. More like when you cool down after you run. Every night, I watch the water on my knuckles and think, *No TB. No cussing. No meds.*

Because a couple months after I started YA, I would holler at the kids, "Take your meds."

"Flintstones, Mama," Danae would say.

Fred looks up at the security videos. "Tika still single, huh?"

"Yeah."

She has a gallery downtown, and she was at the school to show African art. She said to me, "Doesn't it hurt your soul? How can you stand it?"

I didn't say anything at first. I was watching Rey Jr. talk to his teacher. He's tall now, fourth grade, and he smells different to me when he wakes up in the morning.

I told Tika, "I work seven to three. I'm home when the kids get off the bus. I have bennies."

She just looked at me.

"Benefits." I didn't say the rest. Most of the time now Rey and Lafayette stay out in Sarrat, hanging out at the barn, working on cars. Rey hasn't had a plastering job for months. He says construction is way down, and when somebody is building, they hire Mexican drywallers.

When I got this job, Rey got funny. He broke dishes, washing them. He wrecked clothes, washing them. He said, "That ain't a man. A man's job." He started staying out with Lafayette.

Tika said, "Doesn't it hurt your soul to see the young brothers?"

For my New Year's resolution, I told myself, *Silence is golden*. Like that old Maze song—Glorette's favorite jam. I bet she still plays that every day, if she can keep a radio. And some quiet jazz song—"Poinciana." She used to have a boom box, and she lived so bad it always got stolen.

But I saw her last week at Rite Aid—she was buying lotion—and she was humming it. "That's the golden time of day."

At work, cause me talking just reminds them I'm a woman. With Rey and my mother-in-law and everyone else except my kids. I looked at Tika's lipstick and shouted in my head: *I make twenty-nine grand a year! I've got bennies now!* Rey never had health care, and Danae's got asthma. I don't get to worry about big stuff like you do, cause I'm worrying about big stuff like I do. Pay the bills, put gas in the van, buy groceries. Rey Jr. eats three boxes of Cheerios every week, okay?

But I said, "Fred Harris works out there. And JC and Marcus and Beverly."

Tika said, "Prison is the biggest growth industry in California. They're determined to put everyone of color behind a wall."

*Five days a week*, I was thinking, *I drive past the chainlink fence and past JC at the guard gate*. Then Danae ran up to me with a book. They had a book sale at Back-to-School Night. Danae wanted an American Girl story. $4.95.

Tika walked away. I went to the cash register. Five days a week, I park my van and walk into the walls. But they're fences with barbed wire and us watching. Everything. Every face.

"Nobody in the laundry?" I ask, and Fred shakes his head. Laundry is where they've been fighting this week. Black kid got his head busted open Friday in there, and we're supposed to watch the screens. The bell rings and we get up to stand in the courtyard for period change. We can hear them coming from the classrooms, doors slamming and all those boots thumping on the asphalt. The wind moving their stiff pants around their ankles, it's so hard right now. I watch their heads. Every day it's a scuffle out here, and we're supposed to listen to who's yelling or, worse, talking that quiet shit that sets it off.

All the damn heads look the same to me, when I'm out here with my stick down by my side. Light ones like Alfonso and the Chicano kids and the Vietnamese, all golden brown. Dark little guys, some Filipinos, and then the white kids so pale they're almost green. But all the tattoos like scabs. Numbers over their eyebrows and *fuck you* inside their lips when when they pull them down like clowns.

The wind whips through them, and they all squint but don't move. My head is hurting at the temples, from the dust and wind and no sleep. Laundry. The wards stay in formation, stop and wait, boots shining like baby black foreheads. I heard muttering and answers and shit-talking in the back, but nobody starts punching. Then the bell rings and they march off.

"Youngblood. Stop the mouth," Fred calls from behind me. He talks to the wards all the time. Old-school. Luther Vandross loving and hair fading back like the tide at the beach—only forty-two, but acts like he's a grandpa from the south. "Son, if you'da thought about what you were doing last year, you wouldn't be stepping past me this year." They look at him like they want to spit in his face. "Son, sometimes what the old people say is the gospel truth, but you wasn't in church to hear." They would knock him in the head if they could. "Son, you're only sixteen, but you're gonna have to go across the street before you know it, you keep up that attitude."

Across the street is Chino. Men's Correctional Facility. The wards laugh and sing back to Fred like they're Snoop Dogg: "I'm on my way to Chino, I see no reason to cry..."

He says, "Lord knows Mr. Doggy Dogg ain't gonna be there when you are."

The Chicano kids talk Spanish to Reyes, and he looks back at them like a statue wearing shades. The big guy, Michaels, used to play football with Rey. He has never looked into my face since I got here. My nephew Alfonso used to play football, too. He used to say, "Come on, Michaels, show a brotha love, Michaels. Lemme have a cigarette. You can't do that for a brotha, man? Brothaman?"

Alfonso thought this was a big joke. A vacation. Training for life. Called it the country club. Now he's out riding the streets again.

I never said a damn thing when he winked at me. Now I watch them walk domino-lines to class and to the kitchen and the laundry and the field. *Sleepy* and *Spooky* and *Dre Dog* and *Scooby* and *G Dog* and *Monster* all tattooed on their arms and heads and necks. Like a damn kennel. Nazis with spiderwebs on their elbows, which is supposed to mean they killed somebody dark. Asians with spidery writing on their arms, and I don't know what that means.

"I'ma get mines, all I gotta say, Auntie Clarette," my nephew always said when he was ten or eleven. "I ain't workin all my life for some shitty car and a house. I'ma get mines now."

I couldn't help it. Not supposed to look out for him, but when they changed rooms, when they were in the cafeteria, I watched him. I never said anything to him. But I kept seeing my brother in Alfonso's fool fore-head, my brother and Bettina in their apartment back when Alfonso was a baby, nothing but a couch and a TV. Always had something to drink, though, and plenty weed.

Swear Alfonso might have thought he was better off here. Three hots and a cot, the boys say.

We watch the laundry screens, the classrooms, and I don't say anything to Fred for a long time. I keep thinking about Danae's reading tonight, takes twenty minutes, and then I can wash a load of jeans and pay the bills.

"Chow time, baby," Fred says, pushing it. Walking behind me when we line everybody up. They're all mumbling, like a hundred little air conditioners, talking shit to each other.

It was a year of extra worrying I didn't need, back when Alfonso would line up with his new homeys, lips moving steady as a cartoon. He would grin at me. My brother said, *Take care my boy, Clarette. It's on you.*

*No,* I used to holler back at him. *You had seventeen years to take care of him. Why I gotta do your job? How am I supposed to make sure he don't get killed?*

The wind blows past all those bald heads. So hot. I know the words are brushing the back of the necks in line, the Chicano kids wanting to fight, black kids moving their fingers down by their legs like I can't see gang signs, and I walk over with my stick. "Move," I say, and the sweaty foreheads go shining past like windshields in a traffic jam.

"Keep moving," I say louder. I feel all the feet pounding the asphalt around me and I stand in the shade next to Fred, tell him, "Shut up" real soft, soft as these boys still talking yang in the line.

I HAD A buzzing in my head all day. Since I got up at five to do two loads of laundry and make a hot breakfast and get the kids ready for school. So hot in August—and now because the school downtown's so crowded, they said we had to start year-round schedule. Crazy. I dreamed me and Glorette were running in the groves like we used to. Racing down the furrows after they ran the irrigation, splashing in the water. Bare feet.

When I get home, I start folding the towels and see the bus stop at the corner. I wait for the kids to come busting in, but all the voices fade away down the street like little radios. Where are those kids? I go out on the porch, and the sidewalk's empty, and my throat fills up again like that spicy meat's caught. Rey Jr. knows to meet Danae at her classroom. The teacher's supposed to make sure they're on the bus. Where the hell are they?

I get back in the van and head toward the school, and on Palm Avenue I swear I see Danae standing outside the barbershop, waving at me when I'm stopped at the light.

"Mama!" she calls, holding a cone from the Dairy Queen next door. "Mama!'

The smell of aftershave coats my teeth. And Rey Jr.'s in the chair, his hair on the tile floor like rainclouds.

My son. His head naked, a little nick on the back of his skull when he sees me and ducks down. Where someone hit him with a rock last year in third grade. The barber rubs his palms over Rey Jr.'s skin and it shines.

"Wax him up, man," Rey says, and I move on him fast. His hair under my feet, too, I see now, lighter and straighter. Brown clouds. The ones with no rain.

"How could you?" I try to whisper, but I can't whisper. Not after all day of hollering, not stepping on all that hair.

The barber, old guy I remember from football games, said, "Mmm-mmm-mmm."

"The look, baby. Everybody wants the look. You always working on Danae's hair, and Rey-Rey's was looking ragged." Rey lifts both hands, fingers out, like he always does. Like it's a damn sports movie and he's the ref. Exaggerated. "Hey, I thought I was helping you out."

I heard the laughing in his mouth. "Like Mike, baby. Like Ice Cube. The look. He said some punks was messin with him at school."

I go outside and look at Rey Jr.'s head through the grimy glass. I can't touch his skull. Naked. How did it get that naked was tough? Naked like when they were born. When I was laying there and his head laced with blood and wax.

My head pounding when I put it against the glass, and I feel Danae's sticky fingers on my elbow. "Mama. I got another book at school today. *Sheep in a Jeep.*"

When we were done reading, she fell asleep. My head hurt like a tight swimcap. I went into Rey Jr.'s room and felt the slickness of the wax.


IN THE MORNING I'm so tired my hands are shaking when I comb Danae's hair. I have to take her to Rey's mother, since I pulled weekend shift. "Pocahontas braids," she says, and I feel my thumbs stiff when I twist the ties on the ends. I stare at my own forehead, all the new hair growing out, little explosions at my temples. Bald. Rey's bald now. We do braids and curls or Bone-Strait and half the day in the salon, and they don't even comb theirs? Big boulder heads and dents all in the skullbone, and that's supposed to look good to us?

I gotta watch all these wards dressed in dark blue work outfits, baggy-ass pants, big old shirts, and then get home and all the kids in the neighborhood are wearing dark blue Dickies, Rey is wearing dark blue Dickies and a Big Dog shirt.

Like my sister-in-law Cerise says, "They wear that, and I'm supposed to wear stretch pants and a sports bra and high heels? Give me a break."

Buzzing in my head. Grandmère said we all got the pressure, inherited. Says I can't eat salt or coffee, but she doesn't have to eat lunch here or stay awake looking at screens. Get my braids done this weekend, if Esther got time for me. Feels like my scalp has stubbles and they're turned inside poking my brain.

Here sits Fred across from me, still combs his hair even though it looks like a black cap pushed way too far back on his head. He's telling me I need to come out to the Old School club with him and JC and Beverly sometime. They play Cameo and the Bar-Kays. "Your Love Is Like the Holy Ghost."

"What you do last Sunday? You had the day off, right?" he says.

"I worked an extra shift. My grandmère took the kids to the cemetery." I drink my coffee. Metal like the pot. Not like my grandmère's coffee, creole-style with chicory. She took the kids to see her husband's grave, in the military cemetery. She told Danae about World War II and all the men that died, and Danae came home crying about all the bodies under the ground where they'd walked. Six—they cry over everything. Everything is scary.

I worked the extra shift to pay off my dishwasher. Four hundred dollars at Circuit City. Plus installation.

I told Rey Jr., "Oh, yeah, you gonna load this thing. Knives go in like this. Plates like this."

He said, "Why you yelling, Mama? Ain't no big thing. I like the way they get loaded in exactly the same every time. And I help Grammere Marie-Claire all the time with dishes. I just don't let Daddy know."

He grinned. I wanted to cry.

"USED PIANO IN the paper cost $500. Upright."

"What the hell is that?" Rey said on the phone. Hadn't come by since the barber.

I tried to think. "The kind against the wall, I guess. Baby grand is real high."

"For you?"

"For Rey Jr. He fooled around on the piano at school, and the teacher told him he has natural talent. Now he wants to play like my grandpère did in New Orleans."

Rey's voice got loud. "Uh-uh. You on your own there. Punks hear he play the piano, they gon kick his ass. Damn, Clarette."

I can get louder now, since I got this job. "Oh, yeah. He looks like Ice Cube, nobody's gonna mess with him. All better, right? Damn you, Rey."

I slam the phone down so hard the back cracks. Cheap purple Target cordless. $15.99.

Next day I open the classifieds on the desk across from Fred and start looking. Uprights. Finish my iron coffee. Then I hear one of the wards singing. "Three strikes you're out, tell me what you gonna do?"

Nate Dogg. That song. "Never Leave Me Alone."

This ward has a shaved black head like a bowling ball, a voice like church. "Tell my son all about me, tell him his daddy's sorry..."

Shows us his pass at the door. "Yeah, you sorry all right," Fred says.

The ward's face changes all up. Eyes go little and mean. "Not really, man. Not really."

My grandmère would say, "Old days, the men go off to the army. Hard time, let me tell you. They go off to die, or they come back. But if they die, we get some money from the army. If they come back, they get a job on the base. Now them little boys, they go off to the prison just like the army. Like they have to. To be a man. They go off to die, or come back. But they ain't got nothin. Nothin either way."

Wards in formation now. The wind is still pushing, school papers cartwheeling across the courtyard past the boots. Sometimes I still check for Alfonso, in the back like he used to be every day, like a big damn Candyland game with Danae, and it's never over cause we keep picking the same damn cards over and over cause it's only two of us playing. I still think he's here, even though I saw him in a Navigator last week getting a Coke at Rite-Aid—his friend all Thug Life and spitting right past me.

I breathe in all the dust from the fields. Chino hay fields all dry and turned now, the dirt flying past us. Two more hours today. Wards go back to class. The boy singing lifts his chin at me, and I stare him down. Fred humming something. What is it?

If this world were mine, I'd make you my queen... Old Luther songs.

"Shut up, Fred," I tell him. I don't know if he's trying to hook up with me or not. He keeps asking me about Rey.

"All them braids look like a crown," he says, smiling like a player.

"A bun," I say. He knows we have to wear our hair tight back for security. And Esther just did my braids last night. That's why my temples ache now.

"They went at it in the laundry room again Thursday," Fred says, looking at the screens.

I stare at the prison laundry, the huge washers and dryers like an old cemetery my grandmère took me to in Louisiana once, when I was a kid. All those dead people in white stone chambers with white stone doors. On the monitor, I see the wards sorting laundry and talking, see JC in there with them.

"Can't keep them out of there," I say, watching their hands on the white t-shirts. "Cause everybody's gotta have clean clothes."

At home I stand in front of my washer, dropping in Danae's pink t-shirt, her Old Navy capris. One trip to Old Navy in spring, one in fall is all I can afford. And her legs getting longer. Jeans and jeans. Sometimes they take so long to dry I just sit down on the floor in front of the dryer and read the paper, cause I'm too tired to go back out to the couch. If I sit down on something soft, I'll fall asleep, and the jeans will be all wrinkled in the morning.

But the wards here always press their jeans. In the laundry, that's the big deal. The creases have to be perfect.

SIX HOURS INTO the shift, even after four Advil, my forehead still feels like it's full of hot sand. Gotta be the flu. I don't have time for this shit. I re-do my hair, pull the braids back, put a softer scrunchie around the bun.

Seen Sisia at Esther's last night. She always hated me in high school, hated all of us from Sarrat because we were light. But she started hanging out with Glorette years ago—when they both fell in love with the wrong guys and then they got on the rock. Before I went up on Esther's porch for my appointment, I heard Sisia say, "Glorette ain't never had to get braids. Ain't never had to sit for ten minutes or do shit with all that hair she got. Not her whole damn life. I done spent half my money on my hair and nails."

I was thinking, *You spent the other half on crack,* and she said to me, "You got all that pretty hair, why you scrape it back so sharp?"

"Where I work."

"You cookin somewhere?"

"Nope. Sittin. Lookin at fools."

She pinched up her eyes. "At the jail?"

"CYA. Chino."

Then she pulls in her chin. "They got my son. Two years. He wasn't even doin nothing. Wrong place wrong time."

"Chino wrong place, sure."

She gets up and spits off Esther's porch. "I come back later, Esther."

Esther says, "Don't trip on Sisia. She always mad at somebody."

Shouldn't be mad at me.

"I didn't got her son. I'm just tryin to make sure he comes home. Whoever he is."

Esther nods and pulls those little hairs at my temple. I always touch that part when I'm at work. The body is thy temple. My temple. Where the blood pound when something goes wrong.

My laundry's like people landed from a tornado. Jean legs and shirt sleeves all tangled up on my bed.

"You foldin?" I said last night, and Rey Jr. pulled out his jeans and stacked them in a pile like logs. Then he slapped them down with his big hand.

"They my clothes."

"Don't tell your daddy."

"I don't tell him much."

His hair growing back on his skull. Not like iron filings. Like curly feathers. Still soft.

Now Fred puts his comb away and say, "Give a brotha some time."

"I gave him two years. He's been tripping for two years, okay?"

"That's all Rey get? He just goin through some changes, right?"

"We have to eat. Kids got field trips and books to buy." The wind bashes against the gates and they squeal like my grandmère's chickens. I'm not telling him, but I'm working overtime tonight cause I want a real piano. Not a cheap keyboard.

Two years. The laundry piled on my bed like a mound over a grave. On the side where Rey used to sleep. The homework. Now piano lessons.

Fred says, "So you done?"

"With Rey?" I look right at him. "Nope. I'm just done."

"Oh, come on, Clarette. You ain't but thirty-five. You ain't done."

"You ain't Miss Cleo. You ain't on TV predicting futures."

"You need to come out to the Comedy Club. No, now, I ain't sayin with me. We could meet up there. Listen to some Earth, Wind and Fire. Elements of life, girl."

Water. They missed water. Elements of life: bottled water cause I don't want the kids drinking tap. Water pouring out the washing machine. Water inside the new dishwasher—I can hear it sloshing around in there.

I look out at the courtyard. Rogue tumbleweed, a small one, rolling across the asphalt.

"Know what, Clarette? You just need to get yours. I know I get mines. I have me some fun, after workin here all day. Have a drink, talk to some people, meet a fine lady. Like you."

"Shut up, Fred. Here they come."

Reyes leading in his line and I see two boys go down, start punching. I run into the courtyard with my stick out and can't get to them, cause their crews are working now. The noise—it's like the crows in the pecan grove by Sarrat, all the yelling, but not lifting up to the sky. All around me. I pull off shirts, Reyes next to me throwing kids out to Michaels and Fred. Shoving them back, and one shoves me hard in the side. I feel elbows and hands. Got to get to the kid down. I push with my stick.

I swear I thought I saw Alfonso. His face bobbing over them like a puppet. "Get out of here!" I yell at him, and he's grinning. I swear. But it's not him. I reach down and the Chicano kid is on top, black kid under him, and I see a boot. I pull the top kid and hear Reyes hollering next to me, voice deep as a car stereo in my ear.

Circle's opening now. Chicano kid is down, he's thin, bony wrists, green-laced with writing. The black kid is softer, neck shining, and he rolls over. But then he throws himself at the Chicano kid again, and I catch him with my boot. Both down. Reyes kicks the Chicano kid over onto his belly and holds him. I have to do the same thing with the black kid. His lip split like a pomegranate. Oozing red. Some mother's son. It's hard not to feel the sting in my belly. Reyes' boy yelling at me in Spanish. I kick him one more time, in the side.

I bend down to turn mine over, get out my cuffs, and one braid pulls loose. Falls by my eyes. Bead silver like a raindrop. I see a dark hand reach for it, feel spit spray my forehead. *Bitch.* My hair pulled from my temple. My temple.

My stick. Blood on my stick. Michaels and Reyes take the wards. I keep my face away from all the rest, and a bubble of air or blood or something throbs next to my eyebrow, where my skin pulled from my skull, for a minute. Burning now, but I know it's gonna turn black like a scab, underneath my hair. I have to stand up. The sky turns black, then gray, like always. They're all heading to lockdown. I make sure they all see me spit on the cement before I go back inside. Fred stands outside talking to the shift supervisor, Williams, and I know he's coming in here in a minute, so I open the classifieds again and put my finger on *Upright.*

# SOMETHING LIKE SANCTIFIED

THEY BRING ME a body. They bring her in here and lay her on my couch. Glorette. Like we in Louisiana, when Michel get thrown from the mule and kick him in the head and they bring him to Auntie Viola house and she tell me, *Sit here with me, bebe, so I don't lonely while he don't left alone.*

Marie-Claire crossed herself first. Then she stood looking at Glorette's ribs in the space of skin between the sports bra and the tight exercise pants. The two curved bones on each side of her heart, because she lay on her back. Head awkward without a pillow.

"You cold, Maman?" Reynaldo said.

Marie-Claire looked up at her two sons. She had tucked her left arm under her breasts, and her right arm crossed over them, thumb on the marble of bone atop her shoulder. She felt dizzy for a moment. This was how she'd held herself when she was nervous since she was twelve and grew breasts, and her mother began to hide her from Mr. McQuine. She always thought if she covered her chest with her arms—like a scarf wrapped around her upper body—she would be safe. She always pressed down on that round little bone with her thumb while she tried to figure out what to do.

Reynaldo slid the blanket off the end of the wing chair and put it around her.

She thought, *How I'm cold and it was 109 today? None y'all ever see I do this?* She said, "Quiet. Them kids."

"Oh, shit," Lafayette whispered. "If they come out here and see—" The four grandchildren slept in his old back bedroom.

She nodded.

Reynaldo said, "They'd kill us."

His wife Clarette was working late shift at the prison. Lafayette's wife Cerise, with her nametag and low heels and hair in a bun—she'd gone straight from her job to the movies with a friend.

Glorette dead but still with a face like a pansy, purple and gold and the cheekbones mischevious. Marie-Claire bent to touch her forehead. Gold and unmarked, except two faint lines above her brows from squinting in the sun. She'd been working, too.

They'd all picked oranges. But now Glorette would have been squinting to recognize men. Under a streetlight, in darkness of a parking lot.

"Quo faire?" Marie-Claire said quietly to Enrique. He stood at the foot of the couch. Lafayette and Reynaldo moved to the doorway, looking away from her.

"She get kill in the alley," he said in French. He turned to his sons. "What his name—the one find her?" he said to them in English.

"Sidney Chabert," Lafayette said. "He said he was comin out the taco place and he saw her in the alley. In a cart."

"Cart?" Marie-Claire smelled shit, and for a moment she thought of the huge cane carts the mule used to pull.

"Shopping cart."

Outside the big picture window, past her roses and sunflowers, the truck was parked on the grass, and a man was walking toward the long gravel road that led to the orange groves and the gate. "Him?"

They looked out the door.

Marie-Claire looked at the red fingernails, chipped like squirrels had been chewing on the paint. The thin hand—palm up, curled as if holding a secret. The plump little palm Anjolie used to kiss, then tickle with her fingernails when she wanted to waken Glorette from the nap after kindergarten. All five of the girls in the back of Enrique's truck, going off to the school in the morning, and then napping on blankets here in the living room in the hot September afternoons because Marie-Claire had the only window cooler back then.

When she watched them climb into the truck for the first day of kindergarten, it felt like someone jammed a toothpick into her heart. Five tiny faces. She remembered climbing into the Apache on that frozen winter day in Louisiana with the other four girls, lying on the bags of rice under the tarp, because Mr. McQuine said she was next.

Glorette dead on the couch. These girls were supposed to be safe. "You bring her here? You ain't call the police?"

Enrique was watching the retreating back of the young man with no shirt. "That the one?" Marie-Claire said.

Then her husband turned his head slowly toward her, the way he did. Like his body was a lighthouse and his eyes the light. He never moved his shoulders, just his head, when he was looking over the orange trees to see the color of the fruit, or studying the children to see who'd stolen the piece of chicken she'd set aside for herself on the counter, or thinking he had to kill someone.

She knew that look. He'd killed Mr. McQuine after they were driven away in the Apache. But she'd seen his face, his eyes—that unhurried calculating grace—before she left Louisiana. And she'd seen it a hundred times here, when he was deciding something.

"How you gon bring her here?" she said to her sons, but they were already looking out at the grove road. Their big muscled arms a little soft now, the white tank tops, Reynaldo with two black grease stains along his collarbone. They spent the evening working on someone's car down at the barn, and then they went off to the liquor store. They loved only each other, just as their father loved only his own brother.

Her husband with his clean white t-shirt, his forearms so much darker than his throat, his wrists roped with veins like winter vines stripped of leaves. He was shorter and thinner than his boys. He squinted at Glorette, then at the window. He was already trying to figure out who he was hunting.

He lifted his chin, which moved her sons toward the door, and told them, "Get Gustave."

HE SAID, "ONCE he bring her to Lafayette and Reynaldo, she been move. Police would taken them in."

"If they find out she here—" she said, but he shook his head.

"They don't find out." He sat down on the wing chair and looked at Marie-Claire. She moved the skin over her shoulderbone with her thumb. He said, "Graveyard love."

Graveyard love was what had killed Gustave's father, back in the twenties. Graveyard love—you would kill to keep it, or die to have it.

But Marie-Claire shivered violently, once, down her spine like somebody ripped a cord from a bag of feed. Graveyard. The man her husband had killed to save her was in a graveyard in Louisiana. But the man he'd killed to get this house and these orange trees was buried somewhere here. Enrique didn't know she knew.

And now he looked out the window with that lighthouse gaze. He was planning to kill whoever had murdered this child—who was not a child now. He'd come home after doing it and sleep beside Marie-Claire.

GUSTAVE CAME IN, gray hair long and waved by sweat on the back of his burned neck. His wife Anjolie used to trim it, but she'd passed five years ago.

He knelt beside his daughter. He murmured something to Enrique.

She said, "Law say you call the coroner, say she die here at home. But he take her down there and find she got—"

She didn't want to say anything about the drugs. She could see fingernail scratches on Glorette's collarbone. Anyone could have put them there. She could have scratched herself. The alley—they said she was in the alley.

When they first got to California, she and the other girls, she walked in that alley from the boardinghouse to Archuleta's liquor store for salted plums. The first Spanish word she learned—saladitos. She was seventeen. After a windstorm, hundreds of palm fronds hung from the telephone wires like golden lion tails. Like nothing Marie-Claire had ever seen.

"You need to move her," she whispered in French to Enrique. "Them kids in the back."

But Gustave said, "I tell her son she die here. On the couch. Not in the alley."

Before she could answer, they walked out to the truck.

So if the police came, and she was sitting here, she was the one wrong. Her chest was full of anger, not hot but tight like someone reached in to close fingers around her heart—like the hand that rose from the grave in those scary movies.

But they were going to get the boy.


SO HE DON'T left alone. Can't leave them alone. The dead.

*Cause of spirit?*

*Cause of fly. Rat. Spirit. Thief. Sais pas, who come.*

She had been five. 1947. She sat in the wooden chair beside her aunt's wide soft thigh. Cotton dress so thin she could feel the long hard scar from a cane knife when she kept her hand on the leg to make sure her aunt didn't leave her there with Michel. His mouth held shut with a scarf. Silver half-dollars on his eyes. His hands folded on his chest, a bowl beside his body for money to help pay for the coffin.

She pulled her chair close to Glorette. How long had she been dead? She picked up the right hand, dangling closest to her, and moved the fingers. Rubbery and a little stiff. Like old carrots. What if it took them hours to find her son?

And the smell of her. Poop and pee—her grandchildren's favorite words when they were little. *She poop, grammere. She stinky.*

*On my couch. No.*

Marie-Claire allowed herself the tears now. She wiped her cheeks with the hard edge of her hand and felt the calluses scrape her temples. *God-damn it. Midnight and you bring me a body. I had but five hours sleep last night—Enrique come in late from checkin that irrigation, and then a coyote woke me up howlin.*

*I already washed four loads today. God-damn it! Rey Jr. done throw up twice.*

*Glorette's mouth had fallen open now. Not wide, but as if she were trying to speak. Her eyes still open.*

*Terrible. I should be crying to help Anjolie mourn in heaven. But they bring me a body like I know what to do. Enrique the one left behind two bodies. Who had to wash them?*

*Who he think he kill tonight? Who wash that one?*

*I have to wash this woman who was a baby in the bathtub with Fantine. Two faces turned up from the soapsuds with matching white beards. Call them Santa Babies. I put a shivery little piece soapsud on each head like whipcream.*

12:45. SHE DIALED her daughter's number. The cell phone rang only twice before Fantine's voice said, "Hey, I'm in Zurich—I'll get back to you."

Zurich was Switzerland. Marie-Claire knew because Fantine had been there before. Fantine had brought a magazine with a story about Zurich, with pictures of rivers and hotels and restaurants. Sometimes when she heard Fantine say a city on the voicemail, she had no idea where her daughter was in the world.

Fantine might be home tomorrow. But she would never touch a body.

She heard a small voice. A murmur from the back bedroom. A bad dream.

The grandkids. Cerise had planned to leave them overnight. She called Clarette, who whispered, "I'm not supposed to answer the phone."

"You finish at one?"

"They asked could I stay til three. Somebody's late."

"No. Come straight home at one."

"Home?"

"Here."

Clarette's voice was sharp with fear. "The kids okay?"

Marie-Claire closed her eyes. "Rey Jr. thrown up. Come home fast as you can," she whispered. It was nothing, but it would bring Clarette here.

If the kids heard voices, they'd come toward the light in the living room.

MY COUCH. THAT poop. She went quickly to the kitchen and got out the oldest oilcloth table covering. The one they used outside when she made gumbo in the yard on the electric fire because it was so hot. Hot in here now. The body would start to smell.

And she didn't have much time now before it grew truly stiff. "Wait too long you can't move no arm, no leg," she remembered Auntie Viola saying to someone. "Like you break em."

She stood with the oilcloth rolled up in her arms and looked down at Glorette.

Even with the smell, it was the mouth that hurt more. Because it made Glorette look dumb.

She went back down the hallway. Marie-Claire stopped at the door of Lafayette and Reynaldo's old bedroom but heard nothing. No whispering. No whimpering.

In her room, she got the silk scarf from the top drawer. Fantine had brought it for her from Milan, Italy. She sat beside Glorette and pushed up gently on the chin. The bone so small. She tied the scarf tightly, and Glorette looked like a strange foreign star from an old movie.

She had to close those eyes. Her own eyes stung again like alcohol, with tears. She used to love looking at that face, when the girl came over and her son Victor was just a baby. Never see that color again. Anjolie used to say, *Them eyes, like just when the sun go down. Dark purple. Make Elizabeth Taylor eyes look like nothing.*

What had they put on her own grandmother's eyes? The old people didn't even have money back then. No coins.

Bags of rice.

She quickly put rice in two small baggies and tied them off. Glorette's eyelids were traced with the tiniest veins like red thread. Was that from how she died?

That smell. She was too angry now to cry. The yoga pants tight and black. Was Glorette even wearing panties? Marie-Claire went to the hallway, the old linen cupboard with the drop-down front panel on which she used to fold tablecloths. She'd kept baby supplies in there when the grandkids were small. Those wipes—were they still moist?

*No. I am not doin this.* Had her aunt felt the same way when they brought Michel—a grown man, weighed about two hundred pounds? What had her aunt done with him, on the makeshift cooling board of a door propped on two sawhorses? All the old women had come to help.

*Mo tou soule.* Enrique always said that. *Me, I'm all alone.*

But he had never been, since Gustave.

*Mo tou soule,* she chanted to herself, pulling down the yoga pants, the red bikini underwear. If Gustave was telling her son she'd come here to rest on the couch, and she'd died right here, peaceful and unexpected, she couldn't be wearing anything but what she always wore.

The poop was nothing. Less than a baby. Glorette never ate anything. She smoked whatever it was they smoked. But the pee was sharp and strong, and Marie-Claire's chest heaved. She wiped Glorette's bottom with the moist babywipe, breathing through the neckline of her nightdress pulled up over her mouth and nose. She didn't have time to take off the yoga pants. So tight. She couldn't leave the girl exposed like this on the couch, on the oilcloth of picnics and gumbo, to run back and get perfume. She pulled the wet pants back up, and heard Enrique's truck moving slowly down the gravel road through the trees.

She slid Glorette off the oilcloth, ran to the bedroom and got an ancient bottle of Jean Nate. She left the oilcloth on the floor beside her slippers. Then she sprayed Anjolie's daughter, as if she were going to a dance.

But she wouldn't lie on her back, if she were resting. That looked wrong. She clasped the body to her, bent Glorette's arms, which were resisting now, like those old Barbie dolls with their legs that would move but stubbornly, and pulled her onto her side. She lifted the bags of rice from the eyes, praying. They stayed closed. She pulled the scarf from the jaw and smoothed the hair. She hid those behind the pillow and tucked around Glorette's legs the blanket Reynaldo had draped around her own shoulders.

*Hot as hell. She wouldn't sleep with no blanket. But now her son ain't have to see them wet pants.* The truck headlights lit up the red roses along the flowerbed, the petals burnt black at the edges by the sun.

HER SON'S HAIR was a sunburst of on-purpose tangles. Dreads. His eyes were the same purple as his mother's. He sat on the floor beside her body and didn't move for a long time.

And she couldn't say to him, "You have to go. Them kids come out here..."

Because their mamas didn't want them to scar for life by a dead body. And his mama the body. He was so scarred she couldn't imagine it.

WHEN GUSTAVE TOOK him across the street to his house, Enrique sent Lafayette and Reynaldo down to the barn.

In the kitchen, she whispered, "They make a coffin?" she said. "You serious?"

His eyes were distant and narrowed as shards of brown glass.

She said, "Fantine in a plane. Cerise at the movies. Clarette workin late shift. You ain't sit here. Cause you go lookin for who done it."

He picked up the empty silver coffee pot and she said, "I can't even make coffee for stay up all night, not til you bring somebody sit with her." She went back to the front room and knelt down by the couch. "You go get Archuleta."

"Ramon?" He stared at her.

"The other one. The uncle. The priest. Tell the priest tomorrow. And bring that ice. The one for Halloween. The one make smoke."

"I bring you coffee from Archuleta's."

"Drink no dishwater, me." Her shoulders began to shake, and she was crying now. "The grandkids back there. They see her, all I hear from Cerise and Clarette is 'scar for life.' All they talk about—you let em fall out the tree, you let em eat too much candy. You need to put her in Fantine room. Quiet." She pushed him toward the living room. "Can't scar you. You see dead body before."

He lifted his chin at her, eyes even narrower, just a crescent of glitter in the hallway light. "Been in the war, me," he said. "You ain't see no dead body. You been here."

She turned away, thinking about the night Beto had come here and gotten drunk.


NEVER TRUST NO *smiling man,* her mother had said. *Not one smile all the time.*

Her mother had run the plate lunches and dinners in Sarrat. That way she and Marie-Claire didn't have to go in the canefields.

When Marie-Claire was five, she began by sorting through the dry red beans for stems and sticks, then sifting the rice through her fingers for pebbles. After that she snapped the ends off green beans. Sitting on the two wooden steps that led to the porch where her mother plucked feathers from the chickens she killed three days a week, or stripped the bones from the fish she bought the other three days.

Her mother meant the men who walked casually into the yard from the road, a few men from the canefields but sometimes strangers. Men who smiled and grinned while they talked to her mother about cutting some wood or fixing a fence. They wanted free food.

Every time, her mother said, *Ganlargent, mo* so fast it was like one word. Four words—*make some money, me.*

She whispered to Marie-Claire, "Man better smile tou soule li."

Only for you.

Enrique and Gustave showed up in 1949. They'd been in Sarrat as children. Gustave smiled and nodded sometimes. But when he came in after working the canefields, Enrique kept his eyes guarded, his head slanted to the left while he studied everyone in the front room buying plates of chicken and rice and greens.

She was sixteen. He was over thirty. But after a month, when he came into the yard, he took off his hat in a motion, ducked his head toward her, and smiled so slowly it seemed five minutes before she saw his white white teeth.

Now he came out of his daughter's room with the smell of perfume on his arms, about to go hunt someone.

NO ONE EVER slept in her daughter's daybed now. The chair was still at Fantine's desk, where she had written her first stories. When Marie-Claire moved the chair to sit beside Glorette, two magazines fell off. *Vogue.* The woman's lips glossy as candied apple. A story about Italy. Pictures of narrow stone streets, and hams. Fantine was in Zurich right now, tasting someone else's food, listening to what they said.

*And I have to wash Glorette feet. All them miles, up and down the alley. See the same faces some night, see some stranger. Must be the stranger kill her.*

She took off the high-heeled sandals. The ankles like clay. She tied up the jaw again, and put the baggies of rice back on the eyes. Then Clarette burst through the front door and Marie-Claire heard her say, "Rey Jr. still sick?"

She saw the light in Fantine's room, just off the kitchen, and came inside. Her uniform was black, her boots like military.

"Oh, hell, no. No. No."

"I'm sorry, bebe."

"Sorry?" Clarette twirled and put her hands to her temples. "No. I am not this person. I am not these people."

"She your people."

"I am not the people who get high all night and die and then my kids have to see a dead body. I am not the one who touches a dead body and then the cops find out and I lose my job. No. Oh, hell no. I am not doing this."

"Hush and them kids don't see nothin. Hush! She sleep in here. You pick up them kids one by one and take em Felonise house. You call Cerise and tell her and her maman come home. And then you help me right here."

"Cause you know Cerise ain't gon do it."

"Oui. I know. And baby—" Because Clarette was more like her own daughter now, since Clarette's mother had died when she was only fourteen, and she had never known her father, and her brother was gone, too—"I wish I didn't have to ask you. I wish Lafayette could carry em. And you sleep. But he gotta build the coffin."

"Oh, my God," Clarette said, putting her palms to her temples again, so her elbows looked like wings. "You can't just bury someone out here."

Marie-Claire saw the whole place then, in her head, as if she were in the police helicopter that circled like a hornet over the riverbed, looking at homeless camps. The orange groves laid out in rows where she and these girls had moved up and down in straight lines, picking Valencias, all these years. Enrique's barn, and the eight tiny white houses on the narrow street, and her own larger house right here on the rise, surrounded by bougainvillea. He had bought it with more than money. He'd killed Atwater, slowly, and then buried him somewhere out there.

Clarette said, "I can't believe—"

Marie Claire waited. Can't believe she's dead, can't believe Enrique expected them to bury here here, can't believe—

Then Clarette came closer. "How does she still look beautiful?" she whispered. "All these years and her hair like that." The long black hair cascaded through the wrought-iron curlicues on the daybed. *Take two to do the hair*, Marie-Claire thought. *But I can do her nails.*

"So damn illegal," Clarette whispered. "I'll lose my job if the cops come. Damn! I just finished a ten-hour shift!"

"What you think I done? I got up at six and made breakfast for Enrique and Gustave and your husband."

"Like I'm happy he's staying out here in the barn!"

Reynaldo had left Clarette two years ago. "I ain't happy, me. But here he was in my kitchen at seven. And then I cleaned this house and washed all the sheets, and you brought me them kids at four. Rey-Rey done throw up twice cause he ate too many Otter Pops. The box got fifty and whole thing gone."

"How you let—"

"How I let? You think I can keep a eye on all four of em and it was 109 outside? I try keep everything in the yard alive."

"I'm just so damn tired!"

"I been tired longer than you been alive. You don't want do this, go home. But you gotta take them kids with you." Marie-Claire stood up and went to Fantine's closet so she wouldn't scream at her daughter-in-law. Not a closet. This had been a breakfast nook, not a bedroom. And the armoire filled with clothes Fantine would never look at again, and things she'd left after college.

The dress Fantine had worn to high school graduation. Glorette was still exactly the same size as seventeen. But she'd had Victor the week of graduation. Marie-Claire took out the dress—silky and slippery. What they called the fabric—Qiana?

Clarette twirled twice more and then went toward the door.

"Don't tell Felonise why. Tell her I don't feel good." Clarette closed the door behind her.

Marie-Claire heard her going down the hallway, heard the murmuring, and she heard the heavy footsteps of Clarette carrying the first one.


WHEN SHE CAME back, she said, "Oh, my God."

Marie-Claire had taken off the clothes and put them in a white plastic trash bag with red ties. Glorette's breasts were dappled with scars. Tiny white chrysanthemums. Eight. Someone had burned her with cigarettes. Marie-Claire put the white sheet over her chest.

Clarette said hoarsely, "What you want me to do first?"

"Help me with the diapers."

She remembered vague things about what her aunt had done. There was still more waste in the body. Her aunt had used rags, but there were also four diapers left in the cupboard, from when Teeter was potty-training. They were large, but not large enough. Marie-Claire opened them up and overlapped three. She cut the fourth into pads.

"Push down on her stomach." Not much more pee came out. Not like when you had a baby and they had to push out all the afterbirth and blood poured from you like you'd grown a river inside and not a baby. When she had Lafayette she was eighteen and her mother was back in Louisiana.

Two white nurses at the hospital pushed down so hard on her belly she screamed they were killing her, and one said, "Don't be ignorant."

Clarette seemed stunned. Her braids held back by an elastic, but one came out and brushed against Glorette's shoulder. The bead at the end knocking the bone. She jumped and Marie-Claire said, "Just sit down here. On this chair."

Marie-Claire dumped the diapers into the trash bag. She filled a basin with vinegar and water, and washed out Glorette's privates. She covered the body with the sheet. She threw the wet paper towels in the bag, too. Not like rags, where you had to wash them, burn them, or bury them— back in the old days. Now she said, "Don't move. Sit right there. She don't be lonely."

At the trashcans behind the house, she dropped the lid quietly. Night-birds were singing in the eucalyptus windbreak. One mockingbird in the sycamore at the edge of the yard.

Beto had come one night when the mockingbirds were fighting in the trees, singing longer and longer songs, keeping her awake. He was the Indian man who'd worked here for years before Enrique came to this place after the war. They'd always spent hours in the barn, where Beto sharpened knives and tools in the winter. But that night, he was drunk, and Enrique was gone somewhere with Gustave. Beto said, "How you know he won't get tired of you next? Just find a way to get rid of you. Bury you out there somewhere. On his land."

"Why you say that to me?"

"Cause he got this land the wrong way. He knew that white man wouldn't sell it to him. So he killed him."

"Maybe they have a fight." She remembered Beto sitting in the kitchen holding a cup of coffee, having drunk whiskey with Enrique and Gustave all night.

"A fight that lasted ten days? He took ten days to die. I was there."

"So you help."

Beto shrugged. He had a long braid down his back and a feathery little moustache over his lip. Two hairs at the end touching the corner of his mouth. He said, "I didn't know what your husband was doing at first. But he's stone cold. You thought about that? You're still young. And beautiful."

"And I got a baby in the back. Two years old."

Beto said, "Listen." And they heard the nightbirds through the window screen in the kitchen. "You never thought about Atwater used to sleep in this house? And where he's layin now?"

"Ain't my business."

Beto said, "Spirits everybody's business. My old man's buried over there in Agua Dulce somewhere. I still see him walkin the river at night."

"I sit in here at night," Marie-Claire told him, and took away the coffee cup. "And you can sit down in the barn."

"I ain't comin back," Beto said. "I just wanted to see you again." He stood up. "You sure you ain't part Indian? That hair? Those eyes?"

"I'm whole married. You seen me. Now you go."


THE HOUSE WAS silent. Like never. Felonise or someone in the kitchen, children sleeping in the bedrooms, Enrique snoring softly like a rattle had lodged in his throat.

"You got nail polish?" she said to Clarette, who sat staring out the bedroom window.

"Right now?"

"Right now." Marie-Claire bent to Fantine's small desk. In the drawer she found polish remover, the pink liquid sharper than the vinegar smell. When Enrique came back with the dry ice and the boys were done with the coffin, she would behead all the roses and put the petals around the body, even between the legs when no one saw.

Clarette dug in her purse and came up with a bottle. Pink as pale and shiny as the inside of a shell. "You know who picked this?" she whispered. "Rey Jr. He said it was the prettiest color he'd ever seen. We were at Target. And Teeter punched him and said that was sissy."

She stood while Marie-Claire sat in the chair and began taking off the thick red polish, dirty and chipped. The fingers harder now, the wrist tiny but resisting. The skin like a terrible dough spread over the bones.

All that blood pooling inside. Marie-Claire said, "Rey Jr., he ate too many them red Otter Pops. And I had to sit next to him for a while, make sure he ain't throw up again. He ain't want me to go. We was right here, cause the porch was so hot and them other kids was in the groves."

Clarette said, "Greedy."

"He start talkin about blood."

"What? What did he see?"

"Non. When you a child, you look around you. Not inside yet. You see a flower, and you don't know."

"Know what?" Clarette looked out the window at the sunflowers with their heads hanging.

Marie-Claire said, "Them white flower. Jimsonweed. Rey Jr. said somebody tell him that hell's bells, and you can die if you touch it. I tell him you have to make a drink from it to die, and he say how do I know? Indian man tell me, when I first get here."

Beto said Enrique had boiled the jimsonweed and added the liquid to Atwater's whiskey. He'd killed rabbits and roasted them on spits made of green oleander branches, so the poison entered the flesh.

So she could have this house. So they would be safe. The painting on the wall right here, sent by Fantine from Paris, of a blackbird on a snowy fence in France. The coffee beans from Belize that Marie-Claire had never opened—the package was too beautiful.

She said to Clarette, "You don't remember, but you always want sugarcane. Back when Gustave grow cane in his yard, and you greedy. Suck on that cane until you have a white beard down your face. You bout five. And then Glorette and Fantine go work the sugarcane in Louisiana one time, help Enrique when somebody die, and you get so mad. Your mama won't let you go. She say you never go to Louisiana. Never."

"He got her. That old man."

"He got her and Claudine and Zizi. Broke her wrist when he throw her down. You remember when I knock Fantine down the porch?"

Her eyes stung from the polish remover. Her own flat hand clapping across Fantine's face so hard her only daughter fell against the steps. Fantine had talked the others into walking downtown to a rich white girl's pool party, and the father had touched Glorette on the shoulder, looked at her hard. Glorette told them. And when Marie-Claire told her the story of Mr. McQuine, Fantine had laughed impatiently. As if that could never happen here. As if she never needed to be afraid.

Downtown, where the older houses were, Cerise and Clarette lived a few streets apart. Cerise's house with shingles painted light blue, and a wrought-iron arch over the sidewalk with jasmine vine. Clarette's house with stucco painted yellow, and red geraniums Marie-Claire had started for her in coffee cans.

Every room in the house full except this one. So quiet when she was sitting beside Michel, back then. Auntie Viola's house two doors down the quarter from her mother's. Plate dinners until midnight, when her mother finally locked the door. People in the front room, in the kitchen, and her trying to sleep in the middle room. "Hush—Marie-Claire dor-me." But she couldn't. And now the children here, and the men in the kitchen. Reynaldo fighting with Clarette about money, coming back here to live in the empty stone house deep in the grove. Clarette saying she couldn't believe Marie-Claire let him eat here, making it easy for him.

"Go check on the coffin," she said to Clarette now. "See Lafayette get that wood. I be okay here."

Clarette went out the front door. And Marie-Claire knew she turned her head toward her sleeping children at the little house where Felonise was sitting on her own couch, making sure they had no bad dreams or woke up wanting their mothers, dying to come over here and see what was going on.

Rey Jr. crying after he threw up, saying, "I hate when it comes out my nose!" Saying, "It looks like blood comin out my stomach!" Saying, "How come when we eat steak the blood is gray? If we cooked our blood would it turn black?"

And her saying, "That what color you get when you cut your arm, oui? Get black if you healthy."

She took the old polish from the last, smallest fingernail. Glorette sitting on this daybed when she was ten. Saying, "This my favorite place to take a nap. In the whole world. You wake up at my house, you see the wall. You wake up here, you see the flowers right by your face. Or the moon. Remember you let me sleep until dark once? The moon came up all perfect right there." She'd touched the window glass.

The fingers hard now. The nails would keep growing? Marie-Claire shook the polish. *Need to do that hair. But I don't want touch it yet.*

She studied the pale pink. And Glorette's eyelids, shadowy and purple. *I have to do makeup, too.*

"So you don't be lonely," Marie-Claire said quietly. "I sat in my mama's house look at a magazine, and I wanted nail polish so bad. They ain't had it at the corner store. Just food and cigarettes and beer. She taken me to Baton Rouge once and I got red nail polish. Red as blood. I paint my nails and then Mr. McQuine get Mary. They put us in the truck. I was sixteen. We come here, and then Enrique show up two years later."

She opened the bottle. The smell so strong.

"I paint my nails every Saturday, after we got married, and then I had to pick oranges, and wash them diaper, and kill them chicken. But I paint em anyway. We went to the five-and-dime on Palm. Why not nickel-and-dime? All you girls got candy. I got a new color once a month. They had names on the back. Fantine used to tell me. Candy Apple. Apricot Dream. I wonder who name all them color."

Atwater must have slept in the bedroom she shared with Enrique. He had to be buried somewhere by the river.

All those Saturdays, her boys in the other bedroom playing the radio. Marvin Gaye. Girl you give me good feelin—sugar—something like sanctified.

She pulled Glorette's hand to her, that motion she wished all her life she could do for Fantine, and dropped the first tiny pearl of pink on a fingernail.

# POINCIANA

"WHY YOU WASTE your money here?" she asked Sisia. The smell of the chemicals at the nail salon went through Glorette's eyes and into her brain. Passed right through the tears and the eyeball. Through the iris, she thought.

"Not a waste," Lynn Win said, moving around Sisia's hand like a hummingbird checking flowers. Like the hummingbird that came to the hibiscus in front of The Lamplighter Motel. Mrs. Tajinder Patel's hibiscus. "Only to you," Lynn Win said.

"Please." Glorette walked into the doorway to breathe and looked at the cars roaming past the strip mall. Every strip mall in Rio Seco, in California, in the world, probably, was like this. Nail salon, video store, doughnut shop, liquor, and Launderland and taqueria. All the smells hovering in their own doorways, like the owners did in the early morning and late at night, waiting.

Like she and Sisia hovered. Sundown first, Launderland in winter when it was cold in the alley, taqueria when the cops cruised by. All the standing and waiting between jobs. They were just jobs. Like clean the counter at the taqueria. Take out the trash. Uncrate the liquor.

Wash the sheets. All up and down the street. Lean against the chainlink fence, against the bus stop but you couldn't sit on the bench, shove your shoulder into the cinderblock wall outside Launderland and even sleep for a minute, if the fog settled in like a quilt, like the opposite of an electric blanket, and cooled off the night.

Not now. Hot as hell til past midnight.

The nail polish vapors stung her eyes. Why you couldn't get high off these fumes? So convenient. 7-Eleven was a convenience store. Easy. She could sit here and close her eyes and Lynn Win would paint her like a statue and the vapors would rise up into her mouth and nose and make the inside of her forehead turn to snow. She would pay Lynn Win. Instead of paying for the rock to turn into fumes.

The plant to a powder to a chunk—a clover burr in your hand. And then it turned red and glowed, like a rat's eye in the palm tree when you looked up just as headlights caught the pupils. Did rats have pupils?

Then you breathed in. And behind your eyes, it was like someone took a white-out pen and erased everything. Your whole head turned into a milkshake. Sweet and grainy and sliding down the back of your skull.

Look at all these nail salons. She turned the pages of the advertisements in Vietnamese, the flyer on the coffee table. Massage pedicure chairs. Swirling water. The women with perfect eyebrows and lips and hair. Every other one name Nguyen.

Linh Nguyen. Lynn Win told Glorette she changed her name to make it easier for Americans to write on checks. "Win like money I get."

Glorette breathed again at the open salon door. "Sisia. Please. Tell me you ever heard a man say, 'Girl, I love those nails. That color's perfect with your clothes. The decals are fresh.'"

"Shut up, Glorette. You just cheap."

Lynn Win glanced up at her and frowned, her perfect Vietnamese face sheened with makeup, her eyes encircled by a wash of pale green, her lips pink as watermelon Jell-o. Against her neck, on the left side, was a scar. A healed gash that must have gaped, against tight neck skin.

No one had loose neck skin until forty. *She must be about thirty-five,* Glorette thought. *Just like us.*

Sisia had a scar on her neck, too, a keloid caterpillar, shiny as satin. Curling iron. Sixteen. They'd been getting ready for some high school dance. Back when Sisia still hot-combed her hair and then curled it back like Farrah Fawcett and Jayne Kennedy.

What did the DJ play at that dance? Cameo? She'd have to ask Chess when she saw him next time. Bar-Kays? "Your Love Is Like the Holy Ghost."

The hot air at the door mixed with the cold AC and nail polish fog.

No scars. She had never done anything with her hair other than wash it, comb in some Luster Pink or coconut oil, and let it hang loose in long black ripples. Back then. Now she wore it in a high twisted bun every night, unless a man told her to unpin it. *Put all that hair right here. Hurry up.*

This new woman cruising Palm in the brown van had poked her finger into the bun a few nights ago and then pulled. "Man, I know that shit ain't real," the woman had said, her voice New York like rappers on a video, her words all pushed up to the front of her lips. People from New York kept their words there, just at their teeth, not deep in their throats like Louisiana people. Like her mother and father.

Then the new woman had said, "I-on't-even-care you think you the shit around here. Just cause you light. Cause you got all that hair. Anybody get hair. Bald man get hair if he want to. You need to move your ass off this block. Cause I'm parked here."

She couldn't have been more than twenty, twenty-two. Short, thick-thighed in her miniskirt, her hair in marcelled waves close to her fore-head. Her words moved behind her lips and her lips moved like a camel's, while her eyes stayed still.

"Sound like she said she some pork," Sisia said, hands on her hips.

Glorette just shrugged and looked back over her shoulder at the wom-an near her van. That's where she worked the men. She had a CD player in there, and some silk sheets, she said. And her man stood in the door-way of the liquor store for a long time, watching Chess and Reynaldo and the others who were just biding their time.

"I ain't no crack ho," the girl called, and Sisia laughed.

"I ain't either," she said. "I'm somethin else."

"This ain't the nineties." The girl shot them the finger.

"And I ain't Donna Summer."

Glorette watched Sisia move her head on her neck like a turtle and stalk away, and she followed.


GLORETTE THOUGHT: *1980? Was I sixteen?*

*Damn.*

*Gil Scott Heron said the Revolution will not be televised, brother. You will not be able to turn on or tune out.* But they did. That's what Sere always said. Brothers tuned out. *Green Acres* and *Beverly Hillbillies* will not be so important, Gil Scott Heron said—but they were. *The revolution will not be televised, brothers, the revolution will be live.*

One night Glorette had run into Marie-Therese at Rite Aid. Marie-Therese used to be with Chess, back then when they were girls in the darkness of the club called Romeo's. 1981? Only two clubs in Rio Seco back then—Romeo's for jazz and funk, and Oscar's Place for nasty old blues and knife fights and homebrew.

*That was where I met Sere. A brother with a flute. Didn't nobody in Rio Seco have a flute.*

Gil Scott Heron's band had a flute. Yusuf Lateef had a flute. War had a flute. Herbie Mann had a flute. Sere had loved that Mann song—"Push Push." She could still remember it. Sere's band was called Dakar. His last name.

Where the hell was Sere playing his damn flute now? For Jay Z or 50 Cent? For Ludacris? What else did this girl from New York always have blastin out her CD player when she was waiting?

Nobody said *Hey, brotha.* Nobody but the old ones. Her age. Chess and them. That Sidney, the one ran into her at Sundown. He used to work at the hospital. Chess and them said he burned the body parts after the doctors cut them off. Said he burned up Mr. Archuleta's leg, and Glorette always wondered how heavy that piece of meat would have been. She ran her shoulders up under her ears with the shivers. Piece. *Give me a lil piece, sugar. Just a lil piece.* What the hell was that? What they wanted wasn't no size. You couldn't give anybody just a lil bit of anything.

\* \* \*

SISIA HANDED THE money to Lynn Win. Sisia's skin was so thin over her facial bones that her temples looked stretched from the tight corn-rows, even her nose.

They had been smoking for so long. Chess gave her the first pipe, but then he got done with it. He said he didn't need it.

He had his weed and Olde English.

How was the skin distributed over the bones? How did her buttocks stay in the right place? When did men decide they wanted buttocks and cheekbones and hair instead of something else? Like a big nose or huge forehead or belly? Some caveman picked.

Sisia stood up with her nails purple as grape juice and rings wink-ing. But could a woman kill someone with her nails? Because this new woman from New York looked like she wanted to kill Glorette.

THE MAN STOPPED in his old Camaro. Moved his chin to tell her come on. Glorette knew he wanted head. That's all. He parked in the lot behind the taqueria. Five minutes. A little piece of her lip when he jerked around and her tooth banged on his zipper.

Her piece: $20. She walked back toward Launderland, where Jazen and his boys kept their stash in a dryer.

The rock was so small. Not even a piece. A BB. A spider egg. A grass-hopper eye. But not perfectly round. Jagged edged.

A white freckle, she thought, and started laughing, waiting for the screen like a windshield in front of her eyes when she breathed in hard. Like someone had soaped up her brain. Store was closed.

HEADPHONES. AL B. Sure—"Nite and Day." Switch—"I Call Your Name." All those sweet-voiced men from when she was first walking out here. Not jazz. Jazz was Sere. "Poinciana." April in Paris. And funk. Man-drill and Soul Makossa and Roy Ayers.

But somebody always stole the headphones. And she wanted Victor to have headphones, and they kept stealing his, too. So he slept in them, with a chair against his bedroom door. She tried to make sure only Chess or someone she knew came home with her, but sometimes Sisia begged to let her use the couch or the floor with a man, and then sometimes he stole.

Victor knew everything about music.

"New York rappers, man, I have to listen real careful to understand," he said. "Oakland and LA are easy. St. Louis is crazy—I mean, they mess with the actual syntax like nobody else."

Victor analyzed everything. Sometimes Glorette stared at his forehead while he was talking, at the place where his baby hairs hadn't grown into his dreads yet. His hairline curved like a cove on a map. She had been to a cove once. To the ocean. With Victor's father. Sere.

He'd seen her in the club. He thought she was eighteen. He'd borrowed a car, pulled up in front of the high school and leaned his chin on the crook of his elbow like a little kid. He told her, "I'm fixin to see this place California's supposed to be. What they all talk about in Detroit."

"What you think you gon see?" Glorette had watched the freeway signs above them, the white dots like big pearls in the headlights.

"Remember Stevie singing 'Livin for the City'? Skyscrapers and everythang. I'ma see waves and sand and everythang. Surfers."

"At night?"

"They probably surf at night." He'd turned to see her in the passenger seat. That car was a Nova, and someone had spilled Olde English in the backseat and the smell rose from the carpet sharp like cane syrup. "It's an hour to the ocean and you never been there?"

Glorette had shrugged. She had felt her shoulders go up and down, felt her collarbone in the halter top graze the cloth. He had left a love bruise on her collarbone. He'd said her bones made her look like a Fulani queen. "I bet them sorry brothas call you a Nubian or Egyptian. Cause they don't know the specifics."

She'd touched cheekbone and collarbone and the point of her chin. But after all that it was the soft part they wanted.

No bones.

"It's a hour I ain't never had free," she said.

Sere took out the Cameo cassette from the old stereo and slid in an unmarked tape. "Poinciana," he said. Piano hush-hush and cymbals. Like rain on a porch roof and swirling water.

Then, after they'd driven to the ocean and sat in their car looking at the blackness that was one with the horizon, a cold purple-blue blackness like charcoal, with the waves the only sound and then a plash of white in a long line as if someone were washing bleach clothes in too much detergent, Sere turned to her, and he only wanted the same things as the rest of them.


WHY HAVE BUTTOCKS? What good were they? And hair? If Glorette's great-great-whoever had been Fulani and had gotten with some Frenchman in Louisiana, why all this hair falling down her back? How was that supposed to keep her warm? Hair was fur. Nails were claws. Sisia was ready to kill some damn lion then, now that they were done with Lynn Win's place. Glorette had gotten high off the fumes anyway, waiting for Sisia's toenails to dry. Who the hell was she gon kill with them toenails? Lynn Win's mother sat at the spa chair waiting for the next pedicure. The mother looked old but probably wasn't. She wore knit pants like an old woman, and her hair was in a bun on her head. Black hair with gray threads shot through like moss.

All the blood moving through the pieces of their bodies. When she woke up at noon or so, the already-hot light streaming through the blinds like x-rays on her legs where she lay on the couch, she would see the tops of her feet smooth and golden, her toes dirty from the walking, but her skin still sleeping.

Sometimes Sisia spent the $12 on a pedicure just so she could sit down for an hour, she said.

But Glorette didn't want decals on her toes. She saved $20 a day for Victor. For CDs and Ramen.

She went to the older plaza further up Palm, with the Rite Aid and the auto parts store. The lipsticks stacked in the bin like firewood. Haircolor boxes always started with blonde. Blonde as white taffy and then about thirty more yellows. Saffron and Sunflower. Gingercake and Nutmeg. Black always last. Raven. Midnight.

Black hair ain't nothin you could eat.

There were flowering plants in front of the drug store. Her father always shook his head and said, "Anybody buy plant when they buy cough syrup don't grow nothin. Put that tomato in the ground and throw water on it and wonder why it die, oui."

She walked past the window of the auto parts store. When she was small, in here with her father and Uncle Enrique, she used to wander the aisles touching the oil filters like paper queen's collars, and fan belts like rubber bands for a giant's ponytail. After Victor was born, Chess came to visit from college and said he loved her. Brought her the pipe. The little air fresheners hanging right there by the cash register. Chess brought her here once when he needed Armor All. Chess played ball all day, and loved her all night. But he had to love Marie-Therese and Niecy, too, and she told him *Only me*, and he shrugged and said *Only always too small. Only one dollar. Only one rib. See? I ain't livin only.*

Boxes and boxes of fuel filters near the window. Same size as haircolor. *A lil piece. Only a lil piece.*

Ramen was ten for a dollar. Beef.

Now, when she looked at her hands on the Rite Aid counter, they were smooth and gold. She slid the dollar across and got six cents for tax from the little dish. Take a penny leave a penny. By midnight, when she sat in the taqueria just before it closed, she would study her hands, the veins jagged like blue lightning. Her feet—it looked like someone had inserted flattened branches of coral under her skin. The skin so thin by midnight, at hands and feet and throat and eyelids.

She imagined she was swimming down the sidewalk. The pepper trees in the vacant lot past the strip mall, where the old men used to play dominoes on orange crates, where the city had put a chainlink fence, trying to keep people from loitering. She didn't loiter. The streetlights shone through the pepper branches. She was under the ocean. Sere had brought a flashlight that night they went to the ocean, and he'd found tidal pools where the water only swayed in the depressions of the rocks, and the flashlight beam showed her a forest of seaweed and snails clinging to the leaves—were green blades called leaves, underwater? stems?—and the whole world under the surface swayed.

Like now, when the evening wind moved the whole street. The pepper branches swayed delicate and all at once, the palm fronds rustled and glinted above her, and the tumbleweeds along the fence trembled like the anemones.

She'd gotten a book, a child's book, after that night at the ocean, and learned the names of every animal in the tidal pool. She had waited a year for him to take her back there, but he disappeared when she was eight months pregnant, veins like fishnet stockings all stretched out along her sides.

She swam along the sidewalk now, wondering where Sisia had gone, waiting to see who was looking for her. Maybe Chess. Maybe the brown van, with New York City pissed because Glorette had shrugged and said in front of the woman, "This ain't hot to me. Long as my hair up and my soda cold."

"Pop."

"What?"

"You mean pop."

"I'ma pop you," Sisia said, coming up behind the woman. "Don't nobody care if you from New York or New Mexico. Time for you to step. Don't nobody want to get in no nasty van. Fleas and lice and shit."

The woman spat a cloud onto the sidewalk near Sisia's sandals. "Then why I had five already tonight? Make more in one night than you make all week. This the way in New York. Mens want some convenience. And it's the shit up in there. I got incense and candles and curtains. So you take your raggedly country ass back to the alley."

But all this time she was looking at Glorette. "And your high-yella giraffe too."

THE CUSTODIAN BACK in junior high said, "Just a lil minute, now. Just stand still. Right here. I ain't even gon touch you. But it ain't my fault. Look at you. The Lord intended you for love. Look at you. Hold still. See. See. Lord. See."

The mop was damp like a fresh-washed wig near her arm. The closet. He was behind her. He stood close enough that she smelled Hai Karate, and then the bleach smell of what left his body and he caught in a rag.

"See." His voice was high and tight. His white nametag was small as a Chiclet when she crossed her eyes and didn't focus at all.

SHE WANTED SOME chicharrones. Explosions of fat and chile on her molars.

When she turned back down Palm to head toward Sundown, seeing Chess and two other men now, thinking the chicharrones would give her enough time to let them see the backs of her thighs and her shoulder blades, everything better than what New York had, better than curtains or candles, it was like her thoughts had brought the brown van cruising down Palm, stopping at the liquor store. The woman got out and folded her arms, cocked her head to the side, the tails of her bandanna like a parrot's long feathers curling around her neck.

Glorette turned down the alley and headed toward the taqueria instead.

LOOK HERE, THE custodian said. Mr. Charles. But he was not old. His fade was not gray at the edges. *Look here.* He held out money rolled tight as a cigarette. *I ain't gon bother you no more.*

The five-dollar bill was a twig in her sock all day.

SHE SAT AT the table in the taqueria for a few minutes, feeling the blood move and growl in her feet. No socks. Sandals. Heels. The money not in her cleavage. No money yet tonight. When she got money she put it inside the thick hair at the back of her head, just before the bun.

Chess would give her money. But most of the men just slid a rock into her palm.

\*   \*   \*

THE CUSTODIAN DIDN'T have to touch her after that. He didn't ever give her money again. He watched her walk in the hallway, and she knew he went into his broom closet and stood there and saw her when he moved his hands. Free. A lil piece. He stood facing the mop. The string hair. Then he was gone.

They were all gone.

At the taqueria, the woman behind the counter watched her, waiting patiently. Her mop was already wet. It stood up behind her, at the back door. Her night was almost over. The carne asada was drying and stringy in the warming pan.

Just a lil piece of meat. And a warm tortilla.


SHE STILL HAD the bag of ramen, but Victor would be sleep now. He was seventeen. He was about to graduate. He stayed up late studying and fell asleep on the couch, even though he knew she might bring someone home if she had to. The only one who always insisted on coming to her apartment was Chess. He liked to sit on the couch and drink a beer and pretend they were married. She knew it. He would watch TV like that was all he came for, laughing at Steve Harvey, like this living room was TV, too, and there were sleeping kids in the bedrooms and a wife.

"Look at your feet," he would say, like she'd been working at 7-Eleven all day. Convenience. "You should get your feet done like Sisia. Look like they hurt. And get your toes did. Ain't that how y'all say? 'I done got my toes *did*.'"

Glorette smiled.


VICTOR WAS AFRAID of fingernails. He'd cried when he was little and Sisia came over and Glorette didn't know why. Sisia wasn't pretty. She was dark and her cheeks were pitted like that bread. Pumpernickel. What the hell kind of name was that for a bread?

Sisia was a brick house, though. She liked to say it. A real mamma-jamma. 36-24-36 back in the day. More like 36-30-36 now, but still Glorette heard men say, "Close your eyes, man, and open your hands, and you got something there, with that woman."

But it was the fingernails that Victor cried about. Long and squared-off and winking with gems or even a ring through the nail. Lynn Win bored a hole through the tip and hung the jeweled ring.

Claws. For animals.

But now only women were supposed to fight with them. You could scratch a man's face, but then he'd probably kill you. You could scratch his back—some men wanted you to dig nails into their backs, like you were out of control, and that made them lose it, their whole spines would arch and tremble. But some men, if you dug your nails experimentally into the wider part below their shoulderblades, the cobra hood of muscle, just frowned and elbowed your hands off. "Don't mark me up and shit," they'd say, and then Glorette knew they had a wife or woman at home.

But Glorette just used her regular nails. Her claws. The ones God gave her. The ones Victor said were designed different from apes and chimps, and different from cats and dogs. *I don't think we ever dug,* he'd say. *Not like badgers or rabbits. And we didn't need the fingernails to hold onto food or anything. So it must be just for fighting, but we didn't have teeth like the cats or dogs to bite something on the neck and kill it.*

*I think they're just leftover,* he'd say. *From something else.*

Sere had a vein on his temple, from his hairline toward his left eyebrow, like twine sewn under his skin. When he played his flute or drums, the vein rose up but didn't throb. It wasn't red or blue, under his brown skin, not like the white baby Glorette had seen once at the store whose skin was so pale that blue veins moved along its head and temples like freeways.

But Victor's temples were smooth and straight, though he thought all the time, read and wrote and did math problems and studied for gradua-tion tests and played music and didn't just listen but wrote down all these bands' names and dates and song titles. He asked her once, "This song, the one you like so much. Poinciana. What is it?"

She thought for a long time. "A flower? I don't know."

One crystal of salt from a cracker on her tongue. The cracker explod-
ing like hard-baked snowflakes and pieces of rock salt on her molars.
Then a white sludge she could work at while they walked.

She had to have saltines when she was pregnant with Victor.

Sisia's aunt used to eat starch. White chunks of Argo. Only one she
wanted. That box with the woman holding corn. Indian woman. Corn
turned into knobs of snow that squeaked in the teeth. *Like new sneakers
on a basketball court,* Chess used to say when they were young.

The corn husks were green skin when they peeled off. The milky
white when a fingernail pierced a kernel. How did that turn to starch?

The leaves of the coca wherever those Indians grew it. And how the
hell did it turn to little chunks of white? Baby powder cornstarch flakes of
White-Out powdered sugar not crystals not cane sugar and molasses like
her mother would only use like Louisiana. They cut the cane and crushed
it in the mill, her mother said. Mules going round and round. Then the
juice had to boil and boil and boil, and finally sugar crystals formed. Diamonds of sweet. Diamonds of salt. On the tongue. But this chunk—which
she picked up out of the empty dryer drum while Jazen watched from
outside, her twenty in his pocket—she couldn't eat.

It had to turn to gray smoke inside her mouth, her throat, her lungs. In-
substantial. Inconvenience. The convenience store. Controlled substance.
Possession of a controlled substance, but if you smoke it or swallow it
when they pull up you ain't in possession. It's possessin you. Ha. Sisia
laughing. Chess laughing. *Come on. Let's go home.*

He liked to pretend her couch was home.

Swear he would ask her to make grits. The tiny white sand of corn.
Not crystals. Not chunks.

*Call it cush-cush back home,* her mother used to say. Victor had eaten
grits at his grandmère's house and loved to call it that. Cush-cush.

Victor was sleeping now. His math book open on his chest. Sere's
brain. My brain? He had the third-highest grades in the whole damn
school. His ramen was in her hand. The plastic bag handles were rolled
into pearls by now.

\*   \*   \*

SHE WALKED DOWN the alley behind the taqueria, more for the smell of the put-away beef than anything else. Ain't no charge for smelling. She paused beside a shopping cart parked against the chainlink fence. The slats of vinyl worked through the fence. Sideways world. She smoked her last rock, in a pipe the man had given her. Pipe made of an old air-freshener tube blown larger with a torch.

The chunk was yellow and porous. Small as aquarium rock. The fish in the pet store went in and out of the ceramic castle. Her head was pounding. Maybe he gave her some bad coca. A bad leaf.

Someone was behind her. Sisia. Sisia was ready to quit for the night. Glorette was tired now. She had Victor's ramen in her hand.

She heard a voice kept all up behind front teeth. "Old crackhead bitch," the voice said. "See if that hair real now. One a them fake falls. Drink yo damn soda? You ain't gon pop nobody now."

Not Sisia.

Fingers dug into the hair she'd twisted so tight hours ago, at the base of her skull, and pulled hard enough to launch Glorette backward, and then the silver handle of the shopping cart was beside her eyes, and the girl was tying her loose hair to the handle.

"Real enough," the girl said. "But this ain't the nineties. You ain't Beyoncé. You some old J-Lo and shit. You finished."

She was still behind Glorette. Her footsteps went backward. Was she gone?

Glorette couldn't untie her hair. Her hands shook. She was bent too far. Spine. So far backward that she could only look up at the streetlight just above. She felt pain sharp like a rat biting her heart. Teeth in her chest. A bad leaf? *I taste salt.* A crystal. The teeth bit into her chest again. Just a muscle. Victor says just a muscle like your thigh. *Flex.* She closed her eyes but the streetlight was brighter than the moon. Yellow sulfur. The sun. Like staring into the sun until you were blind, until the thudding of your heart burst into your brain and someone slid chalk sideways into perforated stripes across your vision until you couldn't see anything.

# LA REINA

ON THE FIRST Monday in October, the campus police car rolled to a stop in front of the lot, and the officer got out slowly, eying the four Hondas parked in the trampled grass under the pecan trees. Victor was sitting on the porch, reading the William James book for World Religions class. For the first time, he'd washed crow shit off Irwin's Acura.

On his headphones: Average White Band's "Schoolboy Crush" and Gino Vanelli. Marcus had given him a Black-White-Guys mix. He slid the headphones down.

"How you plannin on protectin these vehicles, son?"

*Big old campus security brother,* Victor thought. *Gotta say vehicles. Like a real cop.*

"Son?" The cop said it again.

*Guarding them with my life, pops,* he thought. *I ain't your son. You ain't my daddy. I'm just doin my job. Pops.*

"With my eyes," Victor said. "Sittin right here. All day."

"And when you have to pee?"

"I don't." He looked at the officer's big shoulders and belly in the uniform. *No prostate trouble for me, dude. Prostate. Prostrate. Prosthetic. Your proboscis. My prognosis.*

The officer walked to the lot's edge. "You got a permit for this?"

"For sittin on my grandpa's porch?"

The man stopped and folded his arms high on his chest, looking at the small house, the peeling yellow paint on the porch pillars, the picture window Victor had just washed. "Your grandfather? He buy this place from old Mrs. Batiste?"

The cop looked vaguely familiar. Light-skinned, eyes hidden behind the requisite shades, but something about his mouth. Victor thought, *So you tellin me you know everything about the street.*

"Yeah."

"You done bought four Hondas and you lived here since September?"

"Nope."

"So these ain't your cars, son?" Now he took off the sunglasses and glared at Victor. His badge said *N. Belarde.*

*They ain't yours either. Uniform don't make every damn car in the college lot yours. And you definitely drivin a Nova or Camry. Somethin old or boring.*

"I take care of em like they're mine." Victor didn't move from the chair. The hoods of the cars faced him, since he had Irwin and his friends back into the spaces he'd marked with chalk in the dirt. He wasn't ready to back the cars in yet himself, because even though he'd be eighteen in December, he'd never learned to drive, which in Southern California meant his life was seriously fucked-up.

THEY WERE ALL of the opinion that what he'd missed was a crib, and then a bed. A bed with a comforter featuring Transformers or Ninja Turtles. Wait—Mutant Ninja Turtles. Vital distinction for somebody. Bedspread, comforter, quilt. How did the middle one comfort you more than the others?

He'd missed Flintstones vitamins, his aunts had said. He had to look up Flintstones on the school computer. Flint was a stone, so the word seemed pointless, but Fred was funny.

The teachers in conference with his mother at school, her sitting all legs in the desk-chair, staring out the window at whatever trees grew in the elementary school courtyard; his aunts in the kitchen of Uncle Enrique's house in the orange groves of Sarrat; the cops in the fluorescent room when they'd taken him to jail after the idiot had shot up the apartment in The Riviera.

His mother knew trees. Showed him how to find bees in the pepper tree trunks, spiders in the eucalyptus bark shedding long flat sheaves.

In fourth grade, they studied California Indians, and Victor found a perfect piece of bark for his project. She took him to the riverbed, where the paddle-shaped cactus grew everywhere, and on the smooth green skin were cottony white insects. Their blood was magenta, a color he'd never seen, even among her eyeshadows and nail polish. She showed him how to paint the bark with designs in bug blood.

She used to keep the bark picture in her trunk. The lock had been busted over and over, when people broke into it, but they threw the bark aside looking for money or rock or jewelry. Then someone got pissed when he couldn't find anything, and he broke the bark in half and threw it on the floor.

So she glued it together, and wrapped magenta ribbon from Rite Aid around each end, and hung it on the wall. No one would care about it then. And he saw her staring at it sometimes, when she lay on the couch. At each apartment, she hung it on the wall near the door.

The bug was cochineal. An SAT word. A fucking SAT word.


IT WASN'T THAT big a deal. She had sex with men who weren't his father.

His father had disappeared before he was born. So she couldn't have sex with him. Sere Dakar, some musician from Detroit.

Other moms had sex with their husbands, whom they hated, according to Bir and Amitav, both of whom told Victor that their parents had arranged marriages back in India before they came to California. Amitav's mother had only hung out with his father for three hours before they got married.

Other moms had sex with other women's husbands, according to all three Logans who actually spoke to Victor after AP Art History. Or they had sex with guys they met at bars downtown, especially Marlo's Place and Greensleeves and So Cal Brewing Company. The guys bought them drinks and dinner. His moms got two or three rocks.

Morsels. Kernels. Nuggets. Pebbles. Not shards—that would be sharp and splintery. Not crystals—that would be glittery and multifaceted. Grains—too miniscule.

Decomposed granite was grainy. Three kinds of rock—igneous, sedimentary, and metamorphic?

On Fridays, she'd had sex only with Chess, who was annoying as hell. Old-school brother with bow legs who had played three years of college ball at UCLA and bragged about his nickname, which apparently came from his ability to move the other players around the court with some skill. As he did now at the YMCA. So Victor rolled his eyes and left to hang out when Chess showed up, promptly at 11 on Fridays, with food and, yeah, rock—even though he acted like he wasn't that guy.

Chess had been shot in the parking lot of Sundown Liquor five days after Victor's mother died, in August, and though the cops never found out who'd done it, Victor's cousin Alfonso had disappeared that night. Whether that was about money or rock, Victor didn't care.

He knew it used to take $100 for Chess to keep Glorette at his crib all night. Even though that meant quiet, and if they had a TV at the moment Victor could watch whatever he wanted, he used to hate Fridays.

The shows were dismal. He sat up with his SAT book and made lists. Dismal, distinctive, dystopian, utopian, Sisyphean. In Oneida, New York, they practiced eugenics in an attempt to create a utopian society. Sisyphus rolled that boulder up every time. His mother put another tiny rock in the pipe.

They weren't even shiny.

But she had the system down, until that night.

\*    \*    \*

BACK ON THE first Saturday in May, he was registered to take the SAT. His high school history teacher, Marcus Thompson, had paid for it—and he'd left ten dollars for Victor to buy the number two pencils and some coffee for that morning.

"Make sure you eat," Marcus said, awkwardly.

Victor said, "We got plenty of food."

He remembered being really hungry when he was three. She didn't come home. He sat on the balcony. Maybe Jessamine Gardens. He couldn't remember anything except his stomach was eating his back-bone. He could feel something creeping up there. Vertebrae. He couldn't breathe and so he sat outside, and his uncle Reynaldo found him because they were looking for his mother.

Kindergarten? When he coughed really hard and finally she came home and put him in the shower with her and they sat in there all night, the moisture beading up on her hair like pearls and then collapsing into noth-ing. The water going inside his lungs and somehow cleaning out the burn.

Memphis. The only name he had for the man. When he was ten. The cigarettes. Memphis lit a new one for each time, and when he was done he left them on the floor of the bedroom.

But now she had it down. He was seventeen. So she left ramen, or-ange juice (and she bought Tropicana, not that Sunny Delight shit), and pistachios in the kitchen. The staples. And most nights, she brought home the scheduled items from El Ojo de Agua. He said to her, "Shrimp burrito from the Eye?"

The Eye of Water. Jesus Espinoza, this guy in AP History, said that was from a town in Michoacan, where his father was born. Some shrine.

The shrimp burrito had beans, rice, cabbage, tomatoes, sauce, and fried shrimp. $3.99. It was the size of a small log. A dusty white log. And Victor ate one every Tuesday. Wednesday was fish tacos. Thursday was tamales.

Friday was Chess, and Saturday she was gone until dawn. Sunday she slept. He ate whatever his grandfather brought from Sarrat—gumbo or beans and rice or ham. Always oranges.

She had her part as down as she could, and Victor had his part down cold. Perfect 4.0. Registered for the May 6, 2000 SAT. Last one of the year. Everybody else would be juniors, but he could finish college apps late and Marcus would help him.

It must have pissed off those other moms, when their kids mentioned him. *This black dude with weird hair and he's really light so he's like, not even really black, and his mom is, like, a crack ho—that's just what everybody says, okay, she is—and he gets like, 97 or 98 on everything. Like, never lower. For reals.*

He had the second-highest grade in the class in AP European History, the second-highest in AP US History, and the third-highest in AP Art History.

No one could beat Logan Maas. He would be number one in the senior class even if he did smoke weed every day, even if he'd told Victor one night that his dad put him in a closet when he was twelve because he brought home a B–, and his dad was pastor at a big church and loved to say *Spare the rod, spoil the child.* No one would get number two away from Amitav Kumar, even though he blazed out with Logan, and loved to joke that his mom was seriously pissed that he was the only number-two Indian at any high school in Rio Seco. Probably in all fucking Southern California. Probably in other states, too.

Logan and Amitav kept asking Victor to blaze, and he'd hang with them in the parking lot at Jack in the Box, where everyone went to get high because it was two blocks from school and the lot was huge, with pepper trees all around the edge where no one paid attention, and the cops never went to Jack. They all ate at Logan Huntsman's father's deli. Every day you'd see squad cars parked there.

The four other Logans—the secondary Logans, who hung out with the two Hunters, the Piper, and the two Dakotas—hated his ass. Two girl Logans and two boy Logans. Brown-haired girl Logan had green eyes like olives, one of those girls who wore her hair in a ponytail and it was thick and long so you could see the reason they called it that. She asked him all casual as often as she could without seeming insecure, "So what'd you get on the test?"

"What I always get." Victor loved saying that. He didn't even have to give her the percentage. It was always 97 or 98. Mrs. Mumbles had to take off two or three points for everyone—even if she had to make up some shit about one word being awkward or you forgot a comma or a space in MLA format.

But he loved Mrs. Mumbles. Mumford. She'd been at the high school for so long she'd had three generations of Logan and Hunter and Piper. She'd had their parents named Ted and Betty in the sixties, and their parents named Horace and Eleanor in the thirties. He'd seen their pictures in the hallways.

But Mrs. Mumbles didn't buy into all the hype, and the old families and fundraisers and the right mom or wrong mom at Back to School Night. She never looked any of them in the face. She stared at some spot in the room and mumbled about funeral art of India and Impressionists and Cubism. She didn't give a shit that Victor's mother, who came to Open House because he'd told her it was the last time she could ever do that, sat in the back like the most beautiful zombie statue in the history of the world.

She was luminous. In winter, the nights shitty and cold, her skin got dulled like the gold-leaf frame of a painting if soot and years laid a patina of darkness or haze. Then she would sleep for two days, and when the sun came out, they'd go out to the orange groves. Eat gumbo and oranges, see the grandparents, and she'd take a long shower and put almond oil in her hair.

She'd be gilt again. And the other moms at Open House hated the way she gazed bemusedly at their fleece vests and mom jeans for two seconds before dismissing them and staring at the paintings on the classroom walls.

The SAT plan was to get number-three scores. Logan had taken it twice, Amitav three times. Logan got a 1500, perfect score, and Amitav 1490, in October. Victor didn't have the money in October, and in November she got pneumonia after a cold windstorm when she stood in the alley too long. His aunt Fantine helped him one weekend with vocabulary words. He chanted to himself all day and most of the night.

Luciferous. Loquacious. Lucid. Lucent.

He listened to Classical KUSC, just to hear adagio and arpeggio and adelante. One program featured the high school students who won national competitions in piano or violin or cello. In the interviews, they sounded like who Amitav's mom wished he was.

He listened to NPR, looked up the SAT word of the day in the school library, and read the dictionary. She'd stolen a pocket dictionary from Rite Aid for him.

She never stole ramen or orange juice or nail polish or lotion or candy from Rite Aid, but she said that same dictionary had been sitting in the same revolving rack for a year. She said she knew that because she folded down one page, at the word *Poinsettia*.

Her favorite song was "Poinciana," and that word wasn't in the dictionary.

If no one was going to use it, and it was $12.99, she said it was fate. And she could put it back when he was done, if he didn't mess up the pages.

But that Friday night, May 5, some idiot came up to the apartment with Sisia and wanted Glorette. Chess was already there. The idiot was from LA. He had green eyes and big heavy cheeks like two burlap bags hanging around his nose. Had dooky braids like you saw on little girls, so he thought he was hardcore, which Victor never understood.

He shot five rounds from his Glock and called it a night. But when the cops came they cuffed his mother and Sisia, he heard them yelling, and then they busted down the bedroom door and took Victor, even though he'd been in bed with his headphones on the whole time, and the gunfire had sounded like the crack of palm fronds falling in the wind and hitting the concrete balcony.


ON A RANDOM night in August, somebody had killed his mother and put her body in a shopping cart behind the Eye. The next morning was supposed to be his assigned registration date for city college.

His uncle Enrique was probably still trying to figure out who'd done it. They'd tried to make him believe she died on the couch at their house, out in the groves. Like she'd walked all that way to take a nap.

But his grandfather didn't care about revenge. He was just sad—so sad his voice went down to the whisper of sandpaper on already smooth wood. They had buried her next to his grandmother, in the cemetery at the edge of the orange groves. Then Victor had slept in his mother's old bedroom for days, smelling the oranges hot on the trees, since his life was over.

But five days later Marcus Thompson shook him out of the sheets and stood there glaring. When Victor was a freshman, Marcus had said, "Man, call me your distant uncle, whatever, just let me get you through school and into the big time. The smartest idiot I've had in ten years."

But Victor knew why. Marcus had been seriously in love with Glorette when they were seventeen. Totally sprung. He was married now and had a stepdaughter, but he still loved her. Chess, Marcus, Sidney Chabert who worked at the video store—they never got over his mother. On the dresser were bottles of perfume, dusty on their round shoulders, and inside one drawer were Valentines from her sophomore year. Queen of My Heart, someone named Narcisse had written. Funky French name.

His mother, in the rusted shopping cart.

He turned over and pressed his cheek against the pillow.

Marcus said, "I got you a new registration date. Get up. Get up."

"Fuck that! Everybody calls it thirteenth grade, man. I ain't goin."

Amitav and Logan were already at Berkeley. Blazing in a dorm room now. The two Hunters were at UCLA.

"Get up." Marcus rolled him out of bed and he fell on the floor. His grandfather and Uncle Enrique stood in the doorway. "He has to go to college," Marcus said. "I mean it. He has to get—"

Victor knew the ending. Marcus wanted to say "—get out of here," but facing the old men who'd picked oranges and shot rabbits and rebuilt trucks, who'd tried to save his mother again and again, he knew better.

"Victor has to get started," Marcus said. "He can transfer after two years to the big time."

His grandfather said, "Take them damn thing off your ear. Put them clothes and books in the truck."


THEY BOUGHT A house in the city, on a narrow street at the edge of the arroyo. His grandfather had met Mrs. Batiste forty years earlier, when they'd come out from Louisiana. Her husband died ten years ago, and she went to live with her son Darnell. The little house was empty, and it was across the street from Rio Seco City College.

"We put in them pecan tree for her back in 1970," his grandfather said. "Nothin across the street back then but a field and some old junkyard."

Now the city college had expanded, building a new stadium and classroom buildings all the way to the edge of the former field. Victor carried his bag up the three steps of the cement porch and leaned against one of the wooden pillars. The house was old, pale yellow peeling paint, black wrought-iron railing around the porch that made his eyes burn with tears for a moment when he touched the rusty pitted metal. Like the railings on every second story of every apartment building he'd lived in with his mother.

The tears descended into his sinus cavities, as always. He never let them out. Sinuses and sinews and secretions and synapses.

His grandfather took one tiny bedroom, and he took the other. The kitchen was dusty, with cracked linoleum tiles and a counter with gold speckles inside. Formosa—that was ants. Formidable. Formica.

Fucking thirteenth grade. Cars racing in and out of Lot 8 across the street. Victor had seen the two girl Logans in cheer squad uniforms, leaning close to a side window on a Blazer and putting on lipstick. Of course.

The night before classes began, Uncle Enrique drove up in his ancient truck. Victor's grandfather had never had a truck—he always rode with Enrique.

They sat on the porch after they ate the red beans Enrique's wife had sent in a huge pot. Victor had spent the day weedwhacking the grass and trimming the lowest branches on the pecan trees, to keep from wanting to kill himself.

They lit Swisher Sweets. It was September 5, and over a hundred degrees. They spoke in French too fast and slurred for Victor to make out more than a few words. His mother's name.

His grandfather hadn't said anything to Victor most of the day. Victor sat on the bottom step. Babysitting. His grandfather should be working the groves with Enrique. He had nothing to do here but sit in his recliner and make sure Victor stayed alive.

"You get them book at the school?" Enrique finally said.

Victor nodded. He'd only gotten into two classes. World Religions and English Composition in a stack on the folding chair.

"You look in that shed there?" Enrique said.

"Maybe a washer," his grandfather said.

Victor went into the big side yard, almost a second lot. He remembered delivering oranges to this woman years ago, and getting a bag of pecans. She used to grow sugarcane, too. A few stalks rustled behind the house. The shed was an old leaning wooden building, narrow and long. He slid the wooden door sideways. There could have been a washer at the back, but all Victor saw was the ancient Impala, pale blue, the windshield full of cobwebs that hung low like ghostly sails.

"INDIAN DUDE SHOWED me how to make these," his mother said that day, crouching in the sandy dirt near the cactus. She pointed to a small tree. "He said that was Indian tobacco. Dude named Beto. He used to smoke it when he was little."

"We part Indian?" Victor had asked her.

"Not that kind. Not California. When I was ten and went down there to Louisiana, the old lady said, 'The first one come from Senegal. Marie-Therese. And some a them was Houma. Indian."

"That's all?"

"She was a mean old lady. Spoke French. The white men was French, back in the day."

He remembered looking at the tobacco tree. "What about my daddy?"

"Sere Dakar. Dakar's a city in Senegal."

"He was African?"

"No."

BACK ON THE second Tuesday of September, Victor was on the porch looking over his notes for World Religions. The class had him tripping. Professor Barr was about fifty, with eyes green as a wine bottle and hair dyed the glistening red of pomegranate seeds. She moved her fingers like she was dancing. Hinduism. Buddhism. Counting karma. Classifying people, animals, in a hierarchy so final even death didn't free you.

It was 8 am. A lowered black Acura, custom muffler, racing car, kept cruising past looking for a parking place on the street. Five times. Six. Cars had been swerving into the narrow gravel drive to turn around, then racing off. Victor closed his book and stood up just when the driver pulled up and said, "Dude! You got parking in your yard?"

He was Asian. He kept the car idling, the speakers bumping Nelly. "Serious, bro, I can't be late for class again or they'll kick me out. How much?"

"How much you pay for the student lot?"

"I didn't get the lottery, bro. Never any spaces anyway. I'm always late to class, less I get here six in the morning."

Victor stared past him. Not a clue what students paid, or how much money they'd spare for an extra hour. "You got class every day?"

"Every day. I got five tickets already on this street cause it's one-hour parking and shit."

"Twenty dollars a week."

"Bro! You rock."

Irwin was his name. Chinese-American. He told his three friends, all of them wealthy kids who were doing their first year at city college to get their grades up for university. By Wednesday, the four Hondas parked in a row, black and dark blue, gleaming.

Thursday morning was Professor Zellman's class, at nine, so Victor got up at dawn to make Louisiana-style drip coffee for his grandfather, who was always awake by sunrise. His grandfather would have to watch the cars, just for two hours.

He carried a load of his grandfather's clothes and bedding out to the old washer. He had used his grandmother's old sifter to lay flour lines in the lot after he'd weedwhacked the grass short. He was raking the few branches he'd trimmed, and when he heard Jazen's voice from the street, the words flew around the leaves for a moment before settling on his head.

"You farmin now, nigga?"

Jazen and Tiquan grinned from the open windows of the Navigator. Country Grammar bumped from the speakers.

"Rakin leaves." Victor waited. "Where's Alfonso?"

"In the wind. He vacated." Jazen studied the house. "You stay here now?"

Victor nodded.

"You heard that old dude Chess got gotted?"

Victor shrugged. If Chess had gotten killed by some fool in love, he didn't want to know.

Jazen said casually, "I'm sorry about your moms. They catch the nigga did it?"

Victor said, "How you know it was a nigga? How you know it wasn't a white dude?"

Tiquan said, "Ain't no white dude been—"

But Jazen's face went cold. "He don't know shit."

Victor stared back. "Don't matter who did it."

"Always matter who did it. Matter who got gotted, matter who gotted em. But you ain't interested." Jazen stared him down.

"No. I ain't." Victor felt a splinter in the wooden handle, and Tiquan looked past him and whistled, high and sharp as a rock thrown at a telephone wire.

"That a six-four?" Tiquan said, pointing at the shed. "Damn. You gon sell me that, right? I give you cash right now."

"Ain't runnin."

"I can see that. I don't care. I know this dude got nothin but six-fo's and he want another one."

"Ain't mine."

"Don't gotta be yours."

"Ain't for sale."

The Navigator moved off like a blue house on wheels, and Victor heard the bass all the way inside his kneecaps.


HE HAD NEVER told anyone—not his mother, not Marcus—about that night a month before his mother died, when he'd taken a ride with

Alfonso and Jazen because he'd been walking back from school in the dark and they saw him. He'd never told Marcus how it felt, the neon lights at Sundown Liquor flickering behind his eyelids. He knew Alfonso had a gun in the glove compartment. The Navigator bumping old-school House of Pain—"Insane in the membrane, insane in the brain"—and the moon hanging low like a damn Mento. Like a commercial. And somebody want to pull up hard at the light—checkin and assessin—and you think, *Hell yeah, step or drive.*

Then they'd passed Launderland, and he'd seen the empty shopping carts parked around the telephone pole at the Lamplighter Motel—like silver ponies with fat bellies waiting all patient. *This ain't the Wild Wild West. And I ain't got a horse.*

How when they dropped him off, the neon still shook in his forehead.

You can't always get what you want. Irwin had been singing that one day when he came for his Honda. But he wasn't riding with Jazen.

"I never kill nobody, me," his grandfather said once when Victor was ten, when he'd asked about the shotgun in the living room. "Enrique kill somebody."

"He kill a man?" Victor said.

"He kill two man. But I never kill nobody, cause he do. He the one."

Victor had looked at his mother, sleeping on the couch, her hand cupped, held upward like she was asking for something from the ceiling. Rock. A fucking eighties drug. Disco bumped into funk and then messed up by his mother and her friends. All of them thirty-five and couldn't grow up. Leggings and tank tops, like *Flashdance* reruns. Moving apartments every three months—pay a deposit, no rent, and stay ahead of eviction. Only thing moved every time was the glass-topped table she loved so much, Victor's futon, and the trunk she'd had since she was nine, a metal box imprinted with the American flag.

His grandfather used to say to her, "Co fa?"

*Quoi faire? What you gonna do?* She sat on the floor, painting her toenails the color of cherry juice. Grandpère would say, "A secretary. They hire all the time at the city."

"And nobody grab my ass, want some for free?"

"You can't run the street toujour. Non."

Then she went back to the strip on Palm Avenue: Launderland, which was always warm in winter when they'd been standing outside; Sundown Liquor, where the men filed in and out, one by one, like the leaf-cutter ants he'd seen on TV, but carrying brown paper bags.

That time someone had stolen her mud-brown Celica from the carport at Hyacinth Gardens, and they had no phone, no breakfast, no spoons. Someone had walked off with their spoons. They ate ramen noodles for lunch and dinner with plastic forks, and Victor drank the broth, telling himself bitterly that the tiny green dots floating in the salty soup were vegetables.

Even though his grandmother used to demand him when he was little, his mother wouldn't give him up.

His grandfather whispered to him, "You think you kill somebody if he hurt you?"

His grandfather wanted to know if it ever got that bad at the apartment.

Victor didn't answer.


WHEN HE WAS little, she couldn't leave him forever at night. Sisia would watch TV for a few hours, and then his mother would come back while Sisia went out. Sisia had a face like a black orange, with pinprick scars, and her fingernails were long and painted.

His futon was always in the only bedroom, always on the other side of the wall where the TV stood if they had one, and he could hear the chunk when the channels changed.

Sometimes his mother had to bring them home. He put pillows over his head, but his ears had the canals that went into his brain. He'd seen a movie about the human body at school.

That Christmas, he asked his uncles for headphones. Uncle Reynaldo said, "Lil man wanna hear some sounds. You think Santa comin down the chimney with some music?" They bought him a Walkman, which he hid inside his shirt while he slept.

When he was eleven, she left him alone for longer. She went out at eleven and came home around four.

He never wore the headphones while she was gone, in case someone broke in.

Only once. Around Christmas then, too, because someone had put winking lights around the palm tree trunks in the courtyard. Some dude jimmied open the front door. Splintered the cheap frame. The lights had stopped blinking. The voice said, "Shit, ain't nothin worth nothin in here." Footsteps into the room.

Victor moved quickly from the futon to the closet. He had practiced this a hundred times, stacking three boxes under his mother's few hung-up clothes. He lifted himself to the shelf above the clothes and lay covered with an old sheet he'd left there.

He heard the man's breath, in the closet doorway, and then the soft kicking of his futon, and then the footsteps went back outside, and the cold air came inside until she returned.


THE THIRD TUESDAY in September, he checked on the Impala at 7 pm. Jazen and Tiquan didn't steal cars. But they could pay someone who did. Not that many 1964 Impalas in minty, dirty condition around—everyone wanted them.

He closed the shed door. "Hooptie," he said to the car, "as soon as I get some dinero, I'm hooking you up for me." Then he'd have to learn to drive, practice where no one could see him.

He walked the six blocks to the tiny Mexican market called La Reina. Rice, bananas, tamarind soda, and some chorizo. He hated taking money from his grandfather, who was napping in his chair, so he spent some of Irwin's cash. On the way back, around eight, he kept to the edges of the college lots around the huge campus. He saw Professor Zellman walking toward him, styling his hornrims, his hair gelled up, his thick-soled shoes. Working it. His black restored '65 Mustang fully sweet. He'd driven it all the way out from Brooklyn when he got this teaching job. Fort Greene, said it all the time. He had them read *Vibe* and *The New Yorker* and *Rolling Stone* instead of just the textbook, then write papers: compare and contrast, persuasive, descriptive. The class was tight.

"Goddamnit!" Zellman was bent near the driver door. Glass sparkled near his feet.

Victor moved the grocery bag to his other arm and stopped near a pepper tree on the sidewalk. Zellman always talked about how he loved NWA. *But I ain't his nigga with attitude. Wasn't even here when the window got broken. Would he even remember me? I got the A and kicked ass on the compare and contrast paper.*

He waited until Zellman scrabbled in his briefcase for the celly, then crossed the street, holding his breath until a campus police car sped past him.


THAT WEEKEND, HE met Mayeli.

She and her aunt were running a booth at the weekly farmer's market downtown. Victor had gone to look for used CDs, but he saw the t-shirts waving like stiff ghosts. T-shirts with flags—Mexico, Italy, Puerto Rico, England. Anywhere people came from before they got here. Tight—who came up with that idea?

She smiled at him. About eighteen, with honey-dark skin and cheekbones so high they were soft pillows under her eyes. Hair pulled back into a bun, gleaming around her forehead like a new vinyl LP. She said, "You got another flag you want, we print it so."

Her voice wasn't California. It wasn't Jamaica. Somewhere between. He leaned on the booth, keeping his hands from the stark white cloth, and said, "Where you from?"

"Belize."

Then, unlike Rio Seco girls who would go on and on, tell you all about themselves in long breaths, more than you wanted to know, so you would want them and want to buy something from them or for them, she closed her lips. Not like she was pissed. Closed them soft over her teeth, like she would rather listen.

Oh yeah.

Victor figured eight or nine hundred dollars to drop a new engine in the Impala and get a life. Maybe he could find a new backseat at

Pick-A-Part, the junkyard. Take Mayeli to the movies. *I ain't askin for much.*

On Monday, leaving World Religions, Professor Barr was complaining to another woman about parking permits. "Thirty dollars a month!" she said. "To park two days a week, where I'm employed! And I can't ever find a space! I don't believe a factory wouldn't charge me to park so I could come to work!"

That night, taking clothes from the washer, he saw the dust raised from his feet against the hard-packed dirt and grass of the lot. The dust hung in the fall air for a moment, in the yellow glow of the old streetlamp against the high blue glare of the college lot lights.

He went to Professor Zellman after class, but he didn't hand him the flyer right away. "I heard you pay thirty dollars a month to park in the faculty lot," he said, trying to appear non-threatening. "I live across the street, on Iris. You could park in the lot next door for twenty dollars a month, and I can get somebody to wash your car once a week. Detail, too, if you want, for ten dollars more."

Zellman squinted. "Picard, right? Victor? You wrote about Memphis Minnie and Led Zeppelin for the compare-contrast? They did the same song? Your paper's right here. Brilliant."

Then he laughed. "You know, my dentist has this service in his parking lot. You sure you're not from Brooklyn?"

Victor smiled. "I'm from here. I got a flyer. People can do two days a week, three, whatever. And I'll watch the cars better than campus security."

Professor Barr had come up beside them. She didn't laugh. Her brows had been drawn on with a pencil. She whispered, "All religion begins with the cry 'Help!'"

"William James?" Victor asked politely. He was still remembering the pictures she'd shown in class of the untouchable man who'd had acid thrown in his face for daring to drink out of the well of a Brahmin family during a heat wave.

Zellman threw up his hands and said, "James wasn't parking, no doubt. Just tying up his horse."

\*   \*   \*

THE CROWS WERE the biggest problem so far, landing purple splotches of shit on a few hoods. So he washed those cars, too. Huddling in the trees, crows were the first to get pecans every year, smart enough to drop them on the street, wait for cars to smash the hulls so they could pick out the raw soft meat.

Victor stood in the empty lot at dusk. Three cars left. He studied the nuts hanging like green mini-bananas, thinking about the slingshot his grandfather had made when he was a kid. Thumping speakers shook the leaves when someone slowed, and he heard laughter. "Aw, nigga, now you the damn scarecrow!"

He turned. Jazen and Tiquan. "I can lend you my nine, you get tired standin there like a fool."

Victor said, "Some fools stand. Some sit."

"Talkin shit now?" Tiquan said, and Victor turned away. *Loquacious-ness isn't an attribute.* Then Tiquan said, "I got five hundred right now. Five bills."

Victor kept walking back toward the shed, and Jazen said, "You can't even drive that ride. A waste."

But Jazen didn't add anything—the car accelerated, and when Victor glanced back, the campus police car slowed at the curb. Beefy arm. Sunglasses pink with sunset. Like a bad movie.

"Friends a yours?"

Victor shook his head.

"You get a permit, son?" the officer said, glasses off. A scar on his arm when he dangled the glasses out the window. "Or I gotta call the city?"

Victor waited for him to add whatever he'd add—threat or boast or more unnecessary information. Like Jazen, or like a girl. But he was silent as long as Victor was, and then the car glided away.

Long horizontal scar. Keloided up, like a fat pink caterpillar made of satin. Like something Victor had seen before.

\* \* \*

ON THE SECOND Thursday in October, the campus cop didn't cruise past, though Victor had watched for him all afternoon. At four, Zellman put his briefcase on the porch steps and said, "What you hearin?" He nodded toward Victor's headphones.

Victor slid them down. "Chili Peppers."

"Red Hot Chili Peppers?"

Ain't no other ones, Victor thought. He lifted his chin.

Zellman frowned. Victor knew he was surprised. White band. "What's up next in the rotation?"

*Tryin to figure me out. Wanna hear me say Nelly. My price Range is Rover. Shimmy Shimmy Coco Pow.*

"Clifton Chenier," Victor said. "His favorite." He nodded toward his grandfather, who sat in his chair in front of the window.

Zellman grooved his shoulders two times. "Zydeco. Love it."

"Yeah," Victor said. "See you Tuesday."

But Zellman shook his head. "I'm coming in tomorrow. Friday. We have a meeting all morning."

"Cool," Victor said. But when Zellman pulled out, Victor opened his notebook. Zellman and Barr—Tuesday Thursday. Monday Wednesday Friday—Patrini, the math lab tutor. Irwin and his friends every day.

If they all came at the same time—shit. The lot could hold about seven cars easily. If he had to move cars—shit. He needed to practice backing in and turning.

His grandfather stood in the doorway and said, "Them pecan gon fall this week. They say the wind come." Victor threw a rock from the stash he kept on the porch and five crows rose up screeching at him. "Me and Enrique used to fight them bird for some pecan."

Victor sat on the porch, highlighting pages about caste systems and religions in India. His grandfather went inside to make coffee. Only two Hondas were left.

Every day he walked across the street to go to class, and he walked home. He was gone only two hours at a time, and his grandfather watched

the cars. He'd been born a mile from here, lived in every apartment building off Palm Avenue, rode a bus to school or walked. Rode in Enrique's
truck to the orange groves. He'd been nowhere. He'd done nothing.

His grandfather had taken epic journeys. He walked a hundred miles
with Enrique when they were little kids. When he came out with his coffee—
so sweet Victor could smell the sugar—Victor said, "You ever eat a crow?"

His grandfather hated chicken. He shook his head. "They sit in them
tree laugh at us after the flood. Nobody eat a crow. We ain't had no gun.
Only them soldier—they shoot Enrique's maman because some meat."

Victor didn't know what to say. He wanted to know what kind of meat.
Was it chicken?

"Then a white man come get us."

"All of the people?"

"Non. Me and Enrique. I was seven. Enrique, he was four. Them people on the levee, they don't know us. He take us to Plaquemines Parish
cause Enrique people there. My peoples gone. He have a mule wagon.
They call him a drummer. He sell pot and pan and scissor, he sharpen
them tool. Some day he let us ride on the wagon, but if he buy some
things and they sit on the wagon then I have to walk. Walk all day. Sleep
at night in the woods."

"What he give you to eat?"

"He buy a chicken sometime. From a farm. Tell us pull them feather.
I hate them little bump in the skin. Close my eyes and pull them feather
and feel em float back in my face."

"That's why you never eat chicken?"

"I don't want no bird. All them feather, all them bone."

"How long did it take you to get there?"

"A long time. It was cold when we get there. He gone to all the place
he always go. People say *you buy two little nigger?* He say *I take them to
Plaquemines.* They say *that a long way south.* He say *I get there when I get
there.*"

His grandfather looked across the street at the new stadium, the
lights up high. "Then one day he stop at a store and say *Where Almoinette
Antoine?* Walk one more day and he leave us at her house."

Victor tried to picture it. Sometimes people in the apartments would say, "I'ma call Child Service on her. She need to leave that boy with somebody responsible." But every day, he put on his clothes and shoes and went to school, so they couldn't say anything. And he never took off his shirt around anyone. Not even her. She never saw the scars.

"She was old?"

His grandfather frowned. "Non. Not old, not young. She never have no children. She just say *Come in here take a bath cause I clean the floor.* She was Enrique's aunt. We work on the oyster boat back then. Marinovich and his people get the oyster, and me and Enrique put in the sack and carry all them sack to the dock. She have oranges, so we pick the oranges when they ready. That how Enrique find this place, when he get out the war. California. He see all them orange on the tree."

"You were in the ocean? On a boat?"

"Oyster boat go all in the Gulf. They know where the oyster bed stay. I can't see nothing but water, and they know where to stop. Pull out them tong and rake them oyster and put em in a sack."

His mother had been to the beach once. Newport. At night. With his father. She told him the story three different times—when she was high and sleepy.

Victor had planned to "Hit the Beach for Senior Ditch Day," with Logan and Amitav, but when they opened the door of Logan's Jeep, he said, "I'm cool. I gotta study." It was a Tuesday, sunny and hot in October, and he kept picturing all the other Logans and Hunters, the blankets and towels and coolers, the words flying around.

His mother was talking half to herself, in the doorway. He was in bed. She said the waves were like white clouds that hissed when they fell over. Black mountains and then like a thousand snakes hissed when the water hit the sand. She said that was the night he was conceived.

Conception. Conceit. Concave.

Con man. He finna run a con on Glorette. You cain't run no con on her. She ain't foolish. She just high. Well, that one dude run a con on her. Seventeen years ago. Left the evidence behind.

\*   \*   \*

THAT FRIDAY NIGHT, Patrini never came back for his Volvo.

Mayeli's aunt dropped her off so he could play her a new CD. The Kuffs. She ate red beans and rice, laughing when his grandfather whispered, "Victor say you from down past Mexico, you used to them refry beans, no?"

"Not true!" she said in that accent. She called it Creole. The Beatles and some Spanish and when she wanted to mess with him, whole sentences he couldn't understand. "We have red beans and rice in Belize. And Sunday dinner—stew chicken. So I cook for you one day, yes?"

Her aunt wouldn't come inside when she picked her up, wouldn't even get out of her old Galant. "She says Belizeans are not the same black as Americans," Mayeli whispered apologetically. "She thinks is perilous for us to speak."

"Say it again."

"What?" She grinned, hand on the old cut-glass doorknob. "Perilous?"

"Yeah."

*Perilous—I ain't got shit, can't drive. She ain't gotta worry. Pitiful.*

When she left, and his grandfather went to sleep, the Volvo was still there. Victor sat in the Impala, shed door open, facing the Volvo. He'd thought it would be funny to sit here with Mayeli and eat drive-thru food, but it was fucking pathetic. And when he'd kissed her, she slid her hands up his t-shirt sleeves and onto his shoulderblades and laced her fingers.

His back.

He heard cars leaving after the football game. SUVs with their huge tires whining, the low-riders and Sentras bumping stereos. The street grew quiet again by midnight, and Victor felt tears running down his face, hot on his collarbone. He didn't raise his hands to wipe them.

He wasn't even crying for his mother. She had scars on her ankles. He didn't know if Memphis did that.

He'd never really seen his own scars until last month, in the bathroom in this house. No matter how he tried to stand on the toilet when he was little, and twist to look in whatever medicine chest mirror, he could see only one or two. But here, the mirror was bigger. He could see all seven.

He was from Memphis. He wouldn't leave. He had light brown skin and whiskers that had embedded themselves like chocolate sprinkles from the Halloween cupcakes at school. His eyes were swimming in red. Like blood.

He drank Cisco, and that meant he didn't pass out like Chess, who drank Johnnie Black, or Sisia's brother who drank tequila. Memphis just got more pissed as the sun fell. He never told them his name. It had been two days. He was waiting for something. To carry back to Memphis. They were his entertainment. He made Victor change the channel. It was back when Urkel was on TV.

*Lil nigga never smile.*

*He don't have to smile.* His mother stayed in her chair at the glass table. Memphis had moved the couch across the door. *That ain't his job. My job. I smiled for you yesterday.*

He turned to Victor, who sat on the floor near the TV, where Urkel was so close his glasses looked like lakes. *You betta smile, lil nigga.*

*I smiled.*

*Not today you ain't. You been in them books.*

Victor had waited for hours, until Memphis fell asleep on the couch and his mother put her head down on her arms and her mouth opened. Then he stood up slowly, legs like Gumby, and went into his room to do his homework. He had missed school.

Memphis woke him by pulling off his t-shirt. He lit a cigarette. Seven cigarettes. Two eyes. One on each shoulderblade. Five times in the center of his back in a curve that must look like a grin. If you saw the whole thing.

Which only Memphis had. Pink buttons now. Black before they fell off. Never seen his back, but in bed three little black discs.


THE STREETSWEEPER WOKE him. His heart dangled in his throat for a moment. When he was little, he thought the streetsweeper was a monster. A Chinese dragon, like he'd seen in a parade on TV. All the lights, whirring brushes, hissing past him now to raise dust that settled on Patrini's Volvo.

He'd fallen asleep in the Impala. Zellman was staring at him, the 'Stang idling in the driveway. Zellman pulled up next to the Volvo and rolled down the window.

"You listening to the radio in there?"

Victor shook his head.

"Wanna hear something?"

Victor got out of the Impala and closed the shed door. He got into Zellman's passenger seat. "You always up this early?" Zellman said.

Victor could smell his aftershave. "Sometimes. Why you here? On a Saturday?" Sun poured through the branches. "You worried I wasn't takin care of the Volvo?"

Zellman frowned. "Hell, who'd steal a Volvo?" He put in the new Outkast CD. "I gotta work on something in the library. A piece about pimpology for this new zine."

Victor closed his eyes. He couldn't think. Outkast. Wearing what his mother said looked like leisure suits. "I was waitin for Professor Patrini."

Zellman laughed. "He met some lecturer from Biology at the meeting. I guess she's got her own car."

Doesn't everybody? Victor studied the dashboard, the old-fashioned instruments.

Zellman said, "I wanted to play something else for you." He took out the CD and put in another silver disc. Victor imagined him spinning them all on his fingers like an entertainer at a fair. Then he heard the opening guitar, and felt like a stick poked him in the breastbone. "Love Rollercoaster." Ohio Players. His mother had danced to that. She showed him one night. The rollercoaster. Swaying her shoulders, moving her feet.

Zellman said, "You write really well. Distinctive ideas, man. You know the Chili Peppers version, right? You could try a piece on black originals and white remakes. Ohio Players were wild. I can send it to this zine."


ONE TIME. HE was twelve, and the Celica was in the carport just under their floor and his mother passed out somewhere, and Sisia came yelling for him to come get her. Victor had pushed down on the gas with his shoe and seen the red light flash—he still had those stupid-ass shoes that lit up when you stepped—and then the car inched back out of the space like a basketball player working the ball into the paint. Back, back, back. He turned the wheel slowly and went off the curb.

He asked Irwin for his keys, so he could move the Honda closer to the porch when he washed it. "Dude, you should put some gravel down here, for the winter," Irwin said, and Victor nodded.

"Yeah, bro, good idea."

He felt the powerful vibrations of the Honda engine under his legs, in his forehead, and moved the car carefully across the dirt. The exhaust felt so strong he pictured a cartoon car, with puffs of smoke behind him, and the stereo system shook his fingers on the wheel.

When he got out of the car, the campus cop was staring at him from the street. "And that ain't your vehicle? You just playin with it, like a toy? Your time about up, son."

"Unless you from Detroit, I ain't your son. I'm Glorette Picard's son." He shut Irwin's door carefully, and kept his back to the cop. He didn't hear the campus security car leave for a long time, but the cop didn't say another word.

MARCUS SAID, "YOU registered for Spring?"

Victor shook his head.

"What? You can't quit."

"I'm not quittin. I just have to keep the lot goin right now, and the scheduling won't work." Victor heard his grandfather inside the screen, breathing noisy in the cold. Victor had built a fire, banked and low.

He said, "In January, I'ma pay somebody to watch the cars while I'm in class. Somebody who don't want to steal a 64 Impala. Every couple days, Jazen and Tiquan cruise by and fuck with me."

"Ah, yeah. Like a piece of steak sittin in front of a dog."

"A Rottweiler."

"A Rockwilder. That's how Jazen would say it."

They laughed, and Victor said, "Nobody would get that except you. Nobody across the street. Zellman might be tight with it, but he doesn't get the six-four. Or Jazen."

"That's his 'Stang?"

"Yeah. Rolling Stones. Rollercoaster. He's messin up my list." He hesitated, even with Marcus. "See, I like makin lists. What cars and CDs and clothes go with each one. Dudes like him, then ones like Irwin with the big cash. Brothas like Jazen."

House of Pain. Insane.

He thought of Zellman. Zine. "I gotta get you guys to hang. Listen to some music."


MAYELI SAT WITH him in the Impala one night. She had taken the bus, because her aunt wouldn't bring her. He said, "You not afraid?"

She laughed, low in her chest. "We didn't even have current in Tea-kettle Village. Was dark all the time. Much darker than here."

Current. He put his arms around her, and her lips tasted of coffee and lipgloss. Was that the slick sweetness?

"Quoi faire?" he whispered. "Means *what you wanna do?*"

"Stay here. Nice and dark, yes."

But hours later, she said, "My auntie think you look like Nelly. She hates Nelly. She say you never work hard and your ideas maybe come to fruition, maybe not."

Victor wanted to tell her to say *fruition* again. But it wasn't funny. Would the woman rather have him out making major cash with Jazen? "Where's your moms?" he asked Mayeli, and her back stiffened under his hands.

"She died. In Teakettle. She was fishing on a boat with my uncle—a wave knock over the boat. Call it a rogue wave." She was silent for a long time, her breath trailing a veil of silver in the cold.

But the next day, she drove her aunt's car to Iris Street, bringing coffee beans from Belize for his grandpère. Victor roasted and ground them like his grandmother had taught him, put them in the big drip pot she had brought from Louisiana forty years ago. His grandmother always said to his mother, "That pot older than you, ti-fille." Pot always be older than her, Victor thought, and shook off the ripple that attacked his shoulder.

The fog hung in the trees now, leaves dripping like thousands of eyelashes. The coffee was darker, stronger than he'd ever tasted, and Mayeli said, "Because in Belize, we grow the food better." His grandfather was on the second cup when Zellman, Patrini, and Jameson all came in at the same time.

Zellman came up to the porch and shouted, "My God. Who's brewing that? Smells way better than Starbucks."

"Me," Victor said.

"Bro, you have got to let me have a taste."

Victor poured him a cup, though his grandfather frowned and went back inside.

Zellman blew on the surface, steam and breath and fog all blending near the porch railing. "Okay, now I'd pay you five dollars for a cup of this to get me started before a stupid faculty workshop like today's. Three hours of tedium and—"

"Tenure issues," Patrini said, grabbing the cup.

Mayeli said, "He brew coffee every morning. He can make extra, certain." She moved her eyelashes, not her eyes, at Victor. He shrugged, but she said, "Five dollar seem steep. Maybe two, yes?"

When Mayeli sat on the porch with him—"Looka the bonnet on the red car—get a bird gift for you!"—he felt like he was wearing his headphones. At night she tasted his neck, she let him pull her hair from the tight elastic, but when things got serious, she said, "I cannot have no baby. And don't say it—nothing failsafe, no? Nothing trustworthy. And you not interested in a real job."

He pulled away and thought he'd be angrier. But all he felt was broke. Finally he said, "I still want the big time. And then I want to get a master's like Zellman."

Mayeli twisted her hair hard into the knot at the back of her skull. She had cooked coconut rice, and he'd watched her wrist when she held the wooden spoon. He'd never seen his mother's wrist or hand move like that.

He walked her back to the farmer's market, where she had to meet her aunt. He said, "So you sayin you ain't got time to wait?"

She kissed him, around the corner, before they saw the tarpaulin and silver frame where the t-shirts flew. "My brother coming next week. He get a tattoo say 'Thug Life,' for preparation. I worry about the money. Every day."

Victor saw the flames from a carnitas stand, a drum barbecue, a Mexican woman heating corn tortillas like full moons amid the smoke. He thought, *My mother never swirled anything into boiling water, never held a wooden spoon. Those tacos from El Ojo de Agua—my favorite food in the world. Carnitas tacos, with pico de gallo. Her fingers like sign language when she opened the bags.*

HE PAINTED A small sign and nailed it to one of the porch pillars. It couldn't get him into trouble, because it didn't advertise anything except where he had begun his journey in life, a mile away at the city hospital.

La Reina.

Queen of somebody's heart.

He had asked Zellman last week. Zellman said, "My favorite food? My mother makes this brisket. If I take a bite, I'm like seven years old."

Victor had no idea what brisket was, but he ate the last bowl of Mayeli's coconut rice.

He sold the coffee in Styrofoam cups printed with beans. He detailed cars. Enrique brought a load of fine pea gravel and they raked it over the dirt. The wind made him nervous. Enrique saw campus security cruising past and said, "Quoi faire? Street a bayou and he fishin. Want to catch you wrong."

The cop must have smelled too much coffee, Victor thought, because he stopped the car, got out, hitched up his belt, and walked into the yard.

He must have seen Patrini and Zellman with cups. Then Victor's grandfather squinted and said, "You. Narcisse Belarde boy, you."

The officer said, "Excuse me, now, sir. I'm thirty-six years old. Not no boy."

"You Narcisse Junior."

Marcus watched the campus cop look past the entire house, to the arroyo, irritated.

His grandfather said, "You know me? This Glorette boy. My Glorette."

Then the man's chest rose and fell under his khaki shirt. Victor saw it. My moms. Queen of the Westside every time she walked. Narcisse. The old Valentine. Damn.

The campus police car idled, big engine humming. "Somebody's gonna catch you without a city permit. I'm not the only one patrollin."

"You the only one keep drive past here," Grandpère said.

"That won't last forever."

Victor waited until Belarde got back into his car, and then he said, "Nothin last forever, right?"

The cop pulled forward a few feet, closer to Victor where he sat on the low stone wall. "Now you sellin coffee? You crazy?"

Victor shrugged. "They got a bank inside Kinko's, man. A Starbucks inside the Cinema Eight. You gotta diversify."


BUT THAT NIGHT, he remembered where he'd seen Belarde's scar.

His mother had just taken their things to Sisia's apartment at El Dorado. A creamy yellow stucco building. Victor said, "I don't know where the bus comes!" He'd screamed at her, the first time. He was in third grade. She was sleeping on the couch, it was early morning, and Sisia yelled at him, "Go out to Palm Avenue and wait!"

When he got there a yellow bus was already leaving, and he ran behind it for three blocks. Then a cop pulled up and said, "Hey, hey, little man, where you tryin to go?"

The scar. Belarde. He'd put Victor in the hot car and Victor said, "My mama moved yesterday and I can't find my school."

"What's your name?" His shirt was pressed stiff.

"Victor Picard."

"Picard?" The cop whistled.

He took Victor to the elementary school, which was only six blocks away. Victor had gotten turned around on the narrow streets lined with pepper trees and apartment buildings. He took Victor into the school office and signed him in late, said the boy's mother had a flat tire and had called him for help.

After that, Victor had seen the patrol car three days in a row, idling at the corner of Jessamine and Palm, heat rising off the hood, Belarde looking up from a clipboard to meet his eyes and raise his chin an inch.

Then they'd moved again.

In the cold, waiting for the 7–10 pm classes to let out, he played his mother's favorite songs over and over. Two cassettes she'd never let anyone take. She had never bought a CD, before she started losing everything. She even kept a damn 8-track once, he remembered, big as a square-cut pizza slice in his hands.

Now he played her music. "Poinciana." Then Kool and the Gang: "Summer Madness," with the organ and synthesizer. Even now, in November, in the stone wall his grandfather and Enrique had helped build for Mr. Batiste, whose Impala still smelled of his aftershave, a few crickets sang from their hollows.


ON VICTOR'S BIRTHDAY, the first day of finals in December, Jazen came for the six-four.

The lot was empty. Patrini had just left in the Volvo, his new girlfriend in the passenger seat, seatbelt tight across her chest like a Mexican bandit's bullet-holder. Bandolier?

Jazen pulled over the curb and into the lot. "I'ma give you six-fifty, nigga. I done drove by here twenty times and you ain't done shit with that ride. Tiquan open his big mouth and told this dude, and he want the ride now. Right now. I owe him."

Victor said, "Ain't—"

"This dude don't play. I'ma give you—"

His grandfather opened the screen door with his foot. "I'ma give you fifteen second get out my driveway else I shoot me some window and tire." The shotgun was a third arm next to his sleeve.

Jazen spat on the dirt and spun the Navigator through the lot and off the sidewalk, spraying gravel into Victor's hair, tearing a chunk from the ancient cement curb.

"Gotta have four-wheel drive," Victor said to his grandfather, "for that kind of maneuver."

"I ain't play word game with you, non," his grandpère said, soft and evil like a serial killer in a movie. "Eighteen make a man."

"Eighteen mean I gotta pull in more than four hundred a month from cars and coffee."

"Not yet."

His grandfather's cheeks were traced with hundreds of lines. Like a broken windshield on an old car—not the new ones with shatter proof glass. Scrutinize. You can scrutinize somebody. Then is he scrutable? What about implacable? When is he placable?

Before dawn, Victor startled awake. He heard a huge engine—the streetsweeper again? Chinese dragon?—and then the rattling of chains.

"I call them last night," Grandpère said in the dark.

A tow truck idled in the driveway. Marcus Thompson's older brother Octavious got out of the cab. Then Uncle Reynaldo and Lafayette.

They were old-school lunatic. Nobody messed with them. They'd been drinking hard for years, and in the garage light, their features looked soft and blurred, like bars of soap with just a few watery rubbings to take the edges off. Their eyes were muddy, the irises rough-mapped.

Reynaldo nodded at him. "We frontin you the work, lil cuddy."

They opened the hood on the Impala, pointed and talked, and then hooked it up to the tow truck. His grandfather had made coffee. Reynaldo drank his on the porch steps. "When we done, I'ma have this dude Nacho paint it candyflake orange, and I got this guy Jaime Becerra in El Monte for a buyer. You'll clear big cash. You can register for whatever. And you won't get shot."

"I might still get shot," Victor said. Fuckin little kid who gotta get rescued. "Might get shot walkin to the store."

"Then buy a ride nobody wants."

"Like your truck?"

Reynaldo crumpled up the paper cup and threw it at him. "Whatever works."

The Impala rode high on the tow truck, flat tires at eye level. His grandfather watched silently.

"I'm still runnin the lot," Victor said, after the street was quiet again.

His grandfather nodded.

HE GOT READY when he saw the Navigator turn the corner two weeks later. It was January. He had three night classes—Indigenous History, Intro to Sociology, and Zellman's English lit class—full of women whose kids were grown, and retired guys, and people who worked all day. Mayeli's younger brother Wilfredo, just arrived from Belize, took the 6:30–10 shift for the cars still parked in the dark.

Wilfredo was late, so Victor was already pissed when he heard the speakers. DMX. He put his books on the porch and ran to open the shed door, pulled the light-bulb string, then waited cool by the sidewalk. It was 6:40, winter night dark purple in the trees.

He had practiced.

"What you want now!" he shouted at Jazen. "You done already got the damn ride!"

"What the hell you talking bout?" Tiquan shouted back when the Navigator pulled into the driveway. "Where the damn car?"

"Wherever you took it to, fool!" Victor moved forward. His eyes were shaking with the headlights' jittery bounce, from the speakers thumping the car, doors trembling.

"Who got it?" Jazen lifted his chin, and Victor saw the hesitation.

"Not you?"

Jazen shook his head, and Tiquan said, "That Pomona motherfucker came and stole it himself. We coulda made a grand offa him."

"Yeah," Victor said, taking another step forward. "What it matter who got it? I ain't got it." He was shouting louder now, feeling the cords in his throat tighten, his eyes burn with the cold. "And fuck y'all two times, cause you know who got my mother and you ain't said shit. Ain't did shit. Ran off Alfonso."

"How he—" Tiquan began, but Jazen cut him off and wheeled the Navigator back, tires spinning in the gutter filled with rainwater.

HE FINALLY BEGAN to breathe once he was in the classroom. The murmur of voices, the shoe soles on tile, the rustle of paper.

When class was over at ten, he walked across the college lots. Wilfredo was sitting on the edge of the stone wall, hunched into his jacket, Irwin's car behind him. Wilfredo said, "I tell you, I not washing the cars. I only wash my own car when I get one. Escalade. Black Midnight, okay? In that I get some thug love."

Then Wilfredo stood up. He was fifteen, hated his own name, and his gold-edged teeth, and his voice. *Everybody wanna be an American,* Victor thought, watching Wilfredo hold out his hand for the cash. *Everybody wanna be 50 Cent.*

Wilfredo walked away, toward the bus stop downtown. Victor sat on the porch. Wilfredo and Mayeli's mom had been drowned by one wave. Not even a storm. Just one wave out the blue. Mayeli was seven and Wilfredo was five. His grandpère was seven when the Mississippi River flood took his mother.

I had mine until last year.

The palm tree sparkler. Better than fireworks. *You could have it every month, baby. Just look. Every month, but winter is the best, cause the moon's all clean. Winter moon like the rain washed it.*

*Every moon got a name. The old lady down in Louisiana told me. Hunter Moon. Harvest Moon. Moon pull all that water everywhere.*

*You always got a moon, right here, and you always got a palm tree, baby. Can't nobody ever change that.* Sitting on her lap, on some balcony. *The Riviera? You got a Riviera in France. You got a Riviera right here.* She put her fingers like visors over his eyes, to block out the apartment lights, and all he saw was the courtyard palm tree, full moon behind it, the fronds tossing in the wind, their fringes throwing off silver fire.

Thanks to Richard Parks, Andi Mudd, Katie Freeman, Jay Neugeboren, James Baldwin, Holly Robinson, Chris Ying, Steve Erickson, Tamara Straus, Michael Ray, Denise Hamilton, Jervey Tervalon, Johnny Temple, everyone at McSweeney's who works so hard, and Dwayne Sims.

Susan Straight was born in Riverside, California. She has published seven previous novels, including *A Million Nightingales* and *Take One Candle Light a Room*, companions in this trilogy. Her novel *Highwire Moon* was a finalist for the 2001 National Book Award.